IF SHE RETURNED

If She Returned is the third novel, featuring criminologist David Dunnigan, by Irish author S.A. Dunphy, who has previously written works of non-fiction.

S.A. DUNPHY

If She Returned

HACHETTE
BOOKS
IRELAND

First published in Ireland in 2019 by
HACHETTE BOOKS IRELAND

1

Cataloguing in Publication Data is available from the British Library

ISBN 978 1 4736 9920 5

Printed and bound in Great Britain by Clays Ltd, Elcograf S.p.A.

Hachette Books Ireland policy is to use papers that are natural, renewable and
recyclable products and made from wood grown in sustainable forests. The logging and
manufacturing processes are expected to conform to the environmental regulations of
the country of origin.

Hachette Books Ireland
8 Castlecourt Centre
Castleknock
Dublin 15, Ireland

A division of Hachette UK Ltd
Carmelite House, 50 Victoria Embankment, EC4Y 0DZ

www.hachettebooksireland.ie

For my little brother, Karl, who left us just as this book was begun, but whose presence I felt throughout its writing. This one's for you, bruv.

When the bitter night is dark and cold,
It's then you might see Mother Joan

You may think you're alone and there's no one else there
Those are the times when you should beware

Look in the places where shadows lie
You might catch the glint in her pale green eyes

All dressed in black, she's long and thin;
Her hair is pure white; pale is her skin.

Look there in that doorway – see how she stands?
Is that a knife she's got in her hand?

At the end of the street where no one else passes;
Can you see how she moves? See how she dances?

She's as old as time and as cold as death
Is that her behind you? Can you feel her breath?

Now that you know her, she'll soon be along.
Just listen out and you'll hear her song.

She knows your secrets, and she knows your lies.
She'll whisper them to you as she helps you to die.

There's no place to hide and there's nowhere to run.
Close the book, child, my tale is done.

Posted by hacker_red
www.wickedwords.com

Creepypasta: noun; horror-related legends, myths or images that have been widely copied and pasted on the internet; brief, user-generated content intended to frighten, upset or disturb readers; the stories habitually feature a ritualistic or habitual element, and often purport to be true.

Urban Web Dictionary

Prologue

WHAT WAITS IN THE SHADOWS

1

WHEN DOCTOR MARK MURPHY GOT TO HIS office in the science building of Bligh University, in Cork, the book, which he had burned to a pile of ashes the night before, was sitting right in the middle of his desk.

He froze with the door still half-open, gazing at it numbly.

Replaying the steps in his mind, he recalled taking the leather-bound volume from his filing cabinet, where he had hidden it for fear one of his students or a colleague might see it and discover what it contained. He had bundled it up in a plastic Lidl shopping bag, and placed that in turn into the satchel he used to bring papers into work.

He had considered putting the satchel on the passenger seat of his Mercedes, but had thought better of it – the idea of having the book so close slightly nauseated him – so he dumped it in the boot and then drove at exactly the speed limit (despite a gnawing sense that reality was coming unravelled, he did not want to draw attention to himself) until he reached the detached four-bedroomed dormer in the Cork city suburb of Glenville, where he lived.

He had bought the materials he needed the previous day –

a box of Zip firelighters, a tin of lighter fuel and some long safety matches. He had a barrel-shaped barbeque in his shed, which had been purchased on a whim two summers ago and never used. *Better late than never*, he thought, somewhat hysterically.

He put the book, still wrapped in its blue, red and yellow plastic shroud, on the grill, piled chunks of the acrid-scented combustibles around it, and then sprayed the whole lot with fuel for good measure. He had to strike the match three times before it caught, so violently were his hands shaking. At first, he did not think it would burn – the bag melted almost immediately, but the book itself seemed to sit, immune to the flames, for several long moments before he saw one of the black leather corners begin to curl, and then smoulder, and then in a glorious puff the whole awful thing burst into a wonderful orange conflagration.

He stood and watched, laughing and crying all at the same time, until it was reduced to a smoking grey pile. Then he went inside, poured himself a large single malt and watched pornography until an uneasy sleep claimed him.

At one point in the wee small hours (he had glanced at the clock and it was 3.33 a.m.) he was awakened by what he thought was someone knocking on his window, but there was no one there when he went to check. The stress of the past couple of days had made him paranoid.

He went back to sleep and was troubled by no more dreams.

But the next morning, the book was sitting on his office desk large as life despite all his efforts, and he knew the nightmare was not over. For a long moment he was frozen by a sense of fear that was almost overwhelming. His mind went completely blank – this could not be. He was a man of science, and these were circumstances that flouted all the laws of logic upon which he had built his life.

But then something in him fought back – a survival mechanism clicked in, and he started to function again. The fact that it was on his desk, this time, in a room to which only he and perhaps three other people had a key, gave him some clues as to who was behind the affair.

He knew he was going to have to respond – it was only right.

And with that thought Doctor Mark Murphy closed his office door behind him.

2

MARK MURPHY WAS NOT SUPERSTITIOUS SO HE did not for a moment believe this was the same book. His enemies had clearly made copies.

He sat at his desk, gazing at the tome as if it were a portent of evil.

The book was slightly larger than A4 in size and bound in real black leather (he had been around old texts for long enough to know the smell and feel of it). There was no lettering or any other kind of marking on either the front or back cover, nor the spine. He reached over and slowly drew the thing to him. He did not want to open it, but he had to be sure: this one might contain revelations even worse than its predecessor, so taking his Parker pen from the breast pocket of his cardigan, he used it to turn the first few pages, all of which were made of thick card.

The text was exactly the same as the previous volume – some kind of children's poem, written in rhyming couplets: *When the bitter night is dark and cold, it's then you might see Mother Joan*, the first verse ran. He presumed it was intended to frighten him – some sort of stupid, juvenile joke. The poem didn't bother him at all.

It was the accompanying photographs that scared him half to death.

There were ten stanzas in all, each given its own page. The plate opposite every verse contained a black and white photograph that had been put through some kind of filter to make it look like vintage daguerreotype. The photos all featured him, Doctor Mark Murphy, doing things he would not wish the world to know about. Private acts.

These were images that, should they ever make their way into the wrong hands, would result in him not just losing his job – prosecution and prison would swiftly follow.

The previous collection had included ten shots, taken from various unusual angles (one looked like it had been captured through a hole in the floorboards, another through a light fitting), of Doctor Murphy's less savoury, but perhaps more *moderate*, extra-curricular interests: one showed him masturbating while watching porn (a smaller photo, set into the corner of the larger one, and taken (impossibly) from just behind his right ear, showed that the film he was enjoying involved a woman, two masked men and a nail gun).

Another page showed a sequence of five images of him viciously beating an elderly lady (a neighbour of his who had complained about how he parked his Mercedes – he had to show her he could park anywhere he damn well pleased, and he had reminded the old dear before taking his leave that if she pointed the finger of blame at him when explaining how she came by her injuries he'd come back, and make sure she didn't have any fingers left to point in the future). Each photo in the set was taken from a different vantage point, and one actually showed a close-up of the old woman's battered face.

The final picture in the first book was of him standing over the body of Tom, a semi-wild cat that had lived on the grounds of the university for as long as anyone could remember. The creature had taken to spraying on the window sill of his office, and the stench permeated the entire room. Murphy had stayed to work late one night, and when the filthy animal had come to mark its territory, he had coaxed it inside with some tinned sardines, and cut its throat while it ate.

This photo showed him straight on, standing with his back to the window, the kitchen knife in his hand stained with blood; the animal, its throat open, was on a piece of plastic at his feet. The peculiar thing about this photo was that there was someone peering through the window – they were clearly visible, but he had not seen them at the time, because his back had been to the glass.

The figure was tall (it must have been well over six feet), and dressed in some kind of black coat with a hood obscuring the face. A wisp of blonde or possibly white hair escaped the hood, but other than that there were no distinguishing features. The text of the final verse on the page opposite read: *There's no place to hide and there's nowhere to run. Close the book, child, my tale is done.*

Common sense told him the ominous-looking person had been Photoshopped in, just to freak him out. But there was a nagging voice at the back of his mind reminding him that he was being watched. This must be one of those surveilling him.

The images in the second book were all worse than the first. Murphy had, over the past five years, killed two people and left a third brain damaged to the point she had virtually no mental functioning to speak of. Pictures of all these were present, as well as some action shots of his visit to a particular club in Kosovo where the guests could vent their more violent fantasies. He didn't think he had actually murdered anyone while he was there, although one of the women he had spent time with probably required reconstructive surgery if she was going to be seen in public again.

And that dark-clad figure was, once again, in the last image in this book, this time as a reflection in a mirror, and Murphy knew it had to be a trick, because that room had been locked, and the only people in it were him and the girl he was torturing.

Distracted as he was, he would surely have noticed a towering figure, dressed in a black cowl, looming over his shoulder.

This, he decided, had been created by someone with an axe to grind.

And he thought he knew who that was.

3

MARTHA WINGARDEN WAS BLONDE, THIRTY-FIVE years old, and Murphy believed she was asking for it.

Martha had started work as a cleaner in the college during his salad days, when everything seemed to be going right and the world was at his feet (those days were *long* gone, but that was another story). She had come into his office one evening to empty his waste basket, and he had suggested that, while she was down there, she might be interested in polishing something as well.

The daft cow had pretended not to know what he was talking about, so he had shown her.

It took five days for the black eye to fade, and a year for Bligh's Committee on Bullying and Harassment to begrudgingly decide they didn't have enough hard evidence to initiate disciplinary action. Anger management classes were suggested, and he went, to show he was willing to play ball. Which was a big fat lie. The only reason he had agreed was because she indicated she would not take things further so long as he sought help – it was her word against his, but there had been one or two outbursts on campus and he didn't want to develop a reputation as difficult.

Despite his effort to show willing, Kieran Byrne, an English postgrad and a liberal hippy bleeding heart of the kind the Arts Department had a habit of attracting, was waiting by Murphy's car one evening to inform him that Martha was a friend of his, and he was convinced she was telling the truth. Poking Murphy in the chest to punctuate each word, the do-gooder informed him he would be watching him like a hawk from then on.

In the years since, the long-haired moron had become the university's Equality Officer and Murphy was convinced this was all part of some grand scheme he had cooked up to screw him over. It all added up: Murphy had found the first book seemingly at random in the poetry section of the library and Wingarden, as a cleaner, would have a skeleton key, which would facilitate getting the second one into his office. The artsy nature of the whole thing, with the fancy, digitally enhanced photography, the fairytale-sounding poem and the looming, death-like figure in the window all suggested Byrne was the culprit.

All that was left to answer was how they'd managed to take the photographs to begin with, but Murphy believed he could get the necessary answers out of Martha Wingarden if he could just have half an hour on his own with her. Byrne was ten years younger than him and six inches taller, so he had no intention of taking him on – he had some friends he would call upon to take care of that once he'd had a little fun with the blonde cleaner bitch.

If he planned it just right, he could have way more than half an hour.

With a little care and forethought, he could have all the time he wanted.

4

MURPHY GRABBED MARTHA WINGARDEN AS SHE
came out of the history building at ten that night and knocked
her out by pressing a rag soaked in methylated spirits over her
nose and mouth. It wasn't chloroform, but it was all he could
get his hands on at such short notice, and it did the job just
fine – she went down without much of a struggle.

He had parked the Merc just below the steps outside the
main door to the building, and he had her bundled into the
back seat and was driving out the gate and onto Consilio Road
before anyone noticed a thing. There was one security camera
over the main porch, but he had removed the fuse from the
box that powered it earlier that evening. He was aware from
the photos in the books that he was under surveillance, but
the thought that the person watching was Kieran Byrne made
him less afraid. And once he had Wingarden secure, he would
make a call that would deal with the bleeding heart once and
for all. Feeling ebullient, he put on one of his Ariana Grande
CDs and sang along as he drove across the bridge and turned
left onto the docks. It was a beautiful night and for once the
stars were all aligning in his favour.

Nothing could possibly go wrong, he thought as he sang

about having no tears left to cry. That Ariana surely could sing – and she looked like she knew her way around (he bet he could still teach her a thing or two, though).

Murphy rented a storage locker under one of his aliases at the eastern end of the docks. It was set among a network of derelict buildings, and the closest neighbour was a quarter of a mile away. He parked between his lock-up and a dilapidated shed that was right beside it so the car was completely obscured from view. It took him a little longer than he might have liked to drag Wingarden inside (in the movies the bad guy always throws the lady over his shoulder and carries her into his lair as if she weighs nothing, but reality is a little different). Once she was safely indoors he placed her on the carpenter's table that he kept there in case of emergencies and secured her hands and feet with packing tape, then ran some more over her forehead to stop her from trying to bite him or knocking herself unconscious, as a girl he had played with last year in Bangkok had done at a most inopportune moment.

When his guest was safely stowed, he stripped naked and laid out his tools, starting with the smaller, more precise items like scalpels and tweezers, and finishing with what he liked to think of as his 'shock and awe' implements: hacksaws, hammers, and not forgetting the power tools, always good for a spectacular finish.

When everything was ready, he used some smelling salts to bring Wingarden back to the land of the living. He loved seeing the sense of horror dawning on his playthings' faces, the realisation that something truly terrifying was about to be visited upon them. Martha impressed him, though. Rather than becoming hysterical, she kept it together.

With her head secured, she could only see the ceiling directly above her and he let the slut struggle for a bit, allowing the panic to really settle in her gut, then peered over her, a long filleting blade in his hand.

'Doctor Murphy,' she said, her voice hoarse and ragged from the fumes he had used to knock her out.

'Hello, Martha,' he said, smiling sweetly. 'How do I find you, this evening?'

'Please let me go,' she said, a tear trickling from the corner of her eye, but her voice still quite steady.

'Why would I do that?' Murphy asked. 'You and your friends have made my life very, very uncomfortable. You've gone to some lengths to frighten and upset me. I would go so far as to say I am *entitled* to a little payback, wouldn't you?'

'But that was *ten years ago!*' Martha pleaded. 'We haven't spoken since then! I don't even work in your building.'

He felt anger twitch in his gut, and held up a finger, silencing her.

'Do you think I'm an idiot?' he asked, running the blunt edge of the blade down her cheek so she could feel the coldness of it.

'No!'

He reached over to where his tools were laid out and picked up the book, which he had brought along as evidence of his guest's crimes.

'Was it Byrne's idea to create this little masterpiece?'

Her eyes narrowed. 'I don't know what that is.'

'Don't lie to me!'

Somewhere outside on the empty waterside a strange melody had started playing. There were no buildings close by, so he assumed it was a radio on a boat passing by. It was an odd tune, though: almost like a hymn or a lullaby, and played on a single instrument, a cello, perhaps.

'I'm not lying, I swear I'm not!'

'How did you get these photographs? I know you paid someone to follow me, but I want to know who. This can go easy or it can go hard, and I promise you, I will have you begging to die by the end if you force me to go hard on you.'

The melody had become louder. Murphy could now hear that it was not being played by an instrument but was instead a human voice. He was reminded of a recording he had heard once of a *castrato*, a singer who had been castrated at adolescence to preserve a high vocal range, but with all the power of an adult. He thought he recognised the song now. But he couldn't place it.

'You know, I liked you,' he said, stroking her cheek. 'We didn't have to be enemies.'

'We could still be friends,' she said, and he saw hope in her eyes. 'If you just let me go, we could be really good friends.'

He grinned. 'You want me to cut the tape?' He placed the knife point at her wrist.

'Yes. I'll be good. I'll do whatever you want.'

'I know you will,' he said, and pushed the tip of the blade into the flesh between her thumb and forefinger.

Three things happened all at once.

Martha Wingarden screamed a full-throated, anguished howl, the door to the locker exploded inwards and all the lights went out.

Murphy stood in the darkness, grasping the knife and breathing shallowly. The room seemed full of the sound of the strange song, and he realised that, although he was looking in the direction of the door, all he could see was darkness. There should have been light streaming in from the lamps outside, but the place was pitch black.

'Who's there?' he shouted. 'I swear, if you come any closer, I'll gut her from chin to groin. I mean it!'

There was a movement in the darkness in front of him, like the swarming of insects or the swirling of smoke, and suddenly he realised why no light was coming in the hole where the door had been – somebody or some*thing* very tall was standing in the space. The song got louder, and he could just discern a jerky movement, and something pale, like a long, thin limb, was revealed for a moment, and then it was gone again.

'Keep away! I'm going to cut her if you move one more inch!'

The song stopped all of a sudden, and Murphy heard a deep, throaty sound, somewhere between a laugh and a cry, and then there was a whooshing and he was struck full force in the chest and knocked off his feet.

Something cold and bitter covered his mouth and he couldn't breathe, and then all was black.

*

A very shaken Martha Wingarden was back at work the following day, and it was six months before a strange detective named David Dunnigan came asking about Mother Joan. Until that day, she thought (hoped) it had all been a nightmare.

Part One

LITTLE GIRL LOST

I don't know why I looked up, but when I did I saw her there. She was standing right against my window. Her long black cloak brushed against the glass, and the darkness inside that hood, pointed, like the beak of a foul bird, seemed blacker than the blackest night.

And she just stood there in the window.

My wife was upstairs sleeping, my son was in his crib and I couldn't move. I froze and watched her looking past me through the glass.

Oh, please no. In the name of everything sacred, not her.

She seemed to be slowly swaying, as if she were a serpent, and she put a pale, clawed hand up and slid it down the glass, watching me. A wisp of the whitest hair escaped through the folds of the cowl.

And still she watched me. Mother Joan.

I couldn't do anything. I just stayed there, frozen, feet still in the bushes I was pruning, looking into my home.

And she stood against my window.

Posted by hacker_red
www.wickedwords.com

1

THE TEAM FROM THE NATIONAL BUREAU OF
Criminal Investigation (Ireland's equivalent to the FBI) were
anxious to get back to Dublin. They had been working on a
case involving people trafficking in Faringen, the last outpost
in Greenland before the North Pole, and were waiting for
the first of the four flights on their long journey home when
David Dunnigan, the team's criminologist, received the call
from Father Bill, his friend and mentor, to say he thought he
had found Beth.

Beth.

Dunnigan's niece, for whom he had been searching for
eighteen years.

'I have her in a hotel room in Ballsbridge,' the priest told
him over the static-filled line. 'She's waiting to see you.'

Dunnigan sat on the tiny metal bench, watching the small
plane he and his friends would soon be boarding being
refuelled. He knew he should be feeling an overwhelming rush
of joy and relief, but there was nothing. It was as if everything
had shut down.

'Are you saying what I think you're saying?' Dunnigan
asked, his voice level.

'Yes I am, Davey. Beth has come home.'

The criminologist held the phone to his ear, the hum of the international line a constant drone.

'How?' he said at last. 'I mean ... I don't understand.'

Diane, Dunnigan's recently estranged girlfriend, and Chief Superintendent Frank Tormey, his boss, were gazing at him now.

'What is it, Davey?' Diane asked, concerned.

He held up his hand to silence her.

'It's a long story,' the priest said, 'and I will tell you every bit of it when I see you. Right now, all you need to know is that she is safe and under constant watch, and the second you land I will bring you to her.'

Dunnigan blinked. His mind was racing. So many thoughts were coming in rapid succession, he couldn't process them all. In the end, only one surfaced. 'It should have been me.'

'Perhaps,' Father Bill said. 'I did what I thought was right.'

'I was supposed to find her.'

'Come and find her now. Give me a shout when you know what time you'll be landing. I'll give you the details of where to go.' And he hung up.

All eyes were on Dunnigan, who was still holding the now dead handset.

'What's going on, Davey?' Tormey asked.

'Father Bill says he's found Beth.'

Tormey sighed and shook his head. 'So that's what he's been up to.'

'You knew about this?'

'He told me he was looking into something. I didn't ask him what it was. He has eyes and ears all over the city, and they're not always attached to very nice people.'

'Is he sure it's her?' Diane asked, putting a hand on Dunnigan's shoulder, which he ignored completely.

'He says it is.'

'Do you believe him?'

'I neither believe nor disbelieve him. I don't have enough information. I'll establish the veracity of the situation when we get home.' And, standing up, he began to walk towards the plane.

'You'd think he'd be happy,' Diane said as they watched the scrawny figure move stiffly away from them.

'You don't know him at all, do you?' Tormey said, without irony.

2

BY THE TIME THEY LANDED IN DUBLIN THEY ALL felt as if they had been chewed up and spat out. Dunnigan hadn't uttered a single word since Faringen. He texted Father Bill as they queued for their flight from London: *Boarding Now. Arriving T1 Dublin 3.55 p.m.*

Father Bill responded: *Carton Hotel, Ballsbridge.* And that was that.

Dunnigan and Diane caught a taxi outside the terminal. (Tormey left them at this point, to check in at Garda HQ.)

'How are you doing, Davey?' Diane asked as the cab made its way along the M50.

'I'm fine,' was the terse response.

'No, you're not. Come on, we've been through enough shit together not to have to play these games anymore. Talk to me.'

He was gazing out the window, watching the stream of traffic that flowed past.

'Why? What good will it do? And I didn't ask you to come with me, either.'

'Luckily, I don't require your permission. I'm as invested in this as you are, and you know it. And as a professional therapist, I know a little something about what you're going through. So just shut up and accept my support and friendship. Okay?'

He didn't have an answer for that, so he said nothing.

*

Father Bill – in his mid-fifties, a couple of inches over six feet tall, handsome, with the build of a boxer – was waiting on a couch in the sumptuous lobby of the hotel. He hugged Diane but saw that such an overture would not be welcomed by Dunnigan.

'I want to see this girl,' the criminologist said, without preamble.

'And you will. But please, Davey, she's very delicate. She hasn't yet got her head around the fact that she's safe.'

'Is she safe?' Diane asked. 'Are they looking for her?'

'I don't know,' Father Bill admitted. 'I took a very circuitous route getting here. She's as secure as she can be.'

'But they know it was you who took her?'

'I found her in a brothel in the inner city – apparently, she'd just been trafficked here from somewhere in the Czech Republic. One of my friends in the homeless community tipped me off.' Father Bill was manager of the Widow's Quay Homeless Project. 'They'll know she was taken by now, but I doubt they'll connect it to me.'

'I need to see her,' Dunnigan said again, and the urgency was powerful in his voice.

'And she needs to see you,' Father Bill agreed gently. 'Come on. She's been waiting very patiently.'

The lift took them to the third floor, where a large man was lounging by the ice machine. He nodded as they went past.

'That's Igor,' the priest said. 'A friend of a friend. Lovely chap. Completely lethal, but a nice guy once you get to know him.'

Father Bill had grown up on the streets of the inner city and maintained connections with the criminal underworld. He was not above using these contacts when necessary, which did not always please either the police or his superiors in the church.

He led them to room 324. 'Perhaps you should stay outside – for now, at any rate,' Father Bill said to Diane.

She nodded. 'I'll go and chat to Igor.'

Father Bill put the key card into the lock and opened the door.

3

SHE WAS SITTING ON THE ROOM'S WOODEN CHAIR with her back very straight, gazing out the window. Dunnigan wondered what she was looking at, because the view consisted only of another wing of the hotel and some heating pipes.

'Beth, I have someone here to meet you,' Father Bill said.

The girl turned and looked at Dunnigan with an unflinching gaze, and immediately and beyond any doubt he knew that this was not his niece.

Feelings cascaded over him – pain, disappointment, anger, sadness, relief – it was like he was being beaten up by his own emotions. He reached out and used the wall to steady himself.

They stared at each other for a long moment. His mind raced, taking in every detail, hoping he had somehow got it wrong, that the girl facing him was just so changed it was taking him time to recognise her – it had been eighteen years, after all.

She had dark hair, which was right (although Dunnigan knew a woman's hair colour was not a reliable identifier with all the hair dyes and rinses available), and she was slim to the point of being skinny. But that was where the similarity ended. She was sallow-skinned, whereas Beth had shared his pale complexion, and the eyes were all wrong too. Beth had the grey/blue eyes Dunnigan shared with her mother, Gina, his twin. This girl's irises were more a blue-green.

He gazed at the young woman for another long moment and saw the same realisation in her face – she knew this was not going to be the reunion she had hoped for. He would have felt for her if he was not in so much pain.

Without a word he turned on his heel and walked back out past the priest, closing the door behind him.

*

Father Bill found him sitting on the stone steps outside the hotel's front door. 'She goes by the name Elizabeth,' he said. 'She was taken when she was only small. It all fit. I'm sorry.'

Dunnigan didn't look at him, just stared into the middle distance.

'She told me she had an Uncle Davey. She looked to be the right age.'

'Can you help her find her family?'

'I've already got people looking. I'm just sorry you had to go through that.'

'I didn't ask you to do this, Father. I appreciate it, but it's my responsibility to find her, not yours.'

'We're friends, Davey. I wanted to help you.'

The criminologist sighed deeply, exhaustion taking him in its grip. 'I'm starting to think it's been too long,' he said. 'The trail is too cold. I mean, we learned more in Greenland than we have in years, but it's still like trying to catch smoke. Interpol are following up on some of the information, but who knows if it'll yield anything.'

'I have one other lead, if you've got the stomach for it,' the priest said. 'I've had someone watching a location in Swords, and some information has come to light that might be worth following up. I'd be happy to check it out with you.'

'With the greatest respect, Father, I need to do it myself. I've let this run my life for almost two decades. I need to end it once and for all – for good or bad, regardless of what I learn.'

Father Bill nodded and sat down beside him on the step. 'It could bring you to some bad places.'

'Worse than where I've already been?'

'Maybe.'

'If Beth is gone, she's gone, but at least we'll know and I can say my goodbyes and put her to rest. If she's alive – and I know there's only a microscopically slim chance of that – I can bring her out of whatever hell she's been in and get her help. Please tell me where to look.'

'If you bring the police into it, the bureaucracy will slow you down. I'm worried the entire trafficking organisation is closing ranks. You'll need to move quickly.'

'Father, as a consultant with the Bureau of Criminal Investigation, I am encouraged to conduct preliminary investigations on live cases, of which this is one,' Dunnigan said, smiling wanly. 'I can always get Tormey involved if anything significant comes to light.'

'I suppose that'll have to do.' The priest seemed resigned.

So Father Bill told him about a man he'd been watching, a man who knew the inside workings of the After Dark Campaign, the organisation that had taken Beth.

4

THAT NIGHT DUNNIGAN HAD THE DREAM AGAIN – the one about the day she was taken from him and he had let it happen.

In his mind's eye it was December the eighth, the start of the Christmas shopping season in Ireland. He and Beth were wrapped up against the frigid winter air, scarves about their necks and gloves on their frozen hands, and Grafton Street was thronged with people, all similarly attired and ready to fill their shopping bags with seasonal bounty.

Beth was four – in his heart, despite the passing of time, she was always that little girl – and he held her hand while, rosy-cheeked, she gazed at the store windows resplendent with their festive decoration.

'It's just so pretty!' she said, smiling in childish wonder.

Dunnigan had planned on going into the Stephen's Green Shopping Centre. He'd had this dream countless times and each time there was about it a sickening feeling of helpless dread. He tried to steer his niece towards the double doors of the building, determined to get inside, away from the crowds and towards safety.

But then they heard the music.

In actuality the song the carollers had been singing was 'Little Donkey', but in this dream for some reason it was different – they were performing something choral, a hymn or a plainchant he couldn't quite identify. Beth tugged at his arm and pulled him towards the singers, who were surrounded by a crowd of admiring listeners.

You have to hold on to her, you cannot let go, Dunnigan told himself.

He gripped her hand tightly, determined that, for once, he would leave these benighted minstrels with his niece firmly by his side. He checked behind them and on both sides – all was safe, there was no one nearby who looked suspicious or dangerous. Everyone in the crowd seemed completely transfixed by the music, and for a second he relaxed.

Almost as soon as he did, the sky darkened and the singing took on a sinister pitch. The volume became unbearable, each note threatened to pierce his eardrums, and suddenly, like something from a Hieronymus Bosch painting, a massive, dark figure loomed from behind the group of carollers. It was impossibly tall, dressed in a dark hood and cape that was caked in mud, dead leaves and roots. A gnarled hand reached down, only it wasn't coming for him, it was trying to get Beth. He threw himself in front of her, but it was too late, there was nothing he could do.

A piercing screech cut through the nightmare, dragging him back to a reality that was only marginally less painful. His phone was ringing.

'Yes,' he said, his heart still pounding.

'He's heading for home,' Father Bill's voice said. 'It's time.'

5

TONY MARR PUT HIS BRIEFCASE (HAND-CRAFTED
and made to a design by his wife, who dabbled in fashion in
her free time – which was pretty much *all* her time) on the
bureau just inside the front door of the apartment he kept
near Dublin's city centre. His family home was just outside
Gorey, but when he worked late it seemed more sensible to
stay in town, so he rented a small place for that purpose.

Marr needed a drink. Thursday was his busiest day:
conversations (both face-to-face and via Skype) with
investment brokers and two different teams of fund managers,
planning meetings with the controllers of five subsidiary
companies and a weekly review of the stock portfolios of
three of his biggest clients took up the bulk of his schedule,
but there were always the myriad things that could not be
planned for – phone calls, minor emergencies and the like
that just had to be resolved there and then.

Of course, this was why they paid him the big bucks, and
why he was considered the best at what he did – well, one of
the top three in Europe anyway.

He went into the kitchen and pulled the menu for a new

Thai takeaway from the door of the fridge, where it was held by a magnet, and skimmed it while he went through to the living room. He was pouring himself a large glass of whiskey when he heard knocking on his front door.

Which was puzzling, as the apartment complex had a buzzer system, so unwanted visitors couldn't get in without being permitted to do so by the residents.

He peered through the peep-hole. There was a man outside, holding out an ID card which identified him as a member of the police.

Marr opened the door a crack.

'Yes, detective?'

The cop was skinny and in plain clothes: a long, grey woollen coat over a t-shirt with pictures of superheroes and the words *Justice League* emblazoned on it, paired with ill-fitting black jeans. He looked to be about forty, his long dark hair was shot through with grey and he sported a scruffy beard.

'Could I come in, Mister Marr?' he asked pleasantly. 'I need to ask you a few questions.'

'What's this about?'

'We can do this here, or you can come to Harcourt Street – I really don't mind which.'

Marr stepped back and opened the door, leading the man into his living room. 'What did you say your name was?'

'David Dunnigan. I'm a civilian consultant with the National Bureau of Criminal Investigation.'

'And how can I help you this evening?' Marr asked again, picking up his glass of Scotch and sitting down in one of the armchairs. He motioned at the chair opposite and his visitor followed suit.

'I'd like to know about some of your business associations.'

Marr nodded. So that was it – he'd been involved in some insider trading, but had always been very careful to cover his tracks. Someone had obviously been talking out of turn. He thought he had better play along for a bit, see how much this untidy cop knew.

'Which associations are you interested in – precisely?'

Dunnigan reached inside his jacket and took out a piece of paper – a yellow Post-it Note. He reached over and handed it to Marr. Glimpsing down, the investment specialist saw that it contained three lines of very neatly written script. An address. Suddenly, he thought he was going to throw up.

'You visit that location three times a week,' Dunnigan said. 'Some associates of mine have had it under surveillance, and we have footage of you coming and going quite regularly.'

Marr took a gulp of his drink and said nothing. His mind had gone blank – he knew that he was in trouble, and it was not the kind of trouble he had been expecting. He reckoned speaking would only get him in deeper, however, so he decided to keep quiet until speech was absolutely necessary.

'Not just you, of course – other men come and go too,' the criminologist continued. 'I won't insult your intelligence by pretending I don't know what goes on in that place. I visited there this evening myself, and had a word with Luca, the man who described himself as the caretaker of the operation.'

Marr licked his lips – his mouth seemed to have gone dry, all of a sudden.

'Now, Luca had names and phone numbers of fifteen gentlemen who are regular patrons of the services he provides. After a little gentle persuasion, he gave them to me. I don't expect the names are anything other than aliases, but I could probably get some friends of mine to track down the numbers. On television, they talk about burner phones and how they're untraceable. In reality, it's not quite so simple. Even a pay-as-you-go handset leaves a trail, and we shouldn't forget, I have photos and video footage of the people who visited, which will be a great help in matching names to faces.'

Marr felt a trickle of sweat run down the small of his back.

'Oh, I should probably also mention the two girls – Samantha tells me she is thirteen, and Katya is eleven – who are the real purpose of your calls. They're both in the care of some friends of mine now. Obviously, I'm not going to tell you who or where – suffice it to say, they're safe.'

Marr drained his glass.

'Katya says she was your favourite.'

'She's lying.' The words were out before he could stop them – a reflex action.

'Is that so?'

'I run a financial consulting agency. Luca Dovilla is a businessman. I manage his investments.'

'He must have quite a bit of money in your care to require three visits a week.'

'He does.'

'Do you mind if I have a glass of that whiskey?' Dunnigan asked suddenly.

'What?'

'I usually take a snifter about this time. Do you mind?'

'Help yourself.'

'Thank you.'

The cop stood and walked past him to the drinks cabinet. Marr heard the sound of whiskey being poured.

'Don't you think it's odd Luca operates out of a tiny house in Swords?' Dunnigan continued from behind him.

'He's frugal. Listen, I'm a busy man, and unless you have some kind of concrete proof of these allegations, I'd really like to cut this short.'

Tony never heard the criminologist move, but suddenly he was tipped over backwards in his chair, and there was a boot pressed hard on his windpipe. He struggled for a second, but it was no use. He couldn't breathe, and the pressure was so great he was sure his throat would be crushed. His vision grew dim and he knew he was going to black out when suddenly he was released, and beautiful, wonderful air rushed back into his lungs.

He rolled over, gasping for breath.

'I'm not really very good at violence,' Dunnigan said from somewhere above him. 'I don't like it, and in the past, I've usually allowed other people to do it for me.'

Marr sucked oxygen in and out, feeling life returning by degrees.

'But I have to be honest with you,' the criminologist continued, 'I've been kind of in a bad mood this past year or so, and I'm about ready to get my hands dirty. You seem like a good person to start on.'

'I can get you money,' he rasped, trying desperately to think. 'If you come with me to an ATM there's eighteen hundred I could withdraw right now.'

'You can get that much from a bank machine?' Dunnigan asked, disbelieving.

'I have three accounts. Let's go to the bank in the morning and you can have as much as you want.'

'You're digging yourself in deeper,' the criminologist said grimly.

Marr was almost crying now. 'What do you want, then?'

'Access.'

'To what?'

'The work you do that doesn't get discussed at board meetings.'

And just like that, Tony Marr understood what was going on.

6

TODDY KNEW HE HAD A LAST NAME, BUT HE HAD forgotten it.

At some point in his past he'd had a home and a family and gone to school, and he was sure there had been a job in there somewhere too, but that was all vague. In reality, it didn't matter. When he thought about the time before, which he did not like doing, all that came to him was terrible, crushing anxiety. So he made a conscious decision *not* to think about it.

His world now was manageable and safe. It consisted of a small area of the city around Pearse Street station. He had three different spots where he sat to beg, and two different locations (one for warm weather and a more sheltered place for when it got colder) where he slept. Some of the local shopkeepers were very kind to him and gave him food from time to time. In general, he was left alone.

Toddy had a good sleeping bag and a rucksack that contained two changes of clothes. He liked to read, and there was a second-hand bookshop on Capel Street that was run by a former nun, and she allowed him to swap titles when he was finished with them, so he always had something good to escape into.

Toddy didn't bother anyone, and so long as he kept his head down, no one bothered him.

He was sitting on one of the benches on Platform 3 of the railway station, reading Jane Austen, when Dunnigan found him.

'Hello, Toddy.'

He blinked up at the criminologist. He knew him but couldn't remember how. 'You're Davey.'

'I need your help,' the man he thought he knew said.

'Nobody needs Toddy's help.'

'I do,' Dunnigan reiterated, and opened his hand to reveal a USB stick.

7

DUNNIGAN BOUGHT A CHEAP LAPTOP AT A PAWN shop, then booked a room in a boarding house in Finglas – the criminologist knew enough about computers to know IP addresses could easily be traced and he wanted to make that as difficult as he could.

'Not sure Toddy can still do this,' the homeless man said as he sat down, cross-legged on the floor, the laptop open on his knees. 'Not sure he *wants* to.'

Dunnigan had purchased some essentials – sandwiches, beer, water, crisps and chocolate – and he spread them out on a towel on the floor within easy reach. Toddy had suggested the task might take a while.

'Of course you can. You used to be the best at this kind of thing.'

'The best?'

'Yes.'

'Toddy doesn't remember.'

'I think you do – but it hurts, so you choose not to. And that's okay. But see, this is *really* important.'

'Important how?'

'The drive I've given you contains passwords, dark web

43

locations and files that I'd like to get into,' Dunnigan said. 'No one can do this like you.'

'Okay.'

'Is there anything else you need?'

'Toddy can download all the software for the job. The flash drive is encrypted, but there are lots of key generators out there if you know where to look. Toddy is going to have to use two different routers to make sure no one can track what we're doing, but that's easy.'

'Okay, then,' Dunnigan said. 'Tell me when you're in, and we'll take it from there.'

Toddy ripped open a sandwich and began to clatter at the keys.

The criminologist watched him for a moment, then lay on the bed and went to sleep.

*

'We're in.' Toddy was shaking him gently.

Dunnigan stretched and pulled himself upright. The room was in darkness now, the only light emanating from the laptop screen. 'What time is it?'

'Toddy doesn't know.'

Dunnigan looked at his phone. It was 2.30 a.m. Toddy had been at work for almost twelve hours – the criminologist was surprised at how long he'd slept, but then, he'd barely closed his eyes in days. He probably needed the rest. 'Show me,' he said.

*

Tony Marr, it seemed, had not been as stupid as Dunnigan had taken him for. The flash drive contained thousands of pages of accounts, most of which belonged to businesses that had gone bankrupt during the recession that killed the Celtic Tiger.

'How much of this is there?' Dunnigan asked Toddy after an hour of fruitless scrolling.

'It's a fifteen-gig flash drive,' the homeless man said. 'That's a lot of file space.'

'I'm looking for pages that relate to the movement of people. Shipping records, flight times, letters, emails, that sort of thing. Or anything that mentions an organisation called the After Dark Campaign.'

'Toddy can create an engine to search for that.'

'Is it easy?'

'Toddy can do it.'

'You must be exhausted.'

'No. Toddy is having fun.'

'Oh.'

Dunnigan had been worried about approaching the man, whom he had first encountered during a case involving the transmission of child pornography via mainstream social media sites eight years ago. A programmer for one of the larger social media networks that had set up shop in Ireland during the boom, all too glad to avail of the generous tax incentives the government offered, Toddy had been instrumental in helping the tech squad shut down the pathways being used by the sex industry to peddle their misery in plain sight. The experience had broken him, however: Toddy had always suffered from crippling anxiety and bouts of overwhelming paranoia, conditions that made it difficult for him to hold down a home or a job, and the stress of helping the police had caused a serious breakdown.

The criminologist knew he shouldn't have brought the vulnerable hacker into this, but he needed the skills he possessed, and he needed them quickly. He did not have time for sentimentality. That said, he was glad the demands seemed not to have upset Toddy's delicate mental balance too badly.

Fifteen minutes later, the key-tapping stopped again.

'There are no files like what you're looking for.'

'You're sure?'

'Not on this drive, anyway.'

Dunnigan sighed and sat back, rubbing his eyes. 'Okay, Toddy. Thanks for your help.'

'But there is a portal. They could be through there.'

The criminologist looked up. 'What's a portal?'

'One of the pages has a link to a dark web location. You'd miss it if you didn't know what you were looking for, it's hidden in the middle of a list of other sites and data. Toddy can see by looking at the address that it's a hub site. The dark web is full of them, they're like traffic junctions, banks of information.'

'Can we access it?' Dunnigan asked.

'Toddy has already set up the routers. Just point and click.'

'Do it, then.'

It was as if they had stepped through the looking glass. The page that opened on the laptop's small screen was a constant scrolling stream, lime-green text against a black background. For a moment it looked almost pretty, a random pattern apparently constructed out of ancient hieroglyphs. Dunnigan blinked and the symbols seemed to coalesce into letters and numbers – domain addresses.

'What am I looking at?'

'This is a darknet site,' Toddy told him. Dunnigan noticed his speech seemed to normalise when he was discussing tech matters, as if this was his comfort zone. 'That means people who access it must have a particular type of software, and they have to know where they're going – darknet sites don't leave cookies and can't be stored as favourites like on the mainstream web. It's like a building up a laneway with an access code you have to punch to get in, so only people who have the address and the code can go inside.'

'And can anyone download the software?'

'Some routers, like Tor, are widely available, but they won't get you onto sites like this. It's much more specialised.'

And suddenly Dunnigan understood what he was seeing: moving across the screen in digital procession was the online location of file after file – Ernest Frobisher's kingdom was laid out before them.

Frobisher, the man whose foul empire, built on poverty and pain and human misery, had taken Beth and passed her from one owner to another as soon as she became too troublesome to be useful.

Within half an hour, it was clear that the world they had stumbled upon was vast and terrifying – some of the information available to them touched on truths neither man wanted to consider: services and facilities people with enough money could pay for that spoke of the most foul debasements of human nature.

'I'm looking for any information relating to Faringen in Greenland,' Dunnigan said after a while. 'That's the last place we know for certain my niece, Beth was sent.'

Toddy looked at him steadily for a moment.

'The niece you lost? The one in the papers?'

'Yes.'

'Why didn't you say?' Toddy said, and opened an admin window.

Five minutes later they knew where Beth had been sent next.

8

THE DIAMOND CLUB WAS LOCATED IN PECKHAM, London.

The main bar area was an artless strip club complete with a stage studded with imitations of the gemstone that gave the place its name. Tired-looking young women gyrated on the platform without enthusiasm. The walls were lined with booths where private lap dances could be purchased. The place looked like it had somehow escaped from the 1980s – it was all neon signs and disco balls, and a feeling of vague misery hung in the air like stale cigarette smoke.

Dunnigan had a non-alcoholic lager at the bar before motioning to one of the waitresses.

'How would a person get some ... um ... some private attention?' he asked.

The girl was perhaps twenty, a redhead wearing a black G-string, heels and nothing else.

'All he'd have to do is ask,' she said, winking at him.

'I think I just did.'

'Let me just leave these drinks with their rightful owners, and I'll be with you, okay, my love?'

She returned and led him by the hand to a broom-cupboard-sized cubicle which contained a single chair, upholstered in imitation leather.

'So, what would you like?' she asked, straddling him and putting her arms around his neck.

'Something you are unable to give me.'

'And what might that be? I'm up for almost anything.'

'Let's just say I'd like to be entertained by someone a bit … younger.'

The words resonated between them for a long moment. The redhead eyed him as if she was looking for something she had missed. Finally, she said, 'The fresh flesh is downstairs.'

'How do I get there?'

'You pay for the privilege. I'll send Jethro in. He'll fix you up.'

And she left him without looking back.

*

Jethro was a rat-faced man with a moustache, wearing a cheap suit. 'Five ton up front,' he said, without preamble.

Dunnigan took the five hundred from his wallet and handed it over.

'I'm gonna bring you to the basement, and you're gonna talk to a bloke named Harold. He'll do the paperwork and go through the rules for belowstairs. If you cause a fuss or step outta line, it'll be him you'll answer to.'

'I understand.'

Jethro made a face Dunnigan assumed was his attempt at a smile and led him back out into the club. 'This way.'

A door behind the bar opened onto a narrow stone corridor, which ended in a steep flight of stairs.

'Can't be too careful,' Jethro said conversationally. 'You'd be amazed how many ask for a young 'un, but – and don't take this the wrong way – a lot of 'em just seem plain dodgy. I gotta protect me business.'

At the bottom of the stairs was a grey metal safety door. Jethro rapped on it smartly. 'Which is why I have Harold. Enjoy yourself.'

And he started back up the way he had come. Dunnigan heard a key scraping in a lock, and then the door swung open, revealing one of the biggest men he had ever seen.

'You're Harold, I presume.'

He was perhaps six foot six in height and must have weighed three hundred pounds. He had a shaved head and a thick beard and was dressed in a baggy t-shirt and tracksuit bottoms. His bucket-sized feet were bare. 'If you'd follow me, please,' the behemoth said in surprisingly cultured tones.

Dunnigan was led along a hallway that had doors on each side. He glanced at the ceiling, paying particular attention to the corners. He couldn't see any security cameras – this didn't necessarily mean there weren't any, but he was going to have to risk it.

'My office is just this way.'

'And are these the rooms where the … um … employees work?'

'We'll discuss that in just a few moments,' Harold said, turning slightly and smiling.

Dunnigan took the opportunity and jammed the prongs of a police Taser into the huge man's solar plexus, disabling him immediately.

Harold made a kind of whooshing sound and went rigid. He jerked spasmodically, and when the criminologist released the trigger the big man went down and didn't move. Dunnigan paused for a moment (he had never used a Taser before and was quite pleased with the result) and then stepped over the limp form and walked quickly to the end of the hallway – a door had been left open, revealing a small office with a desk, chair, laptop and printer. Four mobile phones, two of which looked to be veritable antiques, were also on the desk. Dragging the prone Harold inside was not easy, but with no little effort he managed. Using his belt and bootlaces he tied him to the chair, then filled a cup from the water cooler outside and splashed some on the huge man's face to bring him back to awareness.

'I don't know you,' Harold said, when he had taken a few sips to quell the nausea.

'But I know you. Your name is Harold Wallace. You are a pimp, a pornographer and, by all accounts, a very unpleasant person. According to my research, you have been managing the child prostitutes in the Diamond Club for two decades.'

'And?'

'You seem very calm.'

'Struggling isn't going to help. I assume you're here looking for a sister or a nephew or a daughter. You're not the first and you won't be the last. Go on, ask me. I remember them all. You don't need to indulge in the indignity of torture – any information I can give you will be old news, so I'm happy to oblige.'

'Her real name was Beth Carlton – I don't know what you would have called her. She'd have been here in the late nineties, early two-thousands. Irish girl.'

'I think you must mean the problem child. She didn't last long. Came from somewhere in Scandinavia and was damaged goods when we got her. Put one of our regulars in hospital.'

Dunnigan felt something shift in the base of his stomach.

'What do you mean she didn't last long?'

'We sent her on.'

'Where?'

'Where else? Back where she came from, and into the kind of work where she wouldn't be a problem for long.'

*

He sat in his rental car an hour later and watched as the police raided the club. When the first of the children was brought out, a boy who looked to be perhaps six years old, he drove away, wishing he had given Harold Wallace a few more blasts of the Taser.

Then he rang an old friend and organised a raid of his own.

9

DIANE ROBINSON WAS DRESSED IN A BLACK hoody and skinny jeans. Her long blonde hair was tied back in a tight ponytail, and she had a black woollen hat pulled down over her ears. Beside her, similarly attired, was Captain Sean Murtaugh, late of the Irish Army Ranger Wing. Both were sipping coffee from cardboard cups. Over the stereo, Tom Petty and the Heartbreakers were singing about the great wide open.

Dunnigan, dressed as he usually was (in a rare effort to conform he had put a black t-shirt with a line drawing of Darth Vader on under his grey coat), sat behind them, jiggling his leg nervously.

They were in the back of a van with blacked-out windows parked outside the gates of a large mansion house in rural County Galway. It was three o'clock on a Sunday morning, a week after Dunnigan had returned from London.

It had taken him longer than he expected to follow the circuitous trafficking routes to this location, and now that he was here, it filled him with dread.

'This is a bad place,' Murtaugh said in his broad Limerick accent. 'I've asked around, and that house contains women who are worth less on the open market than dogs – and I mean that literally. You would pay more for a Jack Russell.'

Murtaugh had been Diane's commander when she served as a field medic for the Rangers (the Irish Special Forces) in Chad, and he had been stationed in Somalia before that. He was fifty-nine years old, ran a private security company and looked as if he was hewn from solid granite – he was all angles and coarse surfaces, his bald head dark and stubbled, his cheekbones sharp and prominent. Diane believed him to be the toughest man she had ever met.

'I know,' Dunnigan said. 'It's why I asked Diane for help. I didn't want to go in there on my own. I was afraid of what I'd find.'

'You were right to call,' Diane agreed.

'I don't know what we're going to find,' Murtaugh said. 'These poor creatures have been used up by various industries, not just sex, and are rented out to whoever needs them. They're commodities who stopped having an identity years ago.'

'Everyone has an identity so long as people care about them,' Dunnigan said, but the words sounded hollow, even to him.

'Not these women. If some pimp needs a body no one will ever come looking for, he'll be sent one of these. A mushroom farmer needs extra staff to bring in the crop, people who will work twenty-hour days and sleep on sacks on the floor? One or two of these women will arrive. This is the lowest level of the skin trade. They aren't expected to live very long.'

Someone knocked on the vehicle's rear door and the former soldier pushed it open. Stephen, one of Murtaugh's employees, peered in: six feet tall and also dressed for night manoeuvres, he was built like a rugby player and had an Uzi semi-automatic slung across his shoulder. 'There are six men inside, four of them armed, but they aren't expecting a planned assault. We should do this now'

'And the women?'

'Vic has been scoping out the place. He says there are ten of them and three young men.'

'Thank you, Stephen.'

'What kind of shape are they in?' Dunnigan asked as they stepped from the van.

'Impossible to say until we get inside,' Stephen retorted. 'We can have it secured in five minutes if you'd like to wait.'

'No, thank you,' Dunnigan said. 'I'd prefer to come along.'

'You'll be wanting this, then,' Murtaugh said, offering the criminologist a Glock 15 handgun.

Dunnigan looked at the weapon with distaste. 'I don't really like guns,' he said tetchily.

'We are going into a gunfight,' Diane said patiently. 'In my experience, a gun is usually a prerequisite.'

'Thank you, but no thank you.'

'Will I tell my men to put their firearms down too?' Murtaugh asked, incredulous.

'That won't be necessary.'

'So it's okay for them to shoot on your behalf?'

Dunnigan ignored him. 'Can we just get going?'

'Is he always like this?' Murtaugh asked Diane.

'Sometimes, he's worse,' Diane said. 'I'll take responsibility for him.'

Murtaugh gave the criminologist a hard look. 'You'd better not get us killed. Lead on, Stephen.'

A ladder had been placed against the high wall, and once over it they found themselves in a grove of trees, bordering an overgrown lawn. The house itself was vast and crumbling. It had once been a stately home for Anglo-Irish gentry but was now in an advanced state of disrepair – many of the windows were cracked or broken; several boarded up.

'This way,' Stephen said, and jogged along the treeline for a hundred yards.

Eight more men, similarly attired in black jeans and jackets and all armed, were clustered in the shadows.

'What's the plan, gentlemen?' Murtaugh asked in a whisper.

'Go in hard and fast,' a short, wiry, shaven-headed man with an English accent said. 'Give them no time to think.'

'Three through the front door, two apiece through side windows to the east and west and Toby there from the roof.' Stephen nodded at a young man who looked to be no more than five foot three in height.

'Let's do it, then,' Murtaugh said. 'Darth Vader, if you are determined to continue this nonsense about not having a weapon, I strongly recommend you remain at the rear of the action.'

'Agreed,' Dunnigan said, without hesitation.

'Alright. Advance.'

They moved forward in a surge, four men peeling off to create the left and right flank of the pincer movement. Dunnigan watched as the diminutive Toby scaled the drainpipe hand over hand with remarkable ease, pulling himself onto the roof. When he was atop it, he gave a hand signal, and the remaining men, Diane easily keeping pace, charged the front door, which gave with a crash that sounded earth-shattering in the night-time silence.

The entrance hall was in total darkness. The sound of glass breaking and booted feet on tiles echoed throughout the old building. Then there were shouts, and the sounds of gunfire. A light went on at the end of the downstairs hallway, and voices could be heard raised in alarm.

'Deal with that, Stephen,' Murtaugh hissed.

A door was flung open, but before anyone could emerge, Murtaugh's men had sprayed the area with bullets.

With a bellowing roar, a thickly muscled man wearing only a pair of boxer shorts, his upper torso covered in tattoos, charged out of a room to their left. He was waving a hurley, and made a lunge at Dunnigan, who was closest to him. Panicking, the criminologist drove his elbow into the man's stomach, but it seemed to have little effect. With another wordless shout, the thug swung his weapon, connecting with Dunnigan's left shoulder, which went numb immediately. Suddenly, Diane was at his side. With a short, punching motion she lashed out with the heel of her right hand, chopping into his attacker's windpipe. This, thankfully, worked and, gagging, the man fell back, grabbing at his Adam's apple.

Stepping forward, Murtaugh shot him in the forehead.

'Now, did you really need to do that?' Dunnigan asked, vexed.

'Yes,' Murtaugh replied, deadpan, and followed the others deeper into the house.

'It's big boy rules, Davey,' Diane said, and hurried after her former captain.

'We're all clear downstairs,' Stephen said, as they came into a dishevelled-looking kitchen. 'Toby has upstairs secure too. If you hang on here, we'll do a quick recce just to be sure.'

He returned five minutes later. 'All threats have been neutralised.'

'Thank you, Stephen. Get the lads together and make sure the place is clean, I don't want anyone knowing we were here.'

'We've brought the ... um ... the individuals you were concerned about into the dining room for you to have a chat with.'

'How do they seem?' Dunnigan asked.

'They're skinny, but in reasonable health,' the operative said. 'Physically, at least.'

'What are you saying?'

'It's kind of like they don't really give a fuck – begging your pardon, ma'am.'

Murtaugh gave his man a hard look, but Diane waved it off.

Stephen led them through to a room with a long table and chairs. A group of people in flimsy night-gear were huddled together near an unlit fireplace.

'Could someone get us some tea?' Diane asked. 'It'll help put them at their ease.'

'Get Phil to make a pot, will you, Stephen?' Murtaugh said. 'And see if there are any buns or something.'

Dunnigan approached the group. 'Do you all speak English?' he asked tentatively.

Some blank stares, but most of the heads nodded.

'I want you to know that you are not in any danger from us – you're all free to go. My friends and I will help you find your families, if that's what you want. I know you've all had a horrible time, and there isn't much I can do to fix that. All I *can* do is promise that you're safe now.'

This speech was met with silence and wide eyes. Dunnigan

wasn't sure what he had expected, so he just ploughed on. 'I'm looking for someone in particular. Her name is Beth – Beth Carlton, and her family very much want her back.'

More silence. The group looked at one another, and then back at the criminologist. No one moved or said anything.

'I'm sorry,' Diane said. 'Maybe one of them will remember something, given time.'

Dunnigan nodded and sat down on the edge of the table. He was out of ideas. The trail, which he had been following since that awful day eighteen years ago, had finally gone completely cold.

'Davey?'

He looked up. A painfully thin, hollow-eyed young woman with jet-black hair had her hand raised, like a child might in school. He suddenly felt very strange.

'How do you know my name?'

'I'm sorry, but … I think I used to be called Beth.'

Dunnigan stood up and looked at her more closely. Could it be? The colouring was right, as were the eyes.

'I … I think I used to have a family.'

'I don't fucking believe it,' Diane muttered, her hand on Dunnigan's shoulder. 'It can't be ….'

'You were taking me to see Santa,' the girl said, and then, as if something inside her had broken, her face creased up and she fell to her knees, sobs cascading from her as if nothing would ever stop them.

During the summer of 1998, in a quiet village near Dorking, the charred body of a man was found inside the kitchen stove of a small farmhouse. A video camera was also found in the kitchen, standing on a tripod, pointing at the oven. No tape was found inside the camera.

Although the scene was originally labelled as a homicide by police, an unmarked VHS tape was later discovered at the bottom of the farm's well, which had apparently dried up earlier that year.

Despite its worn condition, police were able to view the contents of the tape, after which the decision was made not to share the details of what it contained with the public.

The video depicted a man standing in the kitchen of the farmhouse, apparently recording himself using the same camera the police had found. After positioning the camera to include both himself and the kitchen stove in its view, the man stripped naked and turned on the oven. Then he spoke: 'Mother Joan told me to do this.'

The man then opened the oven door – it could be seen that all shelves had been removed, so he could just squeeze inside – crawled in and closed the door behind him. Ten minutes into the video, a wailing was heard coming from the oven, and the structure could be seen shaking violently. The screaming got progressively worse until at seventeen minutes and fifteen seconds, it stopped. Black smoke began to emanate from the door. For the remaining forty-five minutes of video, until the batteries in the camera died, it remained in its stationary position.

Just before the camera lost all power, a strange figure moved into view. Seemingly very tall, the person was dressed in a long cape with a hood covering the face. The figure was seen to lean down, as if looking through the heatproof glass panel in the oven door, and then back towards the camera, getting closer and closer until nothing but blackness filled the screen. At that point the battery gave out.

The police never released any information about the tape, or even the fact that it was found. Files show that the investigating officers were unable to determine who put the tape in the well, or why the height and stature of the man in the video did not even come close to matching the body that they had found in the oven, meaning this was at least the second death of this kind to have happened at the location. The case remains open, but unsolved.

Posted by hacker_red
www.wickedwords.com

Part Two

THE RETURN

Yuri Chechnik

They told him it would be an easy job.

He had come to Ireland from Romania as a scout for the Volatov family in 2003, and found a land ripe for the plunder. The people were soft and lazy and the biggest gangsters he had to contend with were idiot politicians who thought they were far smarter than they really were.

He spent two years establishing a network, letting the locals know he was serious. The first bit of resistance he encountered was from a Traveller clan in the Ballymun area of Dublin, who thought they had control of the territory. He and three associates visited their halting site one night. They woke the patriarch and his wife and held them at gunpoint while they torched every trailer in the place and shot anyone who made it out of the flames alive.

'I know you have a big family and many friends,' Yuri said to the man, who was weeping and holding his fat wife as they knelt on the tarmac. 'You tell them what you have seen tonight. Tell them that if I have to visit any of them, I will fuck their children before I burn them.'

No one contested their authority after that.

Within three years he had earned his bosses a huge amount of money, and their organisation controlled all the drugs – and, more importantly, all the guns – that came in through the east coast of Ireland. As they became more successful, his role cemented into that of a troubleshooter – where there were glitches within the wider organisation, he would be sent to sort the problems out.

When he was asked to go to Galway, where one of the service agencies was failing to turn a profit, he thought nothing of it – whores, serfs and domestic staff at this level were effectively a disposable commodity. To make money out of them, there needed to be a rapid turnover: send them out, use them up, move them on.

Then restock.

He suspected someone in the front office was getting sentimental. He would have to bang a few heads together and shake things up.

On arrival, Yuri discovered he was absolutely correct.

Records showed that three of the women had been in the Galway shipping centre for three months – they had been sent back with complaints from customers twice.

'This is not good enough,' Yuri had ranted. 'Girl cause you problems, shoot her in the head and get other girl. Simple!'

He informed the men running the place that he would be implementing a rigorous upskilling regimen, starting the next day, and suggested they all get an early night – he had big plans and they would need all their faculties about them.

Gunfire woke him, and, creeping from his room, he found an army invading the house. He saw red (he had always had a temper), grabbed a hurl someone had left lying around, and charged. By the time he realised this was no ordinary group of incompetent Irish criminals, it was too late.

The flash of the gun muzzle was the last thing he remembered.

He should have died, but the devil had other plans for him.

He returned to consciousness an indeterminate amount of time later to find he was secured to a wooden chair with cable ties, and there was a tall, slim man seated opposite him. It seemed this gentleman believed Yuri was involved in the attack on the house and wished to find out who he was working for, so rather than taking their best troubleshooter to a hospital, his superiors felt it was a better plan to torture him.

This was his reward for years of faithful service and for having the temerity to be the only one to survive the attack.

There was a bitter irony to the situation, although it would be some time before he was able to laugh at it.

'I am Yuri Chechnik. I am captain with Romanian Volatov family,' was all he would tell them. He said it repeatedly; he screamed it.

The slim man stayed sitting and watched while his men worked. Occasionally he asked questions, none of which made any sense to Yuri.

Had Yuri told anyone about the After Dark Campaign?

Did Yuri mention the name Ernest Frobisher to his new employers?

Yuri had never heard of the After Dark Campaign, and he did not know anyone with the ridiculous moniker of Ernest Frobisher. But it would have made no difference if he had.

He answered all with his name and his rank.

Like a good soldier.

He laughed when they took his right eye.

He was still laughing when they used crocodile clips to attach him to the electricity supply.

1

FATHER BILL ARRANGED FOR THE SLAVE WORKERS
to be brought to a convent in Galway, and Murtaugh and
his men offered to transport them in their vehicles. Diane
and Dunnigan, with the girl who said she was Beth, booked
adjoining rooms in a hotel a little outside the city.

'Are you sure it's her this time?' she asked him.

'Yes.'

'And you know that how?'

'I can't explain it, other than to say I do. I feel it in my
bones. It's her.'

'Alright. Murtaugh has called Tormey, but he's agreed to
keep it on a need-to-know basis for now, at least.'

'Thank you.'

'I'll be here if you need me.'

'I know.'

*

He knocked on the door of the girl's room. There was no
reply, so he pushed it open gently.

'Um … Beth … it's me. Davey.'

She was sitting on the bed, her knees pulled up to her chin.

'How are you?' he asked, for want of anything else to say.

'You look older,' she said, almost matter-of-factly. 'You have a beard now.'

Dunnigan's hand went to his face. He had not shaved since leaving Dublin over three months ago, and he suddenly realised how different he must look to her. 'Yes. I'm sorry.'

She looked quizzical. 'Why are you sorry?'

He took a step forward, his heart pounding. There was so much he had wanted to say. He had rehearsed this moment a hundred times in his head, but now that it was here his mind had gone blank and his tongue wouldn't work. 'I'm sorry ... for everything,' he said finally.

She sighed and fiddled with the hem of her sleeve, a movement he recognised – she used to do that when she was thinking. She was wearing a pink tracksuit that was several sizes too large, and it made her look even more like a shy child. 'You were going to take me to see Santa,' she said again, as if this fact was all that was grounding her.

'Yes. We were supposed to get presents for ... for your mum and dad.'

'My mum ....' She said the word as if it belonged to a foreign language.

'We should never have stopped to listen to the carollers.' Dunnigan's voice seemed very small in the room.

'Why not?' she asked, still focused on her sleeve. 'The music was pretty.'

He felt as if his throat was constricting. 'That was when ... when they took you. Don't you remember?'

She raised her head. Her eyes were huge and liquid. 'Of course I remember. They told me you didn't want me anymore.'

'That was never, ever true. You know that, don't you?'

She nodded. 'I didn't believe them. They tried to make me say it, but I wouldn't.'

'I really tried to find you. I swear to you, I did.'

'I know that. I always believed you'd come. Every day I waited for someone to bring me back home. It got so there were times I didn't know where "home" was, but sooner or later I was sure it would happen.'

'I'm sorry,' he said again, and it was just a croak now.

'Why?' she asked again.

'I looked and I looked, but I couldn't find you.'

'But Davey, you *did* find me,' she said.

He tried to say something, but no more words would come, and he couldn't see because he was blinded by tears, and then the two of them were holding one another and it didn't matter anymore.

2

TIME PASSED.

The texture of light in the room changed to a dusky grey, but they stayed huddled on the floor beside the bed. Dunnigan was afraid that, if he let her go, she would disappear all over again, and he did not think he could survive that.

'I want to see my mother,' Beth said, after a while.

'Of course. I'll see if we can get her here,' he said, stroking her hair gently.

He told himself he hadn't called his sister because he wanted to be sure this girl really was his niece, but in a deeper part of him, there was a part that wanted some time with her, just for himself. He didn't want to explore that part too deeply, but he knew it was there.

'Soon?'

'Yes. As soon as I can. I promise.'

'And my dad?'

'Of course.'

He didn't tell her that he and her father were on hostile terms (their last interaction involved Clive Carlton physically attacking him while he shopped for fruit at the Henry Street Market), or that her parents were separated. There was time enough for these realities over the days and weeks to follow.

'Davey?'

'Yes, Beth?'

'This is real, isn't it? I'm not dreaming it all?'

'It's real. You're safe, and I am not going to allow anything bad to happen to you ever again. I promise you that.'

Those words would return to haunt him many times as the darkness closed in.

3

TORMEY, WHO HAD RUNG WHILE DUNNIGAN WAS
with Beth, offered to pick up Gina and bring her to Galway.
He told Diane that he had informed the police commissioner
that Beth had been found, and that there was serious concern
for her safety – Murtaugh had left sketchy details of her
rescue, but he made it known that the gang who had held her
might not be happy with the situation and could try to get her
back. A patrol car was duly placed outside Gina's house, and
men from the Rapid Response Unit took up positions about
the hotel. If the After Dark Campaign attempted to reclaim
Beth, they would have to do so while contending with a tight
dragnet of cops.

Gina arrived looking pale and anxious. Hotel management
had given the police a room on the same corridor as Beth's
which they were using as a base of operations, and she came
in without saying a word and dumped her handbag on the
table. She gave Dunnigan a hard look. Gina was slender like
her brother and striking rather than pretty. When it came to
personal grooming she was his polar opposite, dressed in a
crisp white shirt and designer jeans, her dark hair cut short
and tight to her head.

'What's going on, Davey?' she said at last. 'Frank won't tell me anything. He just said to come right away.'

'You should probably sit down.'

All the colour drained from her face.

'She's dead, isn't she? You found the men who took her and she's dead.'

'No. It might be better if I just show you.'

It was a painful reunion. Dunnigan was surprised, and a little frightened, by how these two women, whom he loved more than his own life, seemed so stricken. He sat on the bed as they held one another and his sister wept and he wondered if there would ever be a bottom to this well of grief.

He had thought there would be so much joy, but if there was, he had failed to find it.

'You're mourning all the years you've lost,' Diane said to him later that night when he haltingly mentioned it to her. Beth had fallen asleep, exhausted by the emotional turmoil of the day.

Diane and Dunnigan were no longer a couple (the horrors they had experienced in the hunt for Beth had been too awful for their relationship to withstand), although they both acknowledged (she verbally, he not so much) that they still loved one another.

'You've found her after all these years, which is a miracle in itself. Over time you'd built up the idea that finding her would take away all the pain and fear and dread you'd been carrying around. But of course, it hasn't. You don't have the little girl back. You have a damaged, half-terrified woman who has suffered unspeakable things.'

'Don't say that.'

'You know it's the truth, Davey. This is the beginning of

a long, difficult journey. You can't take away all the dreadful stuff that has to have happened to her. All you can do is be there while she processes it.'

They were lying side by side on the floor, more tired than they could ever remember being, but unable to sleep.

'*Can* she process what she's been through?' Dunnigan asked. 'I mean, do people come back from events like this?'

'That's one of those "yes and no" answers we therapists love,' Diane said. She propped herself up on an elbow and looked at him. Her blonde hair had fallen loose, and he was struck by how beautiful she was. 'With love and support – which she has an awful lot of – she can learn not to be afraid anymore. Will she still have nightmares and the occasional panic attack? Maybe she will, maybe she won't. Is she likely to still harbour some anger? She wouldn't be a normal person if she didn't.'

'She seems so calm – it's like she's a little bit distant from everything.'

'That's normal. She's desensitised – it's a way of protecting herself from emotional and physical pain. I used to see it in soldiers suffering post-traumatic stress disorder. She's basically shut a part of herself down. It'll come back eventually.'

'We just need to take it one day at a time, is what you're saying.'

'There's no other way *to* take it, Davey.'

Sleep finally took them a short while later. At some point during the night, he reached out and she took his hand.

4

TORMEY, ALONG WITH A FEMALE DETECTIVE
Dunnigan knew was named Cindy Byrne, visited Beth for
brief periods over the first few days to try and get a sense of
where she had been, who her captors were and what she had
been forced to do. The girl seemed unable or unwilling to talk
much about any of this, and the chief told the criminologist
that while they would have to get a formal statement at some
point, it could wait until she was feeling more able.

A medical examination was scheduled, and Diane and Gina
drove her to University Hospital Galway. Dunnigan knew
such an appointment was essential – along with malnutrition
there was the risk of sexually transmitted infections. He
had no desire to go along himself and hear about the results
first-hand – there were some things he preferred to keep at a
vague distance.

But that didn't mean he wasn't actively involved.

*

During the years of her captivity, Beth had dreamed about
many things, but the one she wished for more than any other
was to be able to watch *Doctor Who* with her uncle. It had

been a ritual they had shared, and it was one of the first things she asked to do when they were reunited.

Back then the show had been off the air, and she and Dunnigan had watched old video tapes he had collected of the classic series – her favourite had been Tom Baker's Fourth Doctor with his booming voice and fabulous scarf.

Beth was amazed and delighted to discover that this programme, which she had always considered was a secret only she and her uncle shared, was back on television every week, and had become a worldwide phenomenon.

She had missed four new doctors, and (she thought this must be a joke, but Davey promised her it wasn't) the current one was a woman.

'I really like the Twelfth Doctor,' her uncle said. He had his battered laptop, and the two were perched together side by side on the bed in Beth's room. 'The actor who plays him is called Peter Capaldi, and in my opinion he has gone old-school with his performance.'

This Doctor (she told Dunnigan) reminded her a bit of Tom Baker. He was quite old, his clothes were quirky but cool, and he had no patience with anyone. But he was good and kind and he always did the right thing no matter what the cost.

'Where would you go if you had a TARDIS?' she asked Davey during the second episode.

He pushed the space bar to pause the programme. 'I don't know. Where would you go?'

'You first.'

'Okay.' He put his arm around her. 'The TARDIS can take you anywhere in time and space, so mine is a where and a when.'

'Alright.'

'Stephen's Green, December the eighth, 1998.'

She watched him. His voice had become very hoarse, and she knew he was struggling to speak.

'I would stand at the door to the Stephen's Green Centre and wait for you and me to go past.'

'Would you?'

'Yes. I can just see us now: you in your purple jacket and your pink mittens, me holding your hand tightly. We stopped just at that spot, near the newsagent's, and you asked if we could listen to the music.'

'I remember.'

'I'd run over and drag us both into the TARDIS and take us far away until that day was over.'

'What then?'

'That's easy. I'd drop us back down in our lives, and you would have a proper childhood and I could see you grow up and all the bad things would never have happened.'

She laid her head on his shoulder.

'Your turn,' he said. 'Where and when?'

'That's easy,' she said. 'Right here, right now.'

5

THREE DAYS LATER THEY LEFT THE HOTEL, AND Beth returned with Gina to the house she had called home during the four years before that fateful December eighth. Clive was there to meet them. He had visited several times during their stay in Galway, but he seemed to find the whole process deeply unsettling. Keeping the hostility he felt for Dunnigan (not to mention his wife) at bay appeared to require a huge effort, and his anger was regularly all too obvious, even towards Beth.

'I wanted to keep your room just as it was, but we moved to London two years after … after you went away, and your mother had the place redecorated so we could put it up for rent,' Clive said as he brought Beth to where she had once slept.

'It looks so much smaller,' the girl said.

'That'll be the aqua marine paint,' Clive sniffed.

'Or the fact that you're so much bigger than you were the last time you were here,' Gina said gently. 'Now you're back we can decorate it any way you want.'

Beth was standing motionless in the doorway, as if passing

in to her childhood bedroom was a terrifying thing. 'I don't think I want to sleep here,' she said.

'But this is your room,' Clive said. 'Of course you want to.'

'I don't like it,' Beth said and, turning on her heel, she bolted.

'I told you we should never have touched the place,' Clive snapped at Gina, and followed his daughter.

Dunnigan hung back, feeling unhappy and out of place.

*

Gina made spaghetti Bolognese, which had been Beth's favourite, for lunch. They sat at the dining room table, and Dunnigan could not help but remember the last meal they had shared, two days before his niece vanished. The world had seemed so different then – safer and full of possibility.

'What would you like to drink, Beth?' Clive asked. 'We have wine, red or white. Or there's water or juice.'

The girl had her hands resting flat on the table top, eyeing the food nervously. She had put on a little weight in the days since Dunnigan and Diane found her, and Gina had bought her some new, better-fitting clothes. Dunnigan, who was sitting opposite her, was forced to remind himself that she was now twenty-two years old. When he looked at her, though, he still saw the child she had been, albeit wearing the body of a young woman.

Beth was taller than her mother by about three inches and had clever, musician's fingers. Her dark hair reached almost to the small of her back. She had a nervous habit of tucking it behind her ears, and even though she tended to wear a bobbin around her left wrist, Dunnigan had never seen her tie it back

– she tended to drape it over her left shoulder if she needed it out of the way.

The most remarkable thing about the girl, though, were her eyes. They were the same blue as Dunnigan's and Gina's, and there was a steeliness and intelligence about them that was electric to behold. As Diane pointed out, this was a person who had survived, against all odds, things that would have killed most people. That truth lived in those eyes.

'Are you listening to me, Beth?' Clive asked sharply. 'I asked you what you'd like to drink.'

'Um … can I have tea please?'

Her father sniffed. 'Well, we would usually have that after our meal.'

'For God's sake, just give the girl a cup of tea!' Gina snapped, and went to fill the kettle.

'I'd like one too,' Dunnigan said, winking at his niece, who smiled wanly back at him.

Clive snorted and picked up his fork.

*

Beth ate four helpings of Bolognese followed by two bowls of raspberry ripple ice-cream and was sick afterwards.

They sat in the living room, and the sound of the girl retching could be heard from the toilet down the hall.

'I'm going to say something, and I know you're both thinking it,' Clive said, through gritted teeth.

'If we're all thinking it, why say it at all?' Dunnigan said.

'Fuck you,' Clive responded, without missing a beat. 'I don't care what kind of delusions you're both experiencing, but that girl is not my daughter.'

'Yes, she is,' Gina said. 'In your heart, Clive, you know it.'

'I'm not going to continue playing this game,' he said, and stormed out.

'I should have expected that,' Gina said quietly.

'I did,' Dunnigan said. 'There's a sample of her DNA being tested as we speak.'

Gina looked at her brother in disbelief. 'When were you going to tell me that little nugget of information?'

'When I got confirmation of what we both already know.'

They heard the toilet flushing and taps running.

'And do we know?' Gina asked, as the key turned in the bathroom door.

'Yes,' Dunnigan said. 'We do.'

'Then why did you have them run the test?'

'They would have done it anyway,' Dunnigan said. 'I thought I might as well get out in front of it.'

*

Two days later the results of the DNA test, performed by Doctor Georgina Russell in the labs of Forensic Science Ireland in the Phoenix Park, were emailed to Dunnigan. Doctor Russell had compared skin cells swabbed from the girl's cheek with a strand of hair kept on file, a follicle the police had taken from Beth's hairbrush the day after her abduction. The test confirmed that the girl David Dunnigan and Diane Robinson had rescued from a slave den in Galway was a one hundred per cent match for the child that had been taken from Grafton Street on the eighth of December 1998.

There could now be no doubt at all: Beth Carlton had been found.

Gina informed Clive by text, but he did not respond.

Just before midnight, write your full name on a piece of paper, prick your finger with a pin, and let a spot of your blood soak into the paper – names are powerful things, magic spells in themselves. Never forget that.

Turn off all the lights in your house, go to a wooden door, close it, and place the piece of paper in front of it. Light a candle and place it on top of the paper. Knock on the door twenty-two times, and the twenty-second knock must occur at the stroke of midnight. Open the door, put the piece of paper inside, blow out the candle and close the door again. Relight the candle immediately; now the game can begin.

The incantation you have just performed summons an entity called Mother Joan. For the next three and a half hours you and she will play a game of hide and seek, moving throughout your home while making sure you never, ever run into one another.

There are a few protections, which you will need – if your candle blows out, lighting it within ten seconds will keep her at bay; additionally, drawing a circle of salt and staying inside it will keep you safe, as she cannot enter it. Some say that, if she catches you, you can buy your soul back by telling her a secret. The game is over at 3.33 a.m. If you managed to evade capture, congratulations! You win. If you didn't ... I'm sorry. I'm so very, very sorry.

Oh, and lastly? Don't assume that Mother Joan has left the

building when the game is over. In fact, now you've summoned her, don't assume she will ever leave.

Now she knows your name, she'll be with you forever.

Because names are powerful things.

Posted by hacker_red
www.wickedwords.com

6

DUNNIGAN STAYED WITH GINA AND BETH, bringing over a bag of clothes and sleeping in Beth's old room – she seemed happier on the couch, so Gina just made a bed up for her there every night.

The first evening Dunnigan stayed he was woken at two in the morning by a piercing scream. When he got to the living room, Gina was already there.

'She had a bad dream,' his sister said, rocking the girl like a baby.

Gina remained with her the rest of that night. Dunnigan found them, his sister still cradling her daughter, when he got up to make tea at seven thirty.

*

Two nights later he opened his eyes just as it was getting light, to see Beth standing beside his bed.

'Are you okay?' he asked, before realising the girl was still asleep.

He gently led her back to the couch, where she lay down wordlessly.

On another occasion he was awake, reading, when he

heard the front door opening. He caught her as she was walking across the lawn, tears streaming from eyes that were tight shut.

*

Dunnigan called Diane – who as well as having a medical degree was a qualified psychotherapist – to come over and give them some advice. She arrived before work the following morning, and they chatted while Beth was in the shower.

'Sleep disturbance is a pretty standard part of post-traumatic stress,' she told them. 'Frankly, I'm surprised it's so mild.'

'How can we help her?' Gina asked. 'I mean, she wakes up every morning with rings under her eyes – I don't think she's getting any rest at all.'

'You're already doing all the right things,' Diane said. 'You're not making a big deal out of it. You're comforting her, making sure she doesn't come to any harm during her nocturnal rambles. There's not a lot more you can do.'

'Maybe we need to get her out of the house,' Gina said. 'I mean, we're cooped up here like three battery chickens.'

'Tormey says it's as safe as it's going to be,' Dunnigan agreed. 'There's been no sign of anyone watching us.'

'And she needs a load of stuff,' Gina said. 'You know, I think we could all do with a little retail therapy.'

'Could we?' Dunnigan asked nervously.

*

Despite his reservations, they went to Dundrum that afternoon. Dunnigan drove his 1983 BMW 3 Series and they listened to Top 40 radio all the way there. Gina was sad to see that Beth did not seem to know any of the songs, although she gamely tried to sing along. They parked in the underground complex.

'Spring is coming, and you need a whole new wardrobe,' Gina told her daughter as Dunnigan went and got the parking ticket. 'And we should also talk about makeup and hair products. And you could do with a phone.'

'I've never had a phone,' Beth squealed in delight. 'Can I really get one?'

'Of course you can,' Gina laughed, hugging her. 'Davey and I will have to go back to work sooner or later, and I'll want to be able to call you any time I wish.'

'You're going to be leaving me?' A look of deep anxiety clouded Beth's face.

'No one said anything about abandoning you,' Dunnigan said, returning from the parking meter. 'But your mum, as you know, is a schoolteacher, and I teach college and work with the police. We've both been given some time off, but *eventually* we're going to have to go back or they'll stop paying us. You'll probably want to do something during the day too. Maybe take a course, or you could get a job yourself.'

'What kind of a job could I do?' Beth asked, looking interested. 'All I've ever done is … well – you know.'

'And you'll never have to do that again,' Gina said, her voice breaking slightly as she steered her daughter towards the doors of the shopping area. 'But no more about that now. Let the shopping commence!'

*

At first the crowds seemed to overwhelm Beth, but Gina's encouragement, and the fact that Dunnigan held her hand and refused to let go unless she needed to try something on, helped her relax. They stopped after an hour and a half, in which (it seemed to Dunnigan, at least) the two girls bought enough garments to fill twenty wardrobes to capacity, and took refuge in a café.

'Are you sure you wouldn't like something other than tea?' Gina asked as she scanned the menu, while Dunnigan tried to arrange all their shopping bags in the booth around them. 'You used to be a big fan of hot chocolate.'

Beth shook her head vigorously. 'I don't like chocolate anymore.'

'Really? You didn't used to be able to get enough of the stuff.'

'I like tea. They used chocolate as a reward.'

Gina froze. 'The men … I mean, the people who took you?'

Beth nodded.

'If you did what they wanted, you got chocolate or toys or the older kids got clothes – never money, because you weren't allowed to go anywhere to spend it. If you didn't do what they wanted, you got beaten. Or worse.'

Gina looked as if she was about to throw up. Around them in the restaurant people went about their lives and ordered food and had conversations and laughed and chatted as though nothing bad ever happened. Dunnigan cleared his throat loudly. 'Well, I like tea too,' he said. 'Where do you stand on the issue of cake, Beth?'

'Cake is good,' she giggled. 'Lemon is my favourite.'

'Let's see if they have any of that.'

They did – a wonderful, moist lemon drizzle cake. Dunnigan chatted inanely to Beth about the relative merits of Victoria sponge and Battenburg and pretended he hadn't noticed that Gina was crying gently to herself.

7

IF THE PHONE SHOP HADN'T HAD HUGE GLASS windows overlooking the second-floor shopping area, it might never have happened.

They agreed it wasn't a good idea to get Beth a smartphone, primarily because she wouldn't have a clue what to do with one, and also Dunnigan was worried she might work out the benefits of such a device rather quickly and become a safety risk.

To his and Gina's dismay, the staff in the store (both of whom looked as if they should still be in secondary school) seemed not to understand what they meant when they asked for a phone with no internet capacity.

'You could just, like, shut down your social media apps,' the spotty young man said. 'I mean, you don't wanna *uninstall* them – what would you do when you wanna use them again?'

'I had a boyfriend once who came off Instagram for, like, two weeks or something,' the spotty young girl piped up. 'It *totally* decimated his list of followers. I'm telling you, it was *not* worth it.'

'Listen to me,' Dunnigan said, trying to be patient. 'Imagine someone who has never owned a mobile phone before and has no knowledge of the internet, never mind social media. What phone would you give them?'

The pair blinked dumbly at him.

'I don't think a person like that exists, dude,' the spotty young man said. 'I mean, maybe in the furthest reaches of the Amazon or somewhere with really bad Wi-Fi ...'

And then Beth started screaming. There was no warning, no gradual build-up – the girl went from calm normality to terrified frenzy in an instant.

She had been looking at a display of handsets right beside the window. She seemed quite content, seemingly fascinated by the colours and shapes of the devices, and was paying no attention whatsoever to the conversation going on at the counter.

And then she was cataleptic with shock.

Dunnigan whirled. His niece, her face a rictus of terror, hands clutched to her chest, was staring out the window, scream after scream issuing from her contorted mouth.

'Beth! Beth, honey, it's okay – I'm here!' He grabbed her, but the girl was so terrified, she seemed barely aware of his proximity.

'She's starting to hyperventilate.' Gina looked close to collapse herself.

'What's wrong with her?' the spotty young girl asked with barely concealed boredom.

'Give me a paper bag!' Dunnigan barked.

While the teenagers scrabbled around behind the counter for the requested item, he wrapped his arms around her and brought her gently to the ground.

'Here you go, dude,' the spotty young man said.

'You need to breathe into this, Beth, love.' Gina held it to her mouth.

It took a couple of minutes for her to calm down, and five more before she could speak. 'I'm sorry,' she said, when the panic appeared to have subsided somewhat.

'You have nothing to be sorry for,' Dunnigan soothed.

'Was it talking about the chocolate?' Gina wanted to know.

'No,' Beth said. 'I saw *him*.'

'One of the men who took you?' Dunnigan asked.

'He made us call him Uncle Ernest,' Beth sobbed.

Ernest Frobisher.

Dunnigan held his niece close, then took his own phone from his pocket and called Tormey.

8

THE SHOPPING CENTRE WAS SEALED FOR TWO hours. Every shopper was interviewed, and security footage from outside the phone store was viewed from all available angles.

'Beth, I know you're frightened, and you have every right to be,' Tormey said.

He was a tall, rangy man with a crewcut, his mouth covered by a droopy moustache. This look, combined with old-fashioned, crumpled suits and slow, deliberate movements, always reminded Gina of a sheriff from the Wild West – Dunnigan had smiled when she pointed this out to him, and it was an image that came back to him every time he saw his boss after that.

'Can you tell me again what you saw?'

'I've told Davey, and my mam, and the first policeman who came,' Beth said, her eyes fixed on the counter of the phone shop, which she had refused to leave.

'That wasn't a policeman,' Tormey said, patiently. 'He was a security guard from the shopping centre. It would be a big help if you could tell me too. Just one more time, and then I'll leave you alone. I promise.'

'I was looking at the phones over there, and I heard someone knock on the window.'

Tormey glanced at Dunnigan, who shrugged.

'We were at the counter, talking,' he said. 'Just because I didn't hear it doesn't mean it didn't happen.'

'Fair enough. What then, Beth?'

'I looked up, and he was right there, staring in at me. He waved. Then I kind of freaked out.'

'The person you saw was Ernest Frobisher?' Tormey said.

He held up a photograph, showing the head and shoulders of an elderly, bald man with pronounced cheekbones and a beak-like nose. The picture was in black and white, and Dunnigan knew it was at least fifteen years old.

'Uncle Ernest, yes.'

'He looked like this?'

Beth shook her head. 'He was older,' she said. 'He had something wrong with his face – like there was a big sore on his cheek and he had a plaster stuck over it. There was a tube going up into his nose, and he had glasses with a black bit over one of the eyes.'

Tormey glanced at Dunnigan again. The criminologist was one of the last people to see Frobisher before he fled Ireland, and in that encounter, the man had been close to death: bedbound, on a respirator and riddled with cancer.

'The bit about the face fits,' Dunnigan said.

'And he was dressed in a suit?'

'He always wears a suit,' Beth said. 'One of the ones with stripes.'

'Okay. That's been really helpful, Beth. Would it be alright if your mam takes you home now? My people need to give this place a proper search.'

''Kay,' Beth said, and allowed Gina to take her arm.

'One of the lads will drop you home,' Tormey said. 'I'm going to hang on to Davey for a bit. I won't keep him long.'

Gina nodded and left them to it.

'Let's have a chat,' the chief superintendent said, and strolled out of the store.

Dunnigan noticed a large poster in the window of the newsagent's opposite the phone shop, declaring that the *Sunday Independent* would have a special pull-out section focusing on the internationally renowned businessman Wilfred Hubert, who was planning a visit to Ireland to explore the possibility of setting up a branch of his business empire here. People were very excited about it, though the criminologist was only peripherally aware of the event – in the brief news items he had watched featuring Hubert he found the man boorish and vulgar.

There was a bench outside a nearby juice bar and they sat down.

'We've reviewed the tapes fully, and there is no one that matches that description on any of them,' Tormey said. He looked about him as he spoke. It was a casual movement, but Dunnigan knew he was taking everything in. If you asked him later, the chief could tell you how many mannequins there were in each shop window and describe in detail what most of them were wearing.

'That doesn't mean she's wrong,' Dunnigan said. 'What she just told us could have happened in the space of a second. The recordings might have missed it.'

'We have clear views of the area from three different cameras,' Tormey said. 'There was no old man, pinstripe suit or otherwise.'

Dunnigan sat back and rubbed his eyes.

'So let me be clear here – Beth could not have seen Ernest Frobisher.'

'Alright, boss. Thanks for coming over anyway.'

'That wee girl needs help, Davey. Is she seeing anyone yet?'

'She won't talk to a therapist. Not even Diane. I've asked and Gina has begged, but she won't hear of it.'

'That's no good. Have you read the medical report on her?'

'No. And I don't want to.'

'Which is understandable. The thing is, though, it'd give you a picture of what she went through.'

'I don't need the file for that. I know it was bad.'

'I don't think you do.'

'What are you trying to say?'

'I've been a copper for thirty years, and I've sat with a hell of a lot of fathers and brothers and uncles who've had to cope with kids they love being abused in more ways than I want to recall. So I know how it goes.'

'How what goes?'

'The denial. Blokes seem to find facing up to it tougher than ladies do. I always reckon it's the helplessness. Men don't like to feel powerless.'

Dunnigan scowled at his boss. 'I'm not in denial.'

'Yeah, you are. You're a smart guy, maybe the smartest I know. You say all the right things, make the correct noises. You can talk to me about PTSD and victim trauma profiles. Fuck it, Davey, you can cite half a dozen case studies of other missing persons who were returned to their families after a similar period of captivity. But that's not the same as owning what she went through.'

Dunnigan put his head in his hands. 'I don't want to have this conversation, boss.'

'Well, that's a pity, 'cause we're having it. The physical injuries Beth sustained – patterns of scarring which cover about three quarters of her body, broken bones that were either set or healed themselves, burns, puncture wounds – these are all indicative of someone who was regularly physically tortured. Not roughly treated, not neglected, but systematically, sadistically abused.'

'Please stop, boss.'

'I'm not trying to upset you. For her sake, and for that of you and your sister, make her get some help. If you don't, she'll turn that anger onto herself or one of you, and it won't be pretty.'

He stood up. 'Thus endeth the lesson. Go home to your family.'

Dunnigan didn't need to be told twice.

9

HE READ ALOUD TO BETH EACH NIGHT BEFORE bed: *The Enchanted Wood* by Enid Blyton. She had asked him to do this shortly after they all moved to Gina's house. The idea of reading a children's book to a twenty-two-year-old woman had at first seemed ridiculous, but there was a part of her that seemed trapped at the age she had been taken, and as she had always loved the story of three children who discover an ancient tree, the topmost branch of which leads them to magical lands, he thought it couldn't hurt. Before long, he was looking forward to their daily excursions with Jo, Bessie and Fanny.

'I thought of this book all the time when I was away,' she said to him one evening.

'Did you?'

'Yes. I dreamed about finding a doorway into another world so I could escape. There weren't any trees to climb, but I looked in cupboards and behind toilets – I thought a door like that could be anywhere.'

'It's just a story, Beth.'

'I know. But, see, that's the secret.'

He looked puzzled.

'What is?'

'The story *itself* is the magic door. When you read to me about Jo and Bessie and Fanny and old Moonface, it's like I'm there with them, like I've got away from this world and I'm off on an adventure. When I was away and bad things were happening, I'd imagine I was up the Faraway Tree, about to climb to the top branch and through the hole in the clouds to the Land of Birthdays or the Land of Take-What-You-Want. It was as if I left my body behind and I couldn't feel what was happening. I was somewhere else.'

Dunnigan smiled and squeezed her hand. 'So, you found the magic door after all, then,' he said.

'I think I did,' she agreed.

10

DUNNIGAN HAD GONE TO THE SUPERMARKET when Beth tried to kill Gina.

He got back to the house to find his niece curled up on the couch, seemingly asleep.

Thinking nothing of it, he had most of his purchases packed away when Gina emerged from the bathroom at the end of the hall and came into the kitchen, and he immediately saw that one side of her face was swollen and bruised and there was a deep gash across her collar bone. She was holding a breadknife.

'What happened?' he asked.

'I did as we discussed and talked to her again about seeing a therapist. I put it to her that it really wasn't optional, and she seemed to listen quite calmly and rationally. 'Will I make an appointment for you?' I asked her. She nodded, so I went to get my phone from the kitchen. She followed, grabbed a knife from the chopping board and attacked me. Luckily I got the blade from her and managed to lock myself in the bathroom.'

Dunnigan felt that bit of him that could be very cold and extremely clinical stepping to the fore. Clive had been on the phone a lot lately, suggesting Beth needed to be institutionalised – he had proposed a private facility in Scotland, where they specialised in severe trauma.

David Dunnigan wasn't going to have it. Beth was home, and no one was taking her away again.

'I think she just wanted to scare you,' he said, looking at the mark the serrated edge had made on his sister, whom he loved (but, he was starting to realise, not as much as he loved Beth). 'I mean, if you wanted someone dead, you'd hardly go for a breadknife, would you?'

'Jesus Christ, Davey!' Gina shouted in exasperation. 'My own daughter tried to cut my throat! She kept punching me in the face, for God's sake! And do you know what she said? She said I just wanted to have you, her precious uncle, for myself.'

'She's not rational, Gina. You know that.'

Gina sat down on one of the kitchen chairs. 'I can't take any more. I've seen how she looks at me. She hates me.'

'No, she doesn't. You're just tired.'

'You're absolutely right, I *am* tired. We've been doing this for weeks now, and there's no real change. She won't see a therapist, she won't go to any encounter groups or programmes. The three of us are trapped in this house, staring at one another. For fuck's sake, Davey, I don't even blame her for wanting to kill me. Sometimes I want to kill me.'

'It's still early days. We can't give up on her.'

'I'm not giving up. But I need a break.'

Dunnigan nodded. 'Alright.'

He heard footsteps, and then Beth was standing in the doorway. 'What are you two talking about?' she asked, although Dunnigan knew she must have heard the shouting. Her tone betrayed not one shred of stress or worry – it was as if the assault had never happened.

I'm not the only one in denial, Dunnigan thought, and the idea actually kind of pleased him. 'About how it's time for a change of scenery,' he said, grinning. 'You're going to move in with me for a bit.'

There exists a spirit not male but female.

This spirit is wreathed in a cloak of black with a hood that covers its head. She dwells in the shadows at the end of the street and in the dark alcoves at your school and in the places in your home you walk past without ever looking.

She knows and she sees and she waits. She is said to carry an enormous hunting knife, and she has pledged to spend eternity preying on the souls of evil men. They say that the second you know her name, you belong to her, and she to you. Once you've read it in a book, or seen it online, or spoken it to a friend, either directly or indirectly, you have been collected and your body and your soul are the property of the spirit. She may choose never to come for you. But if you are bad, if you do something wicked and you cover it up or lie about it and pretend to be a good person, that's when she will start to stalk you. Many who have witnessed her appearance are said to have gone insane – some take their own lives in the most horrific ways, others realise they will have no peace until she comes for them and seek her out to end their suffering. Because the spirit kills you slowly, a little slice at a time, until you wish for death to claim you. There are those who say she is a myth, an ancient ghost story told to frighten children or keep wayward teens in line, but if you have found this page, please, please take it seriously: this spirit is very, very real. There is only one thing that will stop her, and it is a secret none dare tell. Believe this: a single mention of her name will cause Mother Joan to—

Posted by hacker_red
www.wickedwords.com

Part Three

MOTHER JOAN

Yuri Chechnik

They electrocuted him until he passed out, then they dumped water on him to bring him around, and did it some more, asking the same questions again and again: what had he said about the After Dark Campaign? What did he know about Ernest Frobisher?

Finally, consciousness departed, and did not return for a long while. What felt like a lifetime later, he was awake, and he had no feeling at all in the side of his face. The world was spinning, every joint and limb hurt, and there was a terrible pain in his chest, like something very heavy was pressing on it. He was still attached to the chair with cable ties, and he threw up in his lap, then passed out again.

When next existence careened into being his head was pounding but the room had stopped whirling, and he could take stock of his situation. The house was silent as the grave, and from the texture of the light, he guessed it was late evening. He did not know how many days had elapsed since the attack – they had interrogated him for about forty-eight hours, so he reckoned that at least three days had come and gone.

He tested his restraints but had little strength in his arms.

He tried to move his feet, but they were lashed to the legs of the chair.

Why was he still alive? Why had they not killed him?

Having been on the other end of the torturer/torturee relationship on more than one occasion, Yuri realised that the only reason he had not been shot again was that his interviewers must have believed he was dead already – his heart had stopped.

Obviously, it had started again, but his captors had failed to notice, and left him to rot.

Which, he pondered, was a mistake.

Using his weight, he began to rock back and forth, and within moments the seat was tipping and he managed to topple it over, so he was lying on his back. He slid his legs forward, the ties that held his ankles in place came off the chair and, painfully, he managed to stand.

This made him dizzy, and he had to lean against the wall until the nausea subsided.

When he felt more in control of himself, he stood, took a few steps back and then flung himself into the wall with all the force he could muster. The wooden chair came apart in an explosion of dowels and wooden spokes.

On mangled feet he hobbled carefully down to the kitchen and drank long gulps of water directly from the tap. He found some bread and half a jar of strawberry jam and ate slowly, afraid his stomach would reject it.

When he felt almost like a human being again, he made his way to the bathroom and looked at his reflection in the mirror.

The bullet had cut a groove across his skull, giving his head a misshapen, furrowed look. The hole where his right eye had been was livid and seeping. He had lost most of his upper teeth during the questioning, and they had carved his name into his chest with a carpet knife – if it was all he would say, the slim man had informed him, he would make sure the people who found his body would know who he was.

Yet still he lived.

The weak, pathetic fools had failed to finish him.

But they had posed a question he was suddenly very interested in learning the answer to: who was Ernest Frobisher?

1

WEEKS PASSED.

He was very clear with Beth from the moment she stepped into his flat that her presence was conditional on two things: firstly, she was going to see the therapist Diane had recommended, and secondly, she was going to apologise to Gina.

To his great surprise, she agreed to both these demands with only a modicum of sulking, and their days fell into an easy rhythm. Gina visited most mornings, and Father Bill, whom Beth always greeted with unfettered delight, called the odd afternoon.

Therapy, which she loathed, took three hours out of her week, and she was always tired and cantankerous after it. Dunnigan knew better than to ask her about the sessions, though, and simply waited for her to shake off the melancholy, which she always did.

In the evenings they took turns cooking – Dunnigan was a reluctant and limited chef, but he knew that if his niece was to regain her health he would have to make an effort to feed her something more than breakfast cereal, which he would have lived on if left to his own devices.

'I hate cooking,' he informed her after their first week together. 'And if I have to do it, then so do you.'

They went to Hodges Figgis, bought a cookbook of basic recipes and worked through it together. Barring one or two disasters, they were surprised at how well most of their efforts turned out.

Once they had eaten, they would go for walks through the city. Beth was still uncomfortable in big crowds, but in the evenings the streets were far less populous and they began exploring parts of Dublin they had never been to before. Their home town opened up to them: networks of alleys around the quays, tree-lined avenues in Donnybrook and beautiful Georgian terraces on the northside. The evening strolls took them through the capital's hidden history. Dunnigan realised that by making sure his beloved niece was eating well and getting some exercise, he was actually looking after *himself* better than he ever had before.

And it felt good. In fact, if someone had asked, he would have admitted to being happy. And it had been a long time since he had been able to own that feeling.

Once home they would watch an hour of TV (Dunnigan didn't actually own a television, so they used the old laptop). Working off the premise that Beth was emotionally stuck around the age she had been when she was abducted, he downloaded TV shows she had enjoyed back then – *Scooby-Doo*, *Bear in the Big Blue House*, *Teletubbies* – and introduced her to other things he thought she might enjoy, like *Sesame Street* and *Hey Arnold!*

When their shows were over he would read aloud to her from whichever book they were sharing (the Faraway Tree gave way to Narnia, which in turn brought them to the

Hundred Acre Wood, then down to the river with Ratty and Mole, which meandered into the Secret Garden).

He let her have his bed, and he slept on the couch.

One night he awoke to find her sitting on the floor at his feet, gazing at the framed poster he kept over his fireplace: Patrick Troughton as the second incarnation of Doctor Who. During the years that Beth was missing, Dunnigan had spent many long hours staring at the poster of his hero, and had even started talking to it, sharing his thoughts and hopes and fears.

He reached down and squeezed her shoulder. 'You okay, Beth?'

'I'm fine. Go back to sleep.'

'What are you doing?'

'Keeping watch.'

'Oh. Alright.'

And they sat in the dark together.

2

BETH ASKED DUNNIGAN TO MEET HER THERAPIST, a lady called Harriet Grantham. He had not wanted to speak to *her*, but his niece seemed to feel it was important that he go along for a session with the woman, without Beth being present. So he agreed to go along to the health centre on Saint Peter's Square. It seemed important to the girl that he had some sense of the process, and how tough it could be. And he suspected Beth wanted Harriet to tell him something she couldn't.

In her late forties, Grantham had allowed her thick dark hair to go ashen coloured, which was not unattractive. She wore a brown trouser suit and a pair of wire-framed glasses perched on the end of a nose that had a pronounced Gallic quality to it. 'Beth has asked that I confer with you as her primary support,' she said. 'I am very pleased to finally meet you, Mister Dunnigan.'

Her office was warmly lit, with parchments for a variety of advanced degrees framed on the wall and a bookshelf lined with volumes, mostly written by Freud or Jung, but with a shelf of more modern publications by people like Spotnitz and Williams. Dunnigan noted a box of tissues sitting on a low table within easy reach.

'Please, call me Davey.'

'Davey it is, then. Beth has told me a lot about you. She is very devoted to you.'

Dunnigan shrugged.

'You're her hero. Did you know that?'

'I never really thought about it.'

Harriet Grantham looked at him without expression. 'Why does the thought make you so uncomfortable?'

'I don't think it's productive to waste time considering such things. It took me almost two decades to find the child I had lost in the first place. I'd hardly rate that as heroic.'

'You're still carrying a lot of guilt.'

He sighed and looked at his boots. This was why he hadn't wanted to come here. 'I am not in the market for therapy, Ms Grantham. Why did Beth ask me to come today?'

That elicited a smile. 'Of course. Let's get to the point, shall we?'

'Please.'

'Your niece has memories of much of the first few years of her captivity, the parts relating to her childhood, but virtually none from adolescence onwards.'

'And that's bad?'

'Well, that's the crux of the matter, really. The human mind is a remarkable thing – it is designed to protect its owner from experiences that are too traumatic to be endured, and creates a kind of firewall, blocking off memories that are too distressing.'

Dunnigan looked at her blankly. 'And?'

'The problem with this is that such experiences have their

own kind of survival mechanism – they don't want to stay buried and have a tendency to force their way to the surface. Sometimes this is caused by triggers – something as simple as a familiar smell or hearing a piece of music – but often memories can return for no obvious reason at all.'

'We'll deal with it if it happens.'

'I don't doubt you will. But in the meantime, please be aware your niece is harbouring a lot of anger, a lot of fear, and no small amount of shame.'

'Shame?'

'Most survivors of sexual abuse blame themselves in one way or another.'

'That's ridiculous.'

'Perhaps, but that doesn't make it any less true.'

'There are a lot of people who love Beth,' Dunnigan said, wearily. 'Me, her mother, my friends – many of whom sacrificed a lot to help me find her. We'll get her through this. I'm aware it will be tough, but we are all going to be there, no matter what.'

'I know you will,' the therapist said. 'But please remember, Beth is terrified of what is buried in her subconscious. She seems to think she knows something awful. Something she describes as dangerous.'

Dunnigan was confounded by that. 'I don't understand.'

'I have no doubt that it is a delusion, but she is convinced that if she reclaims some particular memories, she will bring something hideous down on you and those she loves.'

'That doesn't make any sense.'

'It doesn't need to. It's what she believes. Be patient with her, and let her know that, no matter what, regardless of what she remembers, you will still love her.'

'I hope she already knows that.'

'Have you told her?'

Dunnigan shifted uncomfortably in his seat. 'I'm not good with stuff like that.'

'Well, isn't it convenient that I am?' Harriet Grantham smiled.

3

THEY HAD BEEN LIVING IN HIS FLAT LIKE THAT FOR eight weeks when the phone call came.

'Davey, it's Frank.'

'Hello, boss.'

'How's that wee girl doing?'

Dunnigan glanced at the couch, upon which Beth, Gina and Diane were seated, playing the board game *Risk*. It had been four months since he had found his niece in that awful house in Galway. Somehow, it seemed like a lifetime ago, yet the time had passed in the blink of an eye. He wondered for a moment how both could be true at the same time, then turned his attention back to Tormey. 'She's doing very well, thank you for asking.'

'I'm glad to hear it. Have you given any thought to coming back to work?'

Dunnigan went to the window and looked down at the street below, marvelling, as he always did, at the river of humanity that seemed to flow relentlessly down Phibsboro Road.

'No, boss, I haven't.'

'Well, do you think you might feel inclined to start considering it?'

'Are you getting hassle from head office?'

'Davey, you're employed as a temporary consultant – you are not on a retainer, we are not paying you, so your current employment status isn't an issue to anyone but you and me. I'm asking because a case has just come in that I think would benefit from your particular skill set.'

Dunnigan thought about that. 'Could you be more specific?'

'It's really fucking weird.'

Dunnigan looked again at the three women on the couch. A short trip to Garda HQ couldn't hurt. He would only be an hour or so. 'I'll be there in thirty minutes.'

'Good lad.'

And somewhere in the skies above Dublin the clouds started to gather.

4

THE SEX CRIMES UNIT OF THE NATIONAL BUREAU of Criminal Investigation is situated on the fifth floor of Garda HQ on Harcourt Street, and consists of a long corridor, one side of which is made up of small offices, many shared by senior officers, the other by two large bullpens packed to bursting with desks, filing cabinets and stacks of cardboard evidence boxes.

Dunnigan went straight to Tormey's room, which was the last door on the left, and knocked.

The chief superintendent was with two men, one middle-aged and dressed in an expensive-looking suit, the other about ten years younger, resplendent with a fashionably well-groomed beard and soft leather jacket.

'Davey, please say hello to Doctor Leonard Kelly, of Our Lady's College, Limerick and Professor Derek Hynes of South City University, Dublin.'

Dunnigan nodded a greeting and pulled up a chair. With the four of them squashed in, there was barely any room left.

'Doctor Kelly is an English Literature scholar, and Professor Hynes is a chemist.'

The pair smiled modestly.

'Davey here is a criminologist and knows a little something about the more … well, the more *cerebral* aspects of the criminal mind,' Tormey said. 'Maybe it would be best to just show him the book.'

Hynes, the younger of the two, passed a leather-bound tome to Dunnigan.

When the bitter night is dark and cold, it's then you might see Mother Joan.

The first photo showed a man and woman standing at the altar, smiling beatifically, obviously about to be married. Dunnigan turned the page.

You may think you're alone and there's no one else there; those are the times when you should beware.

The next photo showed the pair, seated opposite one another at a table in what seemed to be an open-air restaurant, probably somewhere warm – he was dressed in a short-sleeved shirt; she wore a light, strappy dress. The man was looking at her with a hard expression, and she had her eyes lowered. It seemed the honeymoon was not going well.

Look in the places where shadows lie; you might catch the glint in her pale green eyes.

The third photo showed the man seated on a bed, gripping the woman by the wrist. It looked as if she was trying to pull away. The man's face could not be seen, but the woman was clearly crying.

Dunnigan continued to turn the pages. Each line of verse was accompanied by another photo, charting the descent of the relationship into violence and degradation. The final picture was of the woman, lying in a pool of blood at the man's feet. Looming in the corner of the room behind them, like a medieval depiction of death, was a cowled figure, dressed in what looked like a black cape. A single, pale, claw-like hand was stretched towards the man, who seemed oblivious to its presence.

'What am I looking at?' Dunnigan asked, closing the book. 'It's like a student art project or something.'

'That is, in a way, one of the questions we have come to have answered,' Kelly said.

'I don't understand,' Dunnigan replied.

'The people in the photographs are Doctor Henry Campbell, formerly of South Eastern Institute of Technology, and his wife, Bríd Hennessy, MLitt.'

'They collaborated on this?'

'I haven't spoken to Bríd, but Derek has. And we can assure you they were quite unaware they were the subject of a book at all until Hugh found a copy of it inside the box of a new computer hard drive he had purchased,' Kelly said.

Dunnigan's interest was piqued. 'He found the book boxed up with some hardware he bought in a tech store?'

'He ordered it by post. Directly from the company, in fact. The book had been sealed into the same wrapping as the drive, which appeared not to have been tampered with in any way.'

'Well, someone must have interfered with it – unless a staff member at the distributors is playing a cruel joke on him.'

'I don't think this could be classified as a joke, Mister Dunnigan,' Hynes said.

'Semantics. A prank, then.'

'Of the darkest hue imaginable.'

'It's in bad taste, I'll agree ...'

'Mister Dunnigan,' Kelly said, 'Doctor Campbell really did beat his wife. The photos are not staged, they are genuine.'

'And I can take it that this violence was not consented to by Ms Hennessy?'

'Is violence ever consented to?' Hynes asked.

'You'd be surprised,' Tormey said, deadpan.

'This was an abusive relationship – consent was neither asked for nor given.'

'Why are you using the past tense?' Dunnigan interceded.

'She left him shortly before the book appeared.'

Dunnigan closed the volume and tossed it back onto the desk.

'She's behind it, then. It serves him right for treating her so callously, not to mention having those photos taken.'

'Hugh didn't take the photos. That they exist came as a great shock to him.'

'She obviously set up hidden cameras.'

'Bríd claims she did no such thing. She was too busy trying to stay alive.'

Dunnigan shrugged. 'What difference does it make? I assume you're here asking us to press charges.'

'Tell him the rest,' Tormey said, his hands folded behind his head.

'I also received a book, almost identical to this one,' Kelly said.

'As did I,' Hynes said.

'With pictures of Doctor Campbell beating his wife?'

The two men exchanged glances.

'No. The photographs in our books were … personal to each of us respectively,' Kelly said.

'I don't suppose you'd like to share their content,' Dunnigan asked, although his voice betrayed only the most casual of interests – it was one of his interview techniques, seeming to be almost bored by the conversation, while actually registering every detail. He found people became more expansive in a bid to draw him in.

'We would prefer to keep that confidential.'

Dunnigan shook his head. Tormey was gazing at him, seemingly bemused by it all. 'This is very interesting,' the criminologist said, 'but I fail to see how it is of interest to the police. You all appear to be victims of a well-executed and rather nasty trick. I suggest you have a think about people you mutually know who might have reason to bear a grudge.'

'Mister Dunnigan, five other individuals, not including us and Doctor Campbell, received books like this one. We are all from disparate disciplines and work in different professions.'

'How do you know them, then?' Dunnigan asked.

'They're all people we have encountered at various work functions,' Kelly said, waving it off.

'But you said they're from different professions.'

'Academia brings us in contact with a lot of different stakeholders. Through our research, you understand.'

'And these people you met through your research gave you a ring when they found their books?'

'We kept in contact. It came up in conversation.'

'So these are close friends of yours, then?'

'I wouldn't say that. More acquaintances.'

Dunnigan made a note to revisit that line of questioning at a later date, and asked, 'How did they come across their books?'

'The volumes were found in completely different and seemingly random ways, and all show images we would rather keep private. And, most importantly, they all contain the same threat.'

Dunnigan raised an eyebrow. 'What threat?'

'Didn't you read the text?'

'It's a nursery rhyme of some kind; surely you don't take this seriously?'

'*Look there in that doorway – see how she stands? Is that a knife she's got in her hand?*' Hynes quoted.

'*She knows your secrets, and she knows your lies, she'll whisper them to you as she helps you to die,*' Kelly continued.

'Boss, do you really expect me to listen to this?'

'Mister Dunnigan,' Kelly said, and there was real fear in his voice for the first time, 'Henry Campbell was found stabbed to death three days ago.'

5

'I CHECKED IT OUT BEFORE I CALLED YOU, DAVEY,' Tormey said. 'Frenzied knife attack outside a flat complex in Carlow town.'

'Where was his wife at the time?' Dunnigan asked.

'In a pub with about a hundred witnesses.'

'That doesn't mean she didn't pay to have it done.'

'I agree. The boys in Carlow are checking her web activity, phone records and whatnot, but so far it's all coming back clean. And also, there's this.' Tormey handed Dunnigan a sheet of paper. 'The last email Campbell sent, an hour before his death.' 'Is G. Campbell a father? A brother? A sister maybe?' Dunnigan asked, referring to the email address.

'Brother,' Tormey nodded.

The subject line was blank, and the content of the message was just one line, repeated over and over: *Please beware of Mother Joan. Please beware of Mother Joan. Please beware of Mother Joan.*

'Who or what is Mother Joan?' Dunnigan asked.

'Isn't it obvious?' Kelly said, holding up that final photo and jabbing a finger at the cowled figure.

'That … *person* was Photoshopped in, weren't they?'

'Hugh said only he and Bríd were present at the time, yes.'

'Then I'm still none the wiser.'

'Mother Joan is an internet meme,' Kelly said. 'Sort of an online bogeyman – pardon me, bogey*person*. There are literally tens of thousands of stories about her – she's like the thing hiding under the bed, the monster lurking in the shadows. Some see her as a protector of the weak, a vengeful spirit.'

'So she's a force for good?' Dunnigan asked.

'Arguably.'

'Meaning you two are bad.'

The academics seemed distinctly uncomfortable.

'What do the photos in your books reveal?' Dunnigan asked impassively.

'We would both prefer not to divulge that at this time,' Hynes said without inflection, as if he had rehearsed the sentence.

'We can get a warrant and take them,' Dunnigan retorted.

The lecturers glanced at Tormey, who nodded benignly.

'We knew when we came that we were exposing ourselves to that risk,' Kelly said, and there was a tremble in his voice. 'But you have to understand – we are genuinely afraid. It was a step we were prepared to take, regardless of the consequences.'

'Davey, will you look into this?' Tormey asked. 'I think there's enough to indicate a credible threat. If the lads down in Carlow find out that Ms Hennessy was actually behind the whole business, we can always step back, but it's a bit too elaborate for my taste.'

'Doctor Kelly, your degrees are in literature?'

'Yes.'

'Can you get me any material on Mother Joan?'

'Well, there are pages upon pages about her on various discussion forums on the web.'

'Can you recommend some?'

'It's really not my area of expertise. I'm sorry.'

'Do you know of someone who *would* claim a degree of competence?'

'There's a chap in Edinburgh who specialises in this type of mythology – Ross McSwain. I'd drop him a line if I were you.'

'A friend of yours?'

'Not really,' Kelly said, without pleasure.

'Might he be behind all this, then?'

Kelly and Hynes looked at one another, considering the suggestion.

'Well, he is very eccentric,' Hynes said at last. 'But then, a lot of us are.'

Yuri Chechnik

It took him a week of asking questions to find out that a police consultant – apparently, he was a criminologist, whatever that was – had taken the house along with a private army. He put the name of Dunnigan at the top of the list, and then paid a visit to his own people. He was surprised and disappointed that Petru, the man in charge of Irish operations, gave up Frobisher so quickly.

He only had to take three fingers of his left hand.

'You will not find him!' the man hissed, through clenched teeth.

'Do you doubt my commitment or are you questioning my abilities?'

'I do not know where he is! He disappeared almost a year ago.'

Yuri smiled (a rather daunting sight) and in one rapid movement took the fingernail from one of his former boss's remaining digits. 'But you tell me he runs things?'

'Yes!'

Yuri tutted and shook his head despondently. 'And all this time you led me to believe we were in charge, the Volatovs. How did you let this happen? I handed you Ireland on a fucking platter!'

'They are bigger than us! They had been here for more than a hundred years.'

'I want to speak to him.'

'He will not talk to you.'

'Make sure he does. Tell him I have some important information I will only give to this Frobisher face to face.'

125

'Even I have never talked to him. I send reports. By the email.'

Yuri opened the laptop on Petru's office desk.

'Send an email, then. Tell him it is urgent, and that it is not safe to send information on the web.'

It took a few minutes for Petru to type the message one-handed.

'Good,' Yuri said. 'Now, we wait.'

Three hours later the laptop pinged. The email consisted only of a phone number. He dialled from Petru's landline.

'What is so urgent?'

'I want to speak to Frobisher.'

There was a pause. 'And who is this?'

The voice spoke in fluent Romanian, but with a hint of an accent he did not recognise – French, perhaps.

'A dead man. You are talking to a dead man.'

'Dead men tell no tales, isn't that how the old saying goes?'

'I have a tale to tell, and a debt to collect.'

'Really? And why do you think my employer is beholden to you in any way?'

'You would have to meet me to know that.'

'I see. And you would share your interesting story with us during this visit also?'

'I would.'

'Most fascinating. Well, Mister Dead Person, you are going to have to give me a little hint of what your story might be. Otherwise I am going to hang up the telephone and you will not be hearing from me again.'

Yuri let that hang for a long moment.

'*I have no doubt you would like to know who is responsible for taking the house in Galway.*'

'*Perhaps.*'

'*Does the name David Dunnigan mean anything to you?*'

The line hummed.

'*I will send you an address. Perhaps a conversation would be beneficial.*'

6

LATER THAT EVENING, WHILE BETH WAS COOKING beef chilli with steamed rice and homemade nacho chips, he examined the book closely. Forensics had already gone over it and learned nothing, so Dunnigan had requested a chance to see what he could glean.

It had been made by someone who cared a great deal about what they were doing.

Despite the fact that the photographs depicted such ugliness, whoever had captured them had given thought to angle, lighting and composition – each picture told its story perfectly, leaving no room for interpretation or confusion. In the space of ten images, Dunnigan felt he knew the couple quite intimately, which somehow felt like a terrible violation.

The binding was expertly accomplished. He googled the process, and learned that the technique adopted, which was called 'calf binding', was six hundred years old, and had traditionally been used for the creation of bibles and prayer books. He would have to have it tested, but the leather appeared to be real cowhide, and the pages were some kind of artist's card, pliable but very tough.

The text looked, to his unpractised eye, to have been handwritten by a calligrapher. More online research informed him that the font was an early form of Garamond and had been in use since the end of the sixteenth century.

The poem the scribe had so painstakingly inked was simple and, once again, direct. Its message could not have been more straightforward: Mother Joan is watching you – she knows your sins, and she will make sure you atone. He took a magnifying glass from a drawer in his coffee table and looked closely at the strange image on the last plate.

He didn't know enough about photo editing to be able to tell if the picture had been doctored, but it certainly looked genuine: if it was a fake (which it clearly had to be) it was a good one. He used the glass on each of the other photographs in turn and found something interesting: the figure was in each of them. In the first picture, the one in the church, a hooded person was hunched over among the congregation two rows back. In the second, a diner in the restaurant, seated with their back to the couple, seemed to be wearing a black dress, and a first glance suggested a head scarf; but was that a hood? Each picture featured the Mother Joan character, becoming more and more obvious until the final reveal.

She had, it seemed, been there from the very beginning.

He did a search on Ross McSwain, found an email address for him at the University of Post-Modern Studies in Edinburgh, and sent a short message explaining who he was and that an issue pertaining to an online myth had come up in a case. The academic responded almost immediately (the joys of smartphones, Dunnigan mused), and they agreed to Skype the following morning.

'What's this?'

So engrossed was he, he hadn't noticed Beth coming in and

plonking down beside him. She had picked up the book and was leafing through it.

'It's evidence, so you probably shouldn't be looking at it.'

He wondered if she would be upset by the contents – he knew she had experienced far worse, but since coming home, he, Gina and everyone else had ensured she did not come into contact with anything violent or potentially distressing.

'Why'd you leave it lying around, then?'

'Because I'm not used to having anyone else here when I'm working. And I'm getting old and out of practice.'

'Who's this person meant to be?' She had come to the final page.

'Someone called Mother Joan.'

'Is she going to get the mean man?'

Dunnigan thought about how to answer that. Finally, he said, 'It looks like she got him. He's dead.'

His niece smiled and handed him back the book. 'Good. Dinner's almost ready.'

And she went back to the kitchen.

The Rules of Creepypasta

It must have originated online: a creepypasta isn't a creepypasta if it didn't begin life on the internet.

1. It must be frightening.
2. It must seem believable.
3. It must be shareable.

Beyond that, anything goes.

Posted by hacker_red
www.wickedwords.com

7

ROSS MCSWAIN TURNED OUT TO BE PERHAPS forty years old when they spoke over Skype the following morning, and was, as seemed to be the fashion of the day, heavily bearded.

'What can I do for you?' he asked in a gentle Scots brogue once the necessary introductions and small talk had been dealt with.

'I was hoping you could tell me about Mother Joan,' Dunnigan said.

'The internet meme or the historical figure?' McSwain retorted.

'She is a real person?'

'She was – the online story is based on someone who died in the seventeenth century.'

'Well, that probably rules her out of my investigation, then.'

McSwain laughed. 'Don't be so quick to discount her. Word has it that she didn't stay dead for very long.'

'Why don't you tell me about the more modern incarnation of the tale, and we'll go from there.'

'Okay, then. Do you know what a creepypasta is?'

'I do not.'

'Creepypastas are horror or supernaturally related stories that have been copied and pasted throughout the internet. The phrase itself is a derivation of *copy and paste*.'

'So these are just stories people have made up?'

'It's a bit more complicated than that. Do you remember the craze for chain letters back in the 1990s?'

'Vaguely.'

'They were usually started as a joke, written by bored college students. You know the kind of thing: *If you copy this letter and send it on to ten of your friends, you'll get rich or marry the girl of your dreams*. The ones that really took off, though, were the ones that added a frisson of risk: *If you* don't *send this on to ten people, you'll die a horrible death*. In the days before the World Wide Web, these letters spread like wildfire, and entire urban mythologies evolved around them: stories that suggested a piece of paper, all blurry and indistinct having been copied a hundred times, could make you rich or kill you depending on how you responded to it. As with all good legends, the people passing them on added their own chapters, and the stories grew, developed and evolved.'

'And when the internet became widespread they made the jump online, I suppose,' Dunnigan interjected. McSwain was passionate about his subject, and the criminologist was going to have to work hard to keep him on track.

'Bingo! The origins of creepypasta are texts of some of these chain letters, passed on through discussion forums and chat rooms. Probably the first official meme, in the form fans of the genre would recognise today, is called Ted the Caver.'

'I keep hearing that word: *meme*.'

'I apologise. A meme is an idea, a concept, even a catchphrase, that spreads through online repetition. Ted the Caver is a short story, written in the form of a blog, about a group of friends exploring a cave system that gradually becomes more and more frightening – there are hints that something really awful lives there, hidden in the shadows.'

'Sounds a bit like something Lovecraft might have written,' Dunnigan observed.

'That's an interesting observation. Writers like H.P. Lovecraft generate a sense of fear and dread by suggesting the world as we know it is just a thin veneer under which something sinister is hidden. And an awful lot of people like to buy into that – think how popular conspiracy theories are. And, just like the creepypasta phenomenon, there are people out there who believe Lovecraft was not writing fiction but was documenting things that had really happened.'

'Yes, but those people are a small minority, and are – let's face it – cranks,' Dunnigan said scornfully.

'Google "Lovecraft's Elder Gods" and see what comes up,' McSwain said. 'There are more cranks than you might think.'

'Do these online stories need to have a ring of truth to them, then? Something the readers can identify with?'

'Originally, yes. A lot of the early stories tapped into existing urban myths: one called *Polybius* was about a video game that allegedly appeared in a small number of arcades in Portland, Oregon in the 1980s. The story went that it was dangerously addictive and caused hallucinations, seizures, and ultimately insanity and death. There is a whole subgenre of story about 'lost episodes', either of existing TV shows or fictional ones, in which the author comes across the show completely by accident usually on a satellite channel that suddenly appears on their television late at night, only to discover it contains graphic violence or disturbing imagery. Of course, these 'lost' shows disappear, never to be seen again.'

'So this is really just the internet equivalent of campfire ghost stories,' Dunnigan said. 'Why would anyone in their right mind take them seriously?'

'For me, that's the interesting part, and the answer lies at the root of what a legend really is. There has always been a close link between mythology and religion – if you think about the Celtic and Norse sagas, for example, they deal with humans interacting with gods and doing fantastical things, and people used to take those very seriously indeed. I don't want to tread on your toes if you're a religious man—'

'I'm not.'

'Alrighty, then. Well, the Christian bible, particularly the Old Testament, is no different – heroes and villains mixing it up with the Almighty and having adventures. It all comes back to the fact that stories can be very powerful things. Do you like *Star Wars*?'

'I do, but I'm more of a Trekkie.'

'Me too, but bear with me. Have you ever been to a convention?'

'No, but I'm aware of them.'

'Conventions give fans the opportunity to get actively involved in the world of the stories they love. They can dress up as their favourite characters, meet the actors and producers and writers of the franchise and, in some circumstances, even influence the direction the story will take. Look at the fate of Jar Jar Binks in the second *Star Wars* trilogy if you want a good example of fan power in action – the fans hated him, so George Lucas wrote the character out.'

'How does that relate to what we're talking about?'

'Have you heard of Slender Man?'

'The name rings a bell, I think.'

'Slender Man is, in some ways, the ultimate creepypasta, and illustrates perfectly the group-think aspect of the whole idiom. Slender Man was created by a guy called Eric Knudsen as part of a competition on the Something Awful web forum. The task was to build paranormal images using Photoshop. The original Slender Man post consisted of two photographs – I think one was a group of kids in a park, the other of children playing on a suburban street – into which Knudsen edited a spectral figure with no discernible facial features. He threw in a couple of lines of text (even though the competition didn't ask for them) which suggested this tall, skinny, faceless figure in a black suit was an ancient, demonic evil that targeted children. And that was it. But from such humble beginnings a legend was born.'

'How?'

'I think the secret to Slender Man's success was that Knudsen had created a canvas on which other people could easily work. This was a monster with an immediately recognisable look, one anybody could create with simple online tools. It borrowed from the most commonly talked-about urban bogeyman: the weird guy who hangs around the playground or outside the gates of the school. Tying it all nicely into the zeitgeist, Slender Man had no motive – why did he target these children? Was it sexual? Did he want to eat them? Some users suggested that he didn't have nefarious intentions at all, that in fact he was *protecting* the kids – people projected their own fears, phobias and desires onto the character. And the mythology rapidly grew. Videos started appearing on YouTube claiming to be documentaries about the 'real' Slender Man. One user traced him back to sixteenth-century Germany and found images that bore a close resemblance to Knudsen's original photos on old manuscripts. A series of podcasts were made in which some media students interviewed people who claimed to have seen him, and stories sprang up about deaths and disappearances that had been attributed to the Slender Man.'

'Knudsen had nothing to do with all this?'

'Not at all. His initial idea, which was really just about creating a scary image with some supporting text to put it in context, had gone viral. Within the space of a couple of years, Slender Man was everywhere. And, just like the other stories we mentioned, vast numbers of users – particularly teens and vulnerable young people – seemed to believe he was real.'

'Which is the part I'm still struggling with.'

'Remember what I said about people projecting their own fears? I think Slender Man also fulfilled a need. In 2014 two girls in Wisconsin lured a classmate into the woods and stabbed her nineteen times – they claimed Slender Man had told them to do it, and that he would kill their families if they refused. In 2015, a thirteen-year-old set her house on fire with her mother and nine-year-old brother still inside – again, she said Slender Man was behind the incident. The same year there was an epidemic of suicidal ideation on Pine Ridge Indian reservation in South Dakota. Many of the young people involved admitted they had been reading about Slender Man. The tribal leaders stated that the Sioux believe in a suicide spirit which bears a striking resemblance to the meme.'

'What you're saying is that this monster somehow appeals to the mentally ill?'

'Or perhaps there is something in the idea of him that speaks to the darkness in all of us.'

'Does Mother Joan speak to the darkness too?'

McSwain laughed dryly. 'There are some who would say Mother Joan *is* the darkness,' he said.

It was a year after I made Doris shut up for good, and three months after I found the book, that I noticed the hay bales had started moving.

You spend your life looking but not seeing, I suppose, and I must have walked past the field a thousand times before I spotted that the pattern I had been laying them out in year after year was different.

I walked the perimeter of the field, and I could clearly see the indentations in the earth where they had lain before – it was as if something big had picked them up and dropped them in a new location.

It was so weird I thought I must be seeing things. I tried to ring Bert, who has a farm a mile down the road, close to Ludlow; I was going to ask him to drive over and have a look, tell me I wasn't going nuts. I couldn't get a signal on my mobile, though, so I gave up, fitted the prongs on the tractor and spent the afternoon putting the bales back.

I went to bed satisfied I'd set the world to rights and slept like a baby.

The light coming through my bedroom windows seemed different the next morning, as if I had new curtains. It took me a second to realise what it was: someone has daubed the words Mother Joan on the glass pane, in what I first thought was red paint. It wasn't until I got up and went to feed the

139

animals that I saw my prize bull had its throat cut, and that whoever had done it had collected his blood in a bucket.

And the bales had all been moved again.

There's still no signal on my mobile, and the landline is dead. My car won't start, and when I tried to drive out in the tractor, I saw someone had flattened the two big tyres.

Last night, I sat up with my shotgun and watched the cornfield. At 3.33 a.m. she came out of the woods and stood there among the stalks, singing, watching me watching her.

Mother Joan.

I'm her prisoner. I belong to her now.

Somewhere out there, Doris is laughing.

Posted by hacker_red
www.wickedwords.com

8

'MOTHER JOAN ACTUALLY PREDATES SLENDER Man,' the mythologist continued. 'The first post relating to her appeared on the Wicked Words forum in 2008. The author used the handle hacker_red.'

'Is hacker_red's identity known?'

'No, but there is a good deal of conjecture about who he or she might be. The post was a poem – it's quite famous in creepypasta circles now.'

'*When the bitter night is dark and cold* – I've come across it,' Dunnigan said.

'The verses were accompanied by an image, a cowled figure peering from the mouth of an alleyway on a busy street – people walking past didn't seem to notice this ghostly spectre standing in their midst. And that is, in many ways, the message that is central to the Mother Joan ideology – there is evil all around us but we *choose* not to see it. It's like a conspiracy everyone is party to: we have agreed to turn a blind eye to a myriad of nastiness, from small, seemingly insignificant things like meanness and casual cruelty right up to murder and rape. Mother Joan is that sense of rightness and justice that lives inside us, that bit that can't quite cope with the shame and wants to speak out. She sees all this badness and punishes the perpetrators.'

'Did the character take off in the same way Slender Man did?'

'Not at first. About six months after that initial post, a short story came out on several of the well-known forums, again attributed to hacker_red. It was about a theology student in a big university, a sort of stereotypical alpha male sort, who bullied a shy, socially awkward classmate to the point where the poor lad took his own life. In the story the bully goes to the funeral, puts on a show of being heartbroken, even has the gall to sympathise with the bereaved parents. And that night, as he walks home from the wake, he hears a strange sound.'

'What does he hear?'

'Singing.'

'Mother Joan is a singing monster?'

'It's all in the poem. *Just listen out and you'll hear her song.*'

'How sweet.'

'Well, quite. You see, this is where the mythology starts to kick in. The song is an old hymn. Those whom Mother Joan is hunting report that it is quite terrifying – the sound of it is supposed to come from everywhere and nowhere.'

'People claim to have actually heard it?'

'There have been reports, yes.'

'What happened next? She kills him?'

'Not yet. He does a legger and makes it home in one piece. But you see, that's all part of Mother Joan's MO. She torments her victims first, builds up a sense of terror.'

'Death by degrees.'

'Very much so. Over the next couple of weeks, the bully starts to become paranoid. He begins to believe someone is watching him – he catches glimpses, out of the corner of his eye, of a figure, wreathed in shadow. His phone rings and there is no one at the other end. Somebody knocks on his bedroom door, but there is nobody there when he opens it. He switches on the radio, and instead of the news, on comes that strange song.'

'How'd she make that happen?'

'She's supposed to be supernatural.'

'I see.'

'This goes on until the chap is literally beside himself. And then he finds the book.'

'Tell me about that,' Dunnigan said, fascinated now, despite himself.

'Online, they call it the Black Bible. Mother Joan delivers a leather-bound book to each person she has marked for death. It's kind of a declaration, a dialogue between the huntress and her prey. She lets them know she is coming for them, and why.'

Dunnigan held the book the two academics had given him up to the screen. 'Is this a Black Bible?'

McSwain's eyes grew wide. 'Do you know, I've never seen a real one before. Could you show me some of the pages?'

The criminologist did so.

'The mythos is sketchy about the exact contents of a Black Bible. It's clear each book is tailored to mirror the soul of the evil-doer, and that Mother Joan reveals herself inside. One story talks about the book replaying the worst sins of those meant to read it.'

'This would surely qualify, then.'

'It would. That's – well, it's quite remarkable.'

'Mmm. Once the book has been found, how long before the murder occurs?'

'I don't think there is a set period of time. This isn't like *The Ring*: you watch the cursed video tape and you're dead within seven days. It's a lot more subtle than that. Sometimes the torment can go on for years, getting almost unbearable, and then stopping for months at a time. The book is almost like a challenge – this is what you've done, here it is in all its awfulness, so what are you going to do about it? I've read stories where the bad person changes their life and Mother Joan allows them to live. The vast majority, of course, don't try to change. Being confronted with their darkest selves, many dial their unpleasantness up to eleven, or try to pass the blame onto others.'

'I'd just chuck the book in the bin,' Dunnigan said drolly.

'In some stories people do try to destroy it.'

'Really?'

'It's another important part of the tapestry of the Mother Joan legend. You can't destroy a Black Bible.'

'What do you mean can't?'

'Throw it in a rubbish bin three towns over and it's sitting on your doorstep when you get home. Burn it and flush the ashes down the lav, you'll wake up to find it under your pillow the next morning. Once the book has been given to you, it cannot be cast aside. You see, the Black Bible is a potential death sentence, but it is also the true account of the awful things you've done – very often stuff you've managed to keep secret. The people Mother Joan goes after are successful and respectable. They're doctors or lawyers or teachers or, as in the case of the lad in this story, straight A students and the most popular kids in their class. The book represents their guilt – it cannot be washed away or removed.'

'So this evil bully finds the book. What then?'

'He's convinced his friends have turned on him, or that one of his lecturers has found out the truth and is marking his cards. He barricades himself into his flat, believing that if he stays put it'll blow over in a week or two.'

'Sounds sensible.'

'Indeed – one of those "if I don't get out of bed, the curse can't get me" sort of things.'

'So how *does* she get him?'

'Mother Joan is, you must remember, a twenty-first-century ghoul. On the third day he's hiding out, the bully gets an email, informing him that he has been awarded a scholarship fund he'd applied for. All he has to do is go into town and sign for it.'

'And Mother Joan is waiting.'

'Let's just say he never makes it as far as the bank.'

'And this is the story that set the ball rolling?'

'It's the story that set out the rules and structure of the legend. But what cemented Mother Joan in the consciousness of a whole generation of internet users happened a short time later. About three weeks after the story appeared on the forums, a newspaper article was pasted onto one of the sites' message boards. It was about the unsolved murder of a theology student that had taken place in 2001 – according to the article, this youngster had been dragged into an alleyway right next to a bank in Liverpool and pretty much eviscerated. The person who posted this message claimed to have known him, and said that, about a week before his death, the lad found a book containing private personal information and some sort of veiled threat. The poster wrote that they had seen the book, and that it actually mentioned Mother Joan.'

'And the legend was born.'

'If by that you mean that stories about Mother Joan, most of them purporting to be true, sprang up all over the web, then yes.'

'As part of your research, did you seek out the person who posted that newspaper article?'

'I did of course.'

'Did you find them credible?'

'Sadly, no, I didn't. They were a former classmate of the murdered boy, and I think they were just crippled with grief. Remember what I said about these types of myths being malleable? I think Mother Joan just fit this person's pain.'

'You didn't find a book, then?'

'The chap said he had seen a Black Bible, that his friend had found one purely by accident in a laundrette. I asked him if he knew what happened to it, but he said he didn't. Let me tell you, Mister Dunnigan, you can spend a lot of time chasing ghosts in this area of research. I'm more interested in why people choose to believe a story than in proving their delusions are true.'

'Very sensible,' Dunnigan said. 'I'd appreciate it if you could send me links to some of these forums and sites, all the same.'

'I'll dig them out for you.'

Dunnigan paused for a moment.

'Is there something else?' McSwain asked him.

'I'm a fan of horror movies,' the criminologist said, 'particularly the old Universal and Hammer horror films.'

'Ah, the old classics. I love them too.'

'In those the monster always has a weakness – an Achilles heel, if you like: Dracula is killed by sunlight, the Wolfman can't touch silver, the Mummy loses its power once its bandages are removed.'

'All important things to remember if you happen to be Peter Cushing or Christopher Lee,' McSwain laughed.

'Does Mother Joan have a vulnerability like that?'

'You're asking me what her kryptonite is.'

'I suppose I am.'

'The thing you have to keep in mind with creepypasta is that it's governed by a very nihilistic philosophy. Those old stories tended to be optimistic – good will win out in the end. The vampire, who can only move about at night, is killed by the rising sun – light vanquishing darkness.'

'I understand the symbolism.'

'Of course you do. Creepypasta isn't like that at all.'

'No?'

'In this medium, most readers are rooting for the monsters. The whole point of Slender Man and Mother Joan and their ilk is that they are unstoppable forces of chaos. The only rules they're governed by are the ones they set for themselves, which usually serve their own ends. There's one story that suggests putting yourself in a ring of salt will keep her out, and a few make reference to either speaking her name or *not* speaking her name – it varies depending on the author. But the best way to avoid being killed by Mother Joan is by not being a bad guy.'

'Thank you for your time,' Dunnigan said, and killed the connection.

9

DUNNIGAN SPENT THE NEXT WEEK CHASING UP the five others who had received Black Bibles. Despite the concerns of Professor Hynes and Doctor Kelly, none of them had been murdered since receiving their copies, but neither were most of them happy to receive a call from the police.

'I don't see how any of this is your concern,' Gavin Doyle, a civil servant based in the Department of Agriculture, said over the phone – Dunnigan had called five times without getting a reply and had eventually left a message suggesting he would treat continued radio silence as criminal collusion.

'Some of your colleagues believe the book you found is tantamount to a threat. A man is dead. Murder is usually something the police concern themselves with.'

'Well, it's no concern of mine. I barely knew Henry Campbell.'

'If you are so reluctant to discuss the book, how come you told anyone about finding it at all? How did Hynes and Kelly know you had it?'

The line went silent for a while. 'It just came up in conversation. You know how it goes.'

'I'm afraid I don't.'

'Why does it matter? I'm fine, no one has made any threats against me. I appreciate the call but—'

'Tell me about the photos in your book.'

Another pause. 'I don't have to answer that question.'

'You don't, but I feel it is important to tell you that we can, as part of an investigation, compel you to hand it over.'

'What if I don't have it anymore?'

'Have you given it to someone?'

'Maybe I threw it away.'

'Did you?'

There was another pause, much longer this time. 'Am I under arrest?'

'Mister Doyle, I am speaking to you over the telephone. A person can only be arrested in person.'

'Then I would like to hang up now, please.'

'I may need to speak with you again.'

'I shall look forward to it.'

*

Out of the five, only one was willing to talk. Doctor Liam O'Connor was based in the Dublin Surgical College, but Dunnigan learned that he had not been at work for several weeks. He was forced to jump through the usual hoops to get the man's address, which was in Dún Laoghaire, and called to see him on Wednesday morning.

Doctor O'Connor lived in a large house just off the waterfront, and Dunnigan had to ring the bell five times before he heard steps approaching from the bowels of the building.

The man who opened the door was in his late fifties, short and overweight. He was almost completely bald and wore wire-framed glasses. 'The college informed me you might be calling,' he said, standing back to allow Dunnigan inside. 'Can I offer you some coffee?'

'Tea would be most welcome.'

'Please sit down and I'll be with you in a moment.'

He showed Dunnigan into a sitting room which had far too much furniture. An old-fashioned tube television with the volume low was playing a morning talk show, and a table, which took up the rear half of the space, was littered with books and papers. Dunnigan spotted what looked to be a Black Bible on top of one of the piles. He was tempted to have a look but resisted the urge.

Minutes later tea was served and they sat opposite one another.

'I am not going to beat about the bush, Mister Dunnigan,' O'Connor said without any preamble. 'I am glad you called. I am afraid.'

'What are you afraid of, doctor?'

'Of *her*.' The word was spoken with real fear, but also anger.

'Could you tell me who you mean?'

'The one who watches. Mother Joan. That *is* why you're here, isn't it? I know you've been talking to some of the others.'

'When did you find the book?'

'Three weeks ago on Friday. I had picked up my usual papers and periodicals in Eason's on O'Connell Street, and when I got home and took them out of the shopping bag, *it* was in there too.'

'Were you with anyone in the shop?'

'It was five o'clock on a Friday evening so there were lots of other people around. But I didn't see anyone I recognised, if that's what you mean.'

'And no one else touched the bag between Eason's and your getting home?'

'I took the DART, so once again I was sharing a carriage with many others. I passed numerous people on my way home from the station – believe me, I've racked my brains trying to work out who might have put the thing in there.'

'Alright,' Dunnigan said. 'You are under no legal obligation to tell me, but it might help if I knew: what's in the book?'

'The text is the same as all the others – a child's verse about *her*.'

'And the photos, Doctor O'Connor?'

'The photographs … do you wish to see them?'

'If you want to show them to me.'

The older man got up and fetched the book from the table. He handed it to Dunnigan. 'As you know, I teach advanced medical procedures at the Surgical College. I still practise from time to time, but not as often as I once did – it's a young man's game, really.'

'So what time period do these images represent?'

'The first four show me performing surgeries before my teaching days, the earliest of which dates back twenty-three years – I specialise in gastrointestinal work. Whoever created the book has marked each with a date.'

'Accurately?'

'I have checked my diaries. Yes, they are all correct.'

'And the passport photos in the upper corners of each image?'

'Those are the people I was operating on.'

'And the photos in the bottom right-hand corners of each page?'

'Those are the gravestones of those unfortunate people, yes.'

'The dates on the stones would indicate they all died within a month of you performing surgery on them.'

'Yes.'

'I see. Who is the woman in the series of photos on page five?'

'My wife.'

'You were prescribing her medication?'

'She suffered from abdominal pain.'

'Was it ethical for you to treat her?'

'While not illegal, it is not considered best practice.'

'I see another gravestone.'

'She took her own life.'

'Using the drugs you over-prescribed, I take it.'

'She had become dependent on them. I should have insisted she get treatment, but if I am honest, our marriage had been over for a long time, and it suited me to have her tranquilised and docile.'

'And these other girls? The ones who are performing … favours for you?'

'Students I helped either academically or professionally in return.'

Dunnigan nodded and closed the book.

'You are the only one who has seen fit to share their Black Bible with me.'

'It would be nice to claim that I am braver or more selfless than the others, but the truth is there is nothing in those photos that would result in my being prosecuted – all the deaths were investigated and I was found to be blameless. In my heart I know I was partly at fault – one of those surgeries was performed when I had not slept for two days, and I was using cocaine to stay alert – but there were no drug tests done back then, so there's not a court in the land that would convict me.'

'How nice for you,' Dunnigan said.

'I'm not trying to excuse myself,' O'Connor said matter-of-factly. 'I was not a good man. I had a lot of anger back then – I still do, sometimes, though I have learned to deal with it. I had sex with pretty young medical students – I gave them a better grade or helped them get surgical experience in return, but if they rebuffed my advances, I wouldn't have been angry. No one was coerced.'

'That really is a matter of interpretation,' Dunnigan interjected.

'Some did say no, but I didn't destroy their career or fail them. I'm not that kind of man.'

Dunnigan set his tea cup down on the arm of the chair. 'You said you have learned to deal with your anger.'

'Yes.'

'What do you do?'

'I drink,' O'Connor said. 'I'm not proud of it, but it knocks me out and I don't have dreams.'

'I'm not here to judge you, doctor. I don't like what you've done, and frankly, I question whether a more thorough series of investigations might look upon you so favourably, but that isn't up to me.'

'Of course. I apologise.'

'Other than the book, have you been threatened or otherwise harassed?'

'Yes. That's why I stopped going to work.'

'Tell me about it.'

'I've seen her.'

'You've seen who?'

'Who do you think? She's been in the corridors of the college at night. I've seen her through the window of my classroom, standing in the shadows just beyond the streetlamps. She's been watching me, and I know she has followed me home. Every night she knocks on my door. Things about the house have been moved.'

'Who, doctor?' Dunnigan asked. 'If you tell me, I'll make sure they leave you alone. I am not going to make any promises about the contents of the book – I have no choice but to pass that on to the authorities – but I give you my word, if someone is stalking you, I will put a stop to it.'

O'Connor laughed. It was an odd sound in the cluttered, gloomy room – a short, staccato chuckle. 'How will you make her stop?'

'Give me a name and I'll have a squad car call to her door.'

'Her name,' O'Connor said, leaning forward for emphasis, 'is Mother Joan.'

10

'HE SAYS HE'S SEEN THE FUCKING WICKED WITCH of the West hanging about on Pearse Street?' Tormey said without humour when Dunnigan arrived back at Harcourt Street later that day.

'I think his classroom is at the other end of the building, so if he saw her through the window, it would have been on Magennis Place, but I suppose the end result is much the same,' Dunnigan agreed.

'What are your thoughts?'

Tormey had his jacket off and was sprawled so far back in his chair, he was almost lying down.

'There's only two options,' Dunnigan said. 'Either the book has upset him so much he's had a breakdown, or someone really is pestering him.'

'Dressed up like the Mad Monk?'

'Why not? Think about it – the Dublin Surgical College is maybe a ten-minute walk from the Gaiety Theatre. Those Viking Splash tours, which travel all over the city, feature guides dressed in period clothing. Would anyone really pass comment on a person wearing a cloak and hood?'

'Probably not, at that.'

'I've arranged for a patrol car to do a drive-by a few times a night. If someone is knocking on his door to try and panic him, they'll be spotted soon enough.'

Tormey nodded and yawned loudly. 'Right you be, then. I'm not sure there's a whole lot more we can do with this business. You ready to do something more productive?'

'Do you mind if I stick with it a bit longer?'

'Yes, I do.'

'I'm not happy with how these guys all know one another. It's just too vague. No matter how I look at it, it doesn't add up.'

'Aren't they all college professors or something?'

'No. One is a civil servant, one's a lawyer, another a banker.'

'Maybe they met at a party. Maybe their wives go to the same hairdresser.'

'I still don't like it.'

'Yeah, but you're an anti-social bastard – you don't go to parties.'

'They all insist that they're just casual acquaintances.'

'Maybe they're on these creepy whatsit sites.'

'If they were teenage girls I'd think it a possibility – but middle-aged men? I'm not buying it.'

'People are fucking strange, Davey. You don't need me to tell you that.'

'Can I have a few more days? Please, boss?'

'Alright. We'll revisit it on Monday. But I *do* have other cases that would benefit from your particular talents, and I'd like to get you working on them.'

'You know, I don't remember saying I was coming back to work fulltime.'

'I don't remember you saying you weren't. Now please fuck off and let me do my job, even if you're determined not to do yours.'

'I'm going.'

11

HE GOT HOME AT SIX THIRTY.

Diane had called over earlier to sit with Beth, and was perched on the couch, looking at her phone. His niece was nowhere to be seen.

'How's things?'

'Not so good. Our girl got a bit upset.'

Dunnigan hung his bag on its hook inside the door and went to the kitchen to make tea. 'What happened?'

'I wish I knew. We were reading some magazines I'd brought over – just some teen stuff, nothing heavy. You know how sensitive she is about having such poor literacy skills, which is unsurprising, given never having been sent to school, so I wanted to have a look at something harmless and fun. I was reading some of the articles to her, and she was fine, seemed to be enjoying herself. We came to one of the letters pages, a harmless agony aunt column, and she completely freaked out. Grabbed it off me, ripped the whole magazine up, called me a whore and ran crying into the bedroom. That was two hours ago.'

Dunnigan stood in the kitchen doorway, his arms folded. 'What was the letter you'd been reading?'

'A girl was asking for advice on how to break up with her boyfriend. Her story wasn't sexual, it wasn't exploitative or cruel – she and her guy had just grown apart, and she wanted to let him down gently. I thought it was nice, and kind of empowering, actually.'

Dunnigan nodded. 'I'll talk to her.'

'And say what?'

'I don't know. That it's okay to get upset, that you're not angry with her, that we can get through this …'

'But I am a bit angry. She called me a whore. That's *not* okay.'

Dunnigan heard the kettle switch itself off. 'Would you like a cup?'

'Tea won't solve this, Davey.'

'No, but it won't hurt, either.'

'Ignoring problems doesn't make them go away. I'm delighted she's seeing Harriet, but we have to set some boundaries and parameters here too. Beating up her mother and verbally abusing me aren't acceptable responses to moments of stress. She has to be made see that. I mean, what methods of anger management is Harriet utilising? Because they don't seem to be working. Are you fucking listening to me?'

He had gone into the kitchen and was pouring water over a teabag. She followed him.

'I want – no, I *insist* – that this be a safe place for her,' he said with his back to Diane. 'If she wants to lose it while she's here, then as far as I'm concerned, she can. Beth has every reason to be angry, and letting off a bit of steam now and again seems pretty reasonable, if you ask me.'

'She can let off steam without becoming physically or emotionally violent.'

'She's not violent with me.'

'That's because she's put you on some kind of pedestal and believes her world will crumble if you come down off it.'

'Maybe she just trusts me more than anyone else.'

'Or perhaps you keep things nice and comfortable and don't push her out of her comfort zone.'

Dunnigan walked past her, back out to the living room.

'And will you stop running away from me while I'm trying to talk to you!'

He sat on the couch and gazed at her. 'I don't know what you want me to say.'

'And that, Davey Dunnigan, has always been the problem, hasn't it?' she snapped, and, grabbing her coat, left him to his tea.

12

HE SAT QUIETLY FOR FIVE MINUTES AFTER DIANE left, trying to see things from her point of view, but soon realised it was a pointless exercise, and opened his laptop – he'd been watching the 1970s fantasy/crime series *Randall and Hopkirk (Deceased)*, about a private investigator whose partner is a ghost, and he put on an episode while he drank his first cup of the evening. He wasn't hungry yet, but knew he would be soon, and if Beth had been sulking in the bedroom all afternoon, she would also need feeding sooner or later.

He thought he might just call out for a pizza.

He was dialling the delivery service when the bedroom door opened and his niece, red-eyed and tousle-haired, came out. 'What do you want on your pizza?' he asked. 'Will I just get the usual?'

She nodded and curled up beside him while he ordered a large pie, half plain margherita and half ham and pineapple.

'Fifteen minutes,' he said to her after hanging up.

She nodded and he set the episode playing again.

'What's this one about?'

'A theatre actor is shot during a performance by a prop gun

that someone had loaded with real bullets, so Randall has gone undercover as a stage psychic to find the culprit.'

They watched in silence for a bit.

'The ghost is his best friend, isn't he?' Beth asked.

'Yes.'

'Who's your best friend?'

'You.'

'Other than me. I was gone for years. Who was your friend then?'

He thought about it. 'Well, you know Father Bill.'

'He's your best friend?'

'There's Diane too.'

He watched her in his peripheral vision as he mentioned the recent object of her ire, but she didn't flinch.

'She was your girlfriend, wasn't she? That doesn't really count.'

'Doesn't it?'

'No.'

'Miley, then.'

'Who's Miley?'

'Miley Timoney. He lives in Greenland, now. I suppose he's my best friend, really.'

'Do you miss him?'

'Um … well, yes, sometimes I'd like to be able to talk to him. We email one another now and again – he's thrilled you're back home and safe.'

Beth sighed, a long, painful sigh. 'I don't have any friends.'

'What do you mean? You've got tons of people who would walk over hot coals for you.'

'You're all family, so you *have* to care about me. It's like the law or something.'

'Believe me, Beth, that is not true. We're all here for you because we want to be. And Diane isn't your family.'

'Yeah, but she kind of is, though.'

Dunnigan thought about that, and in a moment of (for him) rare emotional clarity, understood his niece was right. He didn't know what to do with this revelation, though, so filed it for future reference. 'Why did you get upset with her today?'

'I don't wanna talk about it.'

'Yes, but you're going to have to.'

'No. I'm not.'

'I'm not angry with you. I just want to understand what made *you* angry.'

She angled herself away from him, pulling her knees up to her chest huffily, and muttered something, of which he could only discern the word 'stupid'.

'I didn't get that.'

'I said it was the stupid magazine she made me read!'

'Why was it stupid?'

'That dumb bitch of a girl and her thick fucking boyfriend. Who cares if she dumps him or not?'

Dunnigan raised his eyebrows. 'Well … um … you seem to be a bit bothered by it.'

'Am not.'

'I'm afraid you are.'

'Yeah, well, fuck you,' she said, and in a whirl of hair and ill-temper stomped back to the bedroom, slamming the door behind her.

The arrival of the pizza smoked her back out. He made no mention of their previous conversation until she reached for a pineapple-and-ham-laden slice. 'You can have one when you tell me why you got so angry,' he said, closing the lid before she could reach the food.

She glowered at him. 'I said I don't want to talk about it.'

'And I said I want you to.'

She chewed her lower lip, tears welling in her eyes. 'Why are you being like this, Davey?'

'Because …', he struggled to find the words, '… because I love you and you're in pain and I need to know why.'

'That fucking letter,' she said, wiping her eyes with her sleeve. 'The girl wanted to break up with a boy, and I got to thinking – I don't know if I've ever had a boyfriend. I mean, I can kind of remember men who paid to be with me more than once. Were they boyfriends?'

Dunnigan shook his head, and he had tears in his eyes now. 'No, Beth. They weren't.'

'I got angry because I didn't know if that was what she meant, and then I got all confused, because I think you're supposed to *want* to have a boyfriend, and I don't think I ever will, and it just got so I couldn't think straight. I know I said mean stuff to Diane, but it all just came out. Will you tell her I'm sorry?'

'She already knows, but I'll tell her anyway.'

'Thanks.'

He opened the box, and she grabbed a piece and took a ravenous bite.

'Your therapist told me you were having trouble remembering stuff from when you were away.'

'Yeah.'

'Is some of it coming back?'

'Bits and pieces. Not much. I don't want it to.'

'Why not?'

'I don't know.'

'Well, it's obviously really upsetting.'

'There's more than that. I think ... I think I *know* something. Something bad. Something I was told *not* to remember or really scary stuff will happen.'

Dunnigan sat, a slice of pizza halfway to his mouth. 'Someone told you to forget?'

She nodded.

'Who?'

She sniffed. 'I don't know.'

He forced a smile onto his face and patted her on the shoulder.

'It doesn't matter. You're here and you're safe. Eat up before it gets cold.'

And they went back to the show and enjoyed their food and the fact they were together.

Once upon a time, long, long ago, there was a young woman named Jeanne.

Her mother and father were wealthy, and when she was little she believed she would grow up to marry a handsome prince, and they would have beautiful children and be very happy. But that was not to be.

When she was twelve years old she was playing on a dry-stone wall outside her home when it collapsed, breaking her leg in several places. Jeanne would have died if a wise woman from the village had not tended her, but her father, who was a baron and the magistrate for the region, was convinced the old lady had saved his child by making a pact with an evil spirit, and condemned her as a witch. The medicine-woman was banished from the area and Jeanne was sent to a convent, where the nuns beat and half-starved her.

The child was desperately unhappy, and thought often of running away, but the nunnery was surrounded by a vast forest, and when she tried to flee she could not find the path, and grew fearful of the wolves and the wild things that dwelt among the trees.

Jeanne was a clever, resourceful girl, and she knew that if she could not run, she must find another way to make her life tolerable. So she learned her prayers, and worked hard and finally became a nun herself. She bided her time, and took her chances, and as many of the women in that order were ancient crones with black hearts, it was not very long before they died, and as she was so bright and so able, and seemed a pious, humble creature, she was made Mother Superior – head of all the nuns in her convent.

She tried to be a kinder, gentler, sweeter Mother than the ones who had been so horrible to her, and for a while, the convent was a happy, pleasant place to be. But times of peace never last for long.

A new priest came to the village close by – a man whose job it was to visit the convent to say mass and hear the sisters' confessions, and Jeanne was surprised to find she was falling in love with him. His name was Urbain, and he was handsome and clever and well-travelled, and quite unlike anyone she had ever met before.

She told him of her feelings, but he did not return her ardour, and, broken-hearted, she was left to mourn a love that had never been.

When she confided to one of her sisters, a woman she thought was a friend, that she dreamed of her unrequited lover visiting her in the night, the nun made the mistake of mentioning this admission to a visiting member of the Inquisition – the terrifying faction within the church whose mission was to punish heretics – and it was decided that spectral visits for carnal purposes could only be the work of the devil.

Jeanne was tried as a witch, and under torture was forced to confess that she was possessed by a multitude of demons, and that the priest who was the object of her desires was in fact a dark sorcerer who had helped her to commune with evil spirits.

Mother Jeanne knew that, if she did not say what they wanted, they would kill not only her, but all the nuns in her convent. They made her say awful things about them too, but she soon realised that what they really wanted was to get rid of Urbain, who had powerful enemies in Paris, so when she was asked to pass judgement on her sisters, she gave them penances involving fasting and flagellation – painful and uncomfortable punishments, but not deadly.

Her beautiful Urbain was burned at the stake.

And when the flames had died, and all that was left of the priest was scorched meat and ashes, Mother Jeanne cursed the crowd that had watched her beloved die in agony. She cursed them and swore revenge.

Posted by hacker_red
www.wickedwords.com

13

THE NEXT DAY, DUNNIGAN WENT ONLINE IN search of Mother Joan.

He was not a fan of social media, and while a voracious consumer of science fiction and horror in all their forms, he rarely felt the need to share this love with other people. (He had taken Diane to see films he really loved on their first two dates, and the experience had been enough to make her want to give up on the relationship completely.) Thus, his knowledge of the internet and its wider uses was limited, to say the least.

He was, however, an excellent researcher, and when he was on the scent, little could knock him off it.

He spent two days lurking across a range of chat forums and discussion sites. He read close to a hundred stories (of deeply variant quality), listened to a dozen podcasts that tried to make sense of the virtual horror landscape, played some online games based on creepypasta monsters and scenarios, and watched hours of YouTube videos. As difficult to scare as he was, he was certain a couple would give him nightmares.

At the end of the process, Dunnigan had learned some

things, and, as he often did, made a list, placing his discoveries in ascending order of importance:

1. People are really messed up.
2. As Fox Mulder on *The X-Files* might have put it, people *want* to believe there are ghosts and monsters and aliens out there (and that the government is carrying out all kinds of sick and twisted experiments on us).
3. If you can think it (even in your darkest, most depraved imaginings) someone else has thought it too, and probably written a story or made a video about it.
4. The Mother Joan character was, in certain ways, interchangeable with several other creepypasta monsters, most of whom seemed to follow a set of horror tropes that made them more like fictional archetypes than fully rounded characters.
5. The aspect of Mother Joan that *did* set her aside from the other online bogeymen was that she had a past. While Slender Man, Jeff the Killer and The Rake were all variations on urban myths, Mother Joan was of a much older vintage.

According to one of several essays on Mother Joan's origins written by the ubiquitous hacker_red, the paranormal figure had once been a French Ursuline nun, Mère Jeanne des Anges, who had died in 1665, aged sixty-three. The Mother Superior of a convent in Loudun, in western France, Jeanne had been at the centre of one of the most notorious witch trials and cases of mass demonic possession ever recorded.

The case of the Loudun Possessions, which went on for several years, involved the persecution of an entire community and ended with the parish priest, a flamboyantly handsome man named Urbain Grandier (who had made a powerful enemy by speaking out against the infamous spymaster Cardinal Richelieu) being burned alive at the stake.

Mère Jeanne, hacker_red wrote, was used by the Vatican as the hammer of the local witches, despite protesting against this role. She was forced to give evidence against them, to make all sorts of claims about having knowledge of people communing with demons, and on occasion even had to pass sentence – her sentences were always non-lethal and more temperate than those the Inquisition would have doled out, but the process must have been deeply distressing for her, regardless.

Years later, with the trials ended and the Age of Reason well established, Mère Jeanne admitted that she had been given a simple, if unenviable, choice: see her Sisters tortured and put to death, or defame Grandier, who had already damned himself. By the time the scandalous business was over, it was far too late to make amends – a man had been immolated, a community decimated, and the convent at Loudun would be forever linked to satanic rites and pagan sexuality.

The historic Mother Joan died in quiet ignominy. In the final years of her life she took a vow of silence, and those who cared for her spoke of how she spent her last days writing an account of all she had done, desperate to own the sins she had committed, even if she could never atone for them.

She called this confession her Black Bible, a disambiguation of 'bible blacking', the practice (often used by witch-hunters and inquisitors) of using the text of the scriptures to justify cruelty and torture.

The article suggested that the idea of Mother Joan as a

supernatural entity was in some ways rooted in her role in the trial – her inquisitors claimed she was possessed by seven demons, and even when they had been cast out she retained the ability to communicate with them and speak their thoughts and intentions. During the trial Mother Joan herself had said she doubted she would be granted entrance to heaven, and feared she would be damned to purgatory for eternity, or may have to walk the mortal world as a disembodied ghoul.

So, hacker_red proposed, it was no great surprise when, after her death, she became a figure mothers would warn their children about: *Don't stay out after dark, or Mother Joan will get you!* The woods around Loudun, especially those close by the convent of Ursulines de Poitiers, where the possessions had occurred, were said to be haunted by her spectre, which could be seen on clear nights moving through the trees clad in the black, hooded habit of the order, chanting a psalm and begging forgiveness.

Over the years, the essay concluded, the idea of Mother Joan had become more about the avenging angel than the traumatised woman, and in such secular times, the religious basis of the legend, if not forgotten, became secondary.

Yet a vestige remained: while other modern bogeymen were about motiveless evil (bad things can and do happen to good people), Mother Joan held no fear for those who led good lives – what she was about was accepting your shortcomings and making up for them as best you could.

'Mother Joan is the sharp edge of karma,' hacker_red's treatise ended. 'The Christian Bible tells us it is never too late to repent. If one day you find yourself in possession of a Black Bible, however, it might just be.'

Dunnigan sat back and looked at the screen. He realised he

was now more confused than when he had started. He wished Miley Timoney was around – he was the one he usually bounced ideas off.

He picked up his phone and dialled a number. 'Diane, how would you like to meet Beth and me for dinner tonight?'

There was silence for a moment.

'Have you forgotten that I'm supposed to be pissed off at you?'

'I'm buying. Let's call it a peace offering.'

'Good Lord, I don't think you've ever made one of those. Maybe I'm finally house-breaking you.'

'Does this mean you'll come?'

'When and where?'

14

IN HONOUR OF MILEY (WHOM DUNNIGAN FOUND he was thinking about a lot since his and Beth's conversation about friendship), they went to their absent friend's favourite restaurant, Captain America's on Grafton Street.

'What do you think it all means?' Diane said, when he had told her about the bizarre case.

'I genuinely have no idea.'

'Is there any crime to investigate?'

'A man was murdered.'

'A wife-beating piece of scum who got what he had coming,' Beth pointed out, around an enormous mouthful of burger.

'I can't make that distinction,' Dunnigan said. 'I agree he was a criminal, and if he were alive, I would do whatever I could to see him brought to justice. I'm not sure cutting him to shreds with some kind of hunting knife *is* justice, though, at least it isn't what we call justice in Ireland in 2018.'

'Speak for yourself,' Beth said.

'Is it possible some maniac has become obsessed by this Mother Joan character and is using her as a cover to kill a bunch of people?' Diane asked, thinking aloud.

'If more people were dead, I'd say that was a possibility. As of right now, it looks as if the whole thing is just a way of drawing attention to the secrets this group of professionals have been hiding, and Campbell's death could just be a coincidence.'

'I thought you didn't believe in coincidences,' Beth said, pouring tomato ketchup all over her chips.

'I don't,' Dunnigan said, smiling at her despite himself. Every now and again, he had to remind himself how lucky he was to have her back. He could still scarcely believe it.

'Which means someone else is probably going to die,' Diane said, doing her best to eat her buffalo wings with dignity and without getting barbeque sauce all over herself, something she almost managed.

'I'm hoping we can head that off at the pass,' Dunnigan said. 'Doctor O'Connor does seem to be the victim of some kind of harassment, so it makes sense to keep a close eye on him and … um … thwart whoever means to do him ill.'

'And you're doing that by having dinner with two foxy ladies,' Diane said demurely.

'I'm the brains of the operation, you know that,' he said. 'Thwarting is someone else's job.'

'I think you should just leave her alone,' Beth said.

'And why would I do that?' Dunnigan asked.

'Don't you wish there were more out there like her?'

'I wouldn't be a very good police consultant if I thought like that.'

'Yes, you would,' she said. 'You're supposed to catch bad guys, right?'

'When I can, yes.'

'Well, that's what Mother Joan does, isn't it?'

'In a way ...' Dunnigan said.

'You can't argue with that logic,' Diane said, giving Beth a hug.

'I could, but I'm not going to tonight,' Dunnigan said. 'I am having too good a time.'

Yuri Chechnik

Hamburg was a peculiar mix of grim industrial squalor and refined culture.

He had been sent the address of an apartment on the fourth floor of a brownstone building close to the Reeperbahn district.

A man with oddly pink skin, and hair so black it seemed to have blue shadows in it, was waiting when the elevator doors opened.

'I am Doctor Phillipe Ressler,' he said, pumping the Romanian's hand vigorously. 'And you are the oh-so-lively Dead Man.'

Yuri grunted a greeting.

'Please, come to the lounge and we will have the talk and perhaps a small drink. What would you like – I am a Scotch man.'

'I do not drink.'

'Very wise. It is one of my vices – perhaps my biggest.'

Ressler brought him to a long, high-ceilinged room. It was decorated in the Bauhaus style: minimalist furnishings in bold colours, and at the end of the space, surrounded by whirring, buzzing medical machinery, was what had once been a man, lying on an orthopaedic bed.

'You're the boy who lived,' the creature said, through a ragged, scabrous mouth.

Yuri approached him, torn between disgust and wonder: he had never seen anyone so old. The head which was protruding from the sheet seemed to be just skin over bone, all hair and lashes long since vanished. There was something wrong with the flesh of the thing's right cheek, and a thick dressing had been applied to it through which something dark had seeped. The lips had receded to reveal cracked yellow teeth, but it was the eyes that were the most frightening – twin pools of hate, illuminated by a bitter, wicked intelligence.

The room smelt of medicine, antiseptic and human waste.

'This is my employer,' Ressler said. 'Please say hello to Ernest Frobisher.'

'You look almost as bad as I feel,' Frobisher said. 'Someone did a number on you, didn't they?'

'The people you sent to interrogate me were of the opinion I did this to myself. That I had sold you out. The truth is, I did not know I worked for you in the first place.'

Frobisher made a strange, gagging sound, and Yuri thought, for a moment, that he was choking – it took him a few moments to realise the man was laughing.

'D'you want an apology? Is that what this is all about?'

Yuri heard a metallic clicking sound and, turning, saw that Ressler had a large handgun trained on him.

'You stupid inbred Romany,' the old man wheezed. 'It was just business. Nothing personal.'

Yuri blinked in the dim light.

'They took my fucking eye and put electricity through my balls and all the time they ask about you: Ernest Frobisher, Ernest Frobisher! You will forgive me for taking it a little personally.'

'You told my lapdog there you had some information. Are you going to tell me, or do you want me to give you a blowjob first?'

'Your men wanted to know who took the house.'

'We're still a little puzzled about that,' Frobisher admitted. 'Those clapped-out whores didn't seem worth the trouble.'

'I have been doing some investigating, and I know, now, who they were. The women were taken by an agency called Murtaugh International Security.'

'Do we know them?' Frobisher asked Ressler.

'We do not,' Ressler responded, smiling.

'There were two people with them who were not employees of this Murtaugh – a man and a woman.'

Frobisher was incapable of sitting up in bed, but something about him changed, palpably. 'Stop fucking about and give me names.'

'The man was policier. David Dunnigan.'

The room was stiflingly hot, but a chill seemed to creep in the moment Yuri identified the criminologist.

'You mentioned him when we spoke on the telephone,' Ressler said. 'You are certain he was at the house when it was attacked?'

'I have just told you so.'

The two men exchanged glances.

'Would you be so good as to step outside for a moment,' Frobisher said tersely. 'I need to confer with Doctor Ressler.'

The Romanian nodded and returned to the hallway. Several moments later, Ressler bustled past, returning shortly with a bundle of thickly lined papers.

After what felt like an age, he was called back into Frobisher's sanctum.

'I would like to offer you compensation for your pain and suffering,' the dying man said, when Yuri was standing before him again. 'Part of this will be financial, obviously, but I am also going to give you a chance to get even.'

'And why do you think I would want this?'

'Because you are a Volatov. It's your code.'

Yuri shrugged. Frobisher was right.

'David Dunnigan came to the house in Galway to find a girl.'

The Romanian raised the only eyebrow that would now move. 'Girl? Which girl?'

Ressler stepped forward and handed him a thick brown envelope.

'There's a photo inside,' Frobisher said. 'This young lady knows some information about the workings of our operation that could bring a shitstorm down on all of us. She was sent to that particular establishment to be worked to death, and I assumed that had happened. It seems she is more resilient than I gave her credit for. I need her to disappear. As soon as possible, if you please.'

'My argument is with this Dunnigan.'

'Listen to me, you filthy, ignorant fucking gypsy!' Frobisher spat. 'Find one, and you'll find the other!'

'Everything you're going to need is in the envelope,' Ressler said. 'Dunnigan is her uncle – there's a little extra in it for you if you make sure they both suffer.'

'An eye for an eye, as they say in the Bible,' Frobisher said jovially. 'Not that you're likely to know much about that.'

15

DUNNIGAN'S PHONE RANG AS HE AND BETH WERE having breakfast the following morning.

'You'd better get in,' Tormey said. 'Your boy the Doc is here, and he is not a happy chappy.'

'Doctor O'Connor?'

'One and the same.'

'I'm on my way.' He called Gina and asked her to come over. She seemed tetchy over the phone, but he thought little of it – his sister had never been a morning person.

*

O'Connor was in one of the interview rooms when Dunnigan got to Garda HQ.

'What happened?' the criminologist asked Tormey. The chief was standing at the two-way mirror, hands in pockets, gazing at the man in the small room beyond, who was pacing up and down, a large plaster applied to his bald pate.

'He ran out of food and decided to go shopping yesterday evening. Got jumped in the multi-storey car park. The assailant tried to open his skull with a heavy blade – some kind of hunting knife, the medical examiner reckons.'

'Same weapon as was used on Campbell?'

'Yup.'

'How'd he get away?'

'Some other shoppers disturbed them – the attacker fled.

'Did he give us a description?'

'He did.'

'And?'

'He says it was this fucking ghost you've been chasing on the interweb.'

'That doesn't help us much.'

'No. Lucky for us, his rescuers saw it all, and there's half a dozen security cameras on that level. We've got the whole thing on tape.'

Dunnigan glanced at his boss. 'Why don't you look happy, then?'

Inside the room, Doctor O'Connor had come to a standstill and was looking directly at them as if he could see through the mirror. He seemed to be reciting something, his mouth making the same shapes again and again.

'What's he saying?' Dunnigan asked.

Tormey reached over and switched on the speaker.

Please beware of Mother Joan. Please beware of Mother Joan. Please beware of Mother Joan.

He switched it off again. 'Let's go and look at the tapes,' he said.

'Shouldn't I have a word with him?'

'Tapes first.'

'Have you looked at them already?'

'Yup.'

'What did you see?'

'I don't want to ruin it for you.'

And they went upstairs to Tormey's office.

16

THE CHIEF ALREADY HAD THE TAPES CUED UP ON his computer. 'Take a load off.'

Dunnigan sat in his boss's chair, something he had never done before – it had one of those chiropractic covers that looked like they were made of wooden balls tied together with string. Tormey reached over his shoulder and punched a key.

The image showed a large indoor parking garage. Dunnigan could see a concrete path, marked with yellow arrows that had cars on each side. 'Is there any sound?'

'No. Just visuals.'

O'Connor walked into view from the bottom of the screen. He carried a full shopping bag and was dressed in what appeared to be a camel-hair coat, incongruous over a rumpled shirt and tracksuit bottoms. His head was lowered and he was walking at a good pace when suddenly he stopped. His head shot up so he was looking directly ahead. He dropped the bag.

'He's seen something,' Dunnigan said.

'It's easy to see why you've been so successful in the field of detection,' Tormey replied drolly.

The surgeon took two backward steps, looking about him as if for an avenue of escape.

'Wait for it,' Tormey said.

From the top of the screen, a long, sinuous, naked leg appeared. The movement was unnatural and looked almost painful, as if the owner of the limb was contorting themselves or performing an uncomfortable yoga movement. For a moment the leg, complete with an unshod foot, hung on the screen, weird and disembodied.

'What am I seeing?' Dunnigan asked, turning his head, as if looking at the image from another angle might make it clearer.

'Keep watching.'

In a swirl of black, a figure – obviously the person the leg was attached to – spun into shot. At first the criminologist thought he was seeing a huge bird – the folds of a cloak were flung out, creating the sense of two vast wings, and the hood, which came to a sharp point at the top, looked almost like a beak. The cowled figure sank low onto the ground, coming to a stop right in front of O'Connor, seeming to almost prostrate itself. Then, slowly, in jerky, exaggerated bursts of motion, it began to rise.

'Why is it moving like that?' Dunnigan asked. 'Is there something wrong with the tape?'

'Nope.'

'It looks almost like it's dancing.'

The figure really did seem to be performing a bizarre, terrifying gyration before O'Connor, who was frozen to the spot. The movements of the creature looked to be somewhere between an epileptic seizure and a tribal invocation. It suddenly swayed backwards, looking as if it might topple over, then a long, naked arm shot forwards and the person, whom Dunnigan noted was taller than the doctor by a head, lunged to the side, then swayed and wove like a boxer.

'It's in the poem,' the criminologist said suddenly.

'What is?'

'This – don't you remember? *At the end of the street where no one else passes; can you see how she moves? See how she dances?*'

'Poem or not, it is totally fucked up,' Tormey observed.

On the video, the weaving, cowled thing appeared to retreat, and it looked as if O'Connor, who was casting about him for an exit route, might make a run for it. Then a long, pale arm plunged inside the dark robes, and came out clutching a cruel-looking blade.

'That's called a *leuku*,' Tormey said.

'Is it a hunting knife?'

'It's actually more of a woodsman's tool. According to the good people on Google it's traditionally used by the Sami people – nomadic reindeer herders from Lapland – but it's popular in France and Germany as a general survivalist weapon. It's strong enough to be used as an axe replacement, but the edge is fine so can be used for skinning and butchering meat.'

'Ideal to kill someone with.'

'Oh, yes.'

O'Connor seemed to have scarcely noticed the knife, and was hopping from foot to foot in anxiety – the fight-or-flight response was kicking in at last, and he had opted to fly. The cowled figure saw it too, and in a single lunging motion was on top of him. The blade was held high above the hooded head for a moment, then in a vicious arc the long knife sliced downwards.

'And that would have been it for our boy if the cavalry hadn't arrived,' Tormey said, as the bonnet of a car hove into view.

The creature moved with shocking, unnatural speed, and was gone in an instant. A man rushed onscreen from the left, obviously having got out of the car. O'Connor's face was covered in blood.

'Wound looks worse than it is,' Tormey said, reaching over and stopping the tape. 'The scalp bleeds a lot: she didn't get a chance to do much harm.'

'You're sure that's a female?'

'Aren't you?'

'It's very tall.'

'Some women are.'

'Possibly. Statistically, though, crimes like this are far more often committed by males.'

Tormey shook his head. 'Get out of me chair,' he said, and Dunnigan went to his usual seat opposite. 'What do you mean "crimes like this"? There are no other feckin' crimes like this.'

'I wouldn't say that, boss.'

Tormey sighed deeply and ran his fingers through his short salt-and-pepper hair. 'Aren't you even a little bit disturbed?' he asked.

'By what?'

'We've just looked at footage that shows the fucking banshee is real!'

Dunnigan looked back at the chief – who was clearly more than a little appalled at what they had just witnessed – and smiled. 'I disagree,' he said. 'I think that tape proves that she's not.'

'How the hell can you say that?'

'My understanding of ghosts, spirits and supernatural entities is that they are supposedly non-corporeal, meaning not flesh and blood, and that photographic technology does not do well at capturing them. The thing on this recording is one hundred per cent physical – she has weight and height and when she throws herself on O'Connor and knifes him, he is knocked to the floor and cut. There's nothing ghostly about that.'

'I wish I had your certainty,' Tormey growled.

'I'm telling you, boss,' Dunnigan said, standing to leave. 'We are dealing with a person – a strange one, by all accounts, but a person for all that.'

17

OVER THE NEXT THREE DAYS A SUCCESSION OF forensic scientists, computer experts and video technicians pored over the footage in an attempt to prove it had in some way been tampered with.

'If you look here, you can see colour leakage in this frame,' Bagenal, a chubby young man from the tech squad, told Dunnigan.

'What does that mean?'

'It *could* indicate that an image has been laid over the original recording.'

'It could?'

'Yes.'

'You're going to tell me there are other possible interpretations, aren't you?'

'Well, seepage like that sometimes occurs when low-definition cameras are used in poor light.'

'Like the sort often used for security in a poorly illuminated multi-storey car park.'

'That could be one possibility, yes.'

Dunnigan left them to it.

Doctor O'Connor proved to be no help. In the days after

the attack he had become less and less communicative. 'She came for me,' was all he would say to Dunnigan. 'I saw her dance! I heard her song! She whispered my secrets and lies to me.'

'Doctor, you were violently assaulted, and that is certainly distressing, but if we are to catch the person responsible, some more information would be really helpful,' Dunnigan said gently.

They were seated in the visitors' room of Coolmine Priory, a privately run facility in south County Dublin into which O'Connor had booked himself as soon as the police said he could leave. The establishment was, effectively, a psychiatric hospital for those who could afford to pay for some extra luxury while they convalesced – the nurse who had shown Dunnigan in had brought him a pot of tea brewed with proper leaves, and a plate of freshly baked scones.

'Did you see your attacker's face at all?'

'Her hair is white, and pale is her skin,' O'Connor said.

He had not looked at Dunnigan once since the criminologist had arrived.

'I see. So you are clear that it was a woman who attacked you?'

'She will be coming back for me,' the older man said, rocking gently in his chair. 'There's no place to hide and there's nowhere to run.'

'You're in a secure facility, doctor,' Dunnigan said, sipping his tea. 'I think you're safe here.'

'Now that she knows me, she'll soon be along.'

'Not through five security doors and a state-of-the-art alarm system she won't,' Dunnigan said.

But the doctor didn't seem to be convinced.

'How do you know Hynes and Kelly and all the others?' He asked it more out of frustration than anything else – he didn't really expect an answer.

'The group,' O'Connor said.

'Which group?'

'The support group.'

'You all attended some kind of self-help class?'

'To make us stop being angry,' O'Connor said. 'It didn't work.'

Detective Inspector Alfie Jones

It had been a year since the last case like this had come across his desk in the office of the London Metropolitan. He had hoped it was over – God knows, he had given everything in his attempt to solve the blasted thing: his marriage, his career, almost all his friendships.

His desk was toward the end of the bullpen, next to an ancient radiator. He kept the box with all the files on that seemingly disconnected set of cold cases in a large cardboard box just beside that old rad. He pulled it out and sat it on his knees, brushing the dust off with the sleeve of his jacket.

Fifteen cases – all unsolved.

Strike that – the murder of Dick Hargreaves had been pinned on his wife, but pretty much everyone knew that verdict was dodgy as hell. He'd done his best to have it overturned, but all he had managed to achieve was to make himself a pariah within the department.

Fuck them.

Fuck the whole lot of them.

He opened the new file (he'd been allocated it that morning) and skimmed the cover page: Ron Webster, a corporate lawyer found in his office with his throat cut. No sign of forced entry, no sign of a struggle. The man had a reputation for being a mean bastard, and he had one previous arrest – he was present when a brothel in Birmingham had been raided in 2008.

His wife (who stood by him during that unpleasant business) reported that he had recently become nervy and paranoid. He believed someone was following him. They had both been woken several times by knocking on their front door in the middle of the night, and Webster was sure someone was in the house the evening before his death.

The man's secretary told the uniforms that she had arrived to work three weeks previously to find a package sitting on her desk, addressed to her boss. She had opened it, as she did all his mail.

All she would say was that it contained a strange, leather-bound book.

Jones closed the file and went outside for a cigarette.

He wondered if Webster had heard her sing before he died.

Jones had heard that song once.

Sometimes, he still heard it in the dark hours of the night.

Part Four

PAYBACK

I wish we hadn't done it, but he was just so beautiful, and we'd fantasised about it for so long. It's too late now. I'm writing this in the darkness while I wait.

I want people to know why I died.

It was James who found the book, and he was the first to go. He left our room to follow the scraping at the window, and I never saw him again. We'd been together since 1986, and he was gone in the blink of an eye.

I begged him not to go. I knew what it was, you see, from years of studying the creature. Maybe you don't know – why would you? Let me warn you, then.

There is a monster that wanders the dark places preying on those who have tasted the shadows, watching, waiting.

He left me on September fifteenth, 2002, and I remember it like it was yesterday.

That was the year James and I escaped London and the memory of what we had done to live our lives in the beautiful wooded county of Northumberland. We lived happily there for several months, until she found us: Mother Joan.

She took my love, my very reason for breathing, but she did not show herself to me until much later. I almost thought she had been satisfied with James. I was wrong.

I first saw her on June nineteenth, 2004, standing in the shade thrown by the ancient oak tree behind our house. I was in a daze when I descried her, and my destiny beckoned to me: it said, 'follow her, love her, accept her'.

Two weeks later I awoke to a strange tapping noise on my bedroom window, and I knew it was her. I ran out of the house, to see her perched in the tree like a demonic bird, staring down at me, I was about to cry from the majesty of her. I remember her song, so sad and beautiful in the silence of the night. I knew I would do anything for her.

On April third, 2007 Mother Joan arrived at my window again. I was overjoyed. She said it would soon be time, and I was glad. You see, Mother Joan devours the souls of men who have done wrong. It's why she took James and it's why she has come for me.

It's because of what we did to the little boy.

I remember the child so well, oh what was his name? It doesn't matter anymore.

I'm sitting under the oak now, waiting for her.

I brought this on myself.

I hope she makes it quick.

Posted by hacker_red
www.wickedwords.com

1

THE FOLLOWING SUNDAY DUNNIGAN, BETH AND
Father Bill went to Glendalough, an old monastic settlement
that had been built on two beautiful lakes in the sixth century
and now, as was the fashion of the times, had an interpretive
centre to explain how guests should enjoy it. The park also
boasted a nice café and some very pleasant walks that required
varying degrees of effort, and without the need for guided
interpretation.

'Why did you become a priest, Father?' Beth asked as they
strolled beneath the trees, a blackbird trilling and burbling
above them from the canopy.

Beth was linking arms with Father Bill, and they received
some odd glances from passers-by: the handsome, well-built
cleric arm in arm with such a pretty girl. Neither seemed to
care. Beth adored him – she told Dunnigan she felt very safe
when Father Bill was around. The criminologist was a bit
jealous of their relationship, but he knew such feelings were
unproductive, so he pushed them aside.

'When I was a lad it was obvious I could do one of two
things,' Father Bill told her. 'I could join one of the gangs that
ran the inner city, which was the only world I knew, or I could

throw my lot in with the Almighty and become a member of a different kind of club. So I signed on at the seminary.'

'Do you like it?'

'Most of the time, yes.'

'Do you love God?'

'Of course I do. It comes with the job description, Beth.'

They walked on in silence for a bit, listening to the wind among the branches.

'Sometimes God does bad things though, doesn't he?' Beth said after a time.

'Does he?'

'I think so'

'Like the things that happened to you?'

'They didn't just happen to *me*. There were lots of other people in the places I was sent. Kids, women – some men too.'

'God didn't do that, Beth. People did.'

Dunnigan was walking beside them, and he watched his niece from the corner of his eye. She was chewing ferociously on her lower lip and playing with one of her sleeves, as she tended to when she was thinking something over.

'Didn't God let it happen? Couldn't He have stopped it if He wanted to?'

'I like to think He did. You're here in this beautiful place with us now, and the sun is shining and in a little bit, we're going to have tea and cakes. Isn't that just wonderful?'

She hugged him. 'It is. And I know I'm lucky to be alive. My therapist tells me every time I see her. But do you know, I've been thinking about that too.'

'Have you?'

'She tells me I should be grateful to God, or the fates, or the universe or whatever I want to call it. But do you know what I reckon?'

'I have a feeling you're going to tell me.'

'I'm grateful to *me*.' Father Bill raised an eyebrow. 'Is that right?'

'I think I'm alive because I chose not to die. There were hundreds of times when I thought about giving up. I made plans to kill myself more often than I want to remember. But there was always a voice in my head that told me to hold on, that I might escape or that someone might come for me. So I didn't end things and I kept on fighting. That's all down to me.'

'Of course it is,' Father Bill said. 'You're one tough little lady.'

'There's certainly an element of luck in how I got found, but I'm not sure I see God in it.'

'Well, I like to think I played a small part in the whole thing,' Father Bill said, 'and I do come equipped with a dog collar.'

'That's true,' Beth said. 'And how many other badass priests with friends in the Mafia are there? I mean, what are the chances that someone like Father Bill Creedon would find out about me, and use all his skills and resources to look for me? Is there another Roman Catholic cleric in the whole world with an army of homeless people at his disposal and friends in the Mob? You're a fairly major reason I'm here today, and I know luck played a part in you and Davey meeting, but when I look at you, what I see is a wonderful, amazing man. A man who loves God, but still a man.'

'You'll give me a big head, Beth,' the priest said, laughing. 'But can I just remind you that God and me come as a package?'

'I know that. I don't want to offend you.'

'You'll have to try much harder than that if you want to offend me, sweetheart.'

'There's one more reason,' the girl continued. 'And, again,

199

you could call it luck, but I just can't. I have an uncle who happens to work for the Irish version of the FBI.'

'How cool is that,' Father Bill laughed.

'I know, right? And when every single person told him I was dead and to give up on me, he wouldn't. For eighteen years, he never stopped looking, and he chased up every single lead, no matter how small. He faced down paedophiles and killers and the worst people in the world, and he told everyone he met about me in the hope that some of them might look too. That could be called luck, but I don't think it is, either.'

'It's love,' Father Bill said. 'Davey's love for you just wouldn't let him give up. The relationship you had, that energy between you, was so powerful, it kept him going.'

'Yes. Without him, I know for sure I wouldn't be here today.'

'I would say that your Uncle Davey is probably the main reason you're here,' Father Bill said, 'and I know hearing those words means an awful lot to him.'

Dunnigan said nothing – he was fighting hard not to cry like a small child. He reached over and squeezed Beth's hand instead.

'What I'm saying is that I don't know if there's a God or not,' the girl went on. 'But if there is, I think He needs a hand to make good things happen. Sometimes, the good guys need all the help they can get.'

'The Bible tells us we all have a part to play,' Father Bill said.

'Right now, the part I want to play is taking this path back to the café and having some tea and a jam doughnut,' Beth said.

'That sounds like a plan I can get on board with,' the priest agreed.

2

WHEN HE AND BETH GOT HOME THAT EVENING Dunnigan received the news that Doctor Liam O'Connor was dead. They had gone to see the latest Marvel blockbuster after arriving back in the city. (Dunnigan swore never to go to the cinema with Father Bill again – the priest had no idea what was going on, and wouldn't stop asking questions: 'Why does that fella have a hammer – is he a carpenter? What's wrong with the big green lad? Why can the rat talk?') He had switched his phone off in the theatre and hadn't thought to turn it on again until they arrived at the flat.

'I'm sorry to hear that,' he said to Tormey. 'I suppose it just all got too much for him.'

'If it did, it caused him to stab himself twenty-seven times.'

'It wasn't suicide?'

'Six of the wounds were in his back and were delivered at angles even the most flexible person couldn't reach.'

'Another patient, then?'

'He was sharing a room – the great thing about the two-tiered medical system in Ireland is that you pay to still be treated like shit.'

'I'm on my way.'

*

He was met at the hospital door by a besuited administrator in a state of high agitation.

'This is quite impossible,' he said, as he showed Dunnigan to the room where O'Connor had met his demise. 'None of the patients have access to knives – we don't permit it!'

'Well, one managed to find its way in,' the criminologist said.

The room looked as if someone had butchered a sheep in it – crime scene tape barred the door, but beyond that the walls and furniture were bathed in blood, and the coppery scent was heavy in the air. The bed where O'Connor had obviously been lying when he was attacked still had pools of gore congealing on the blankets, and the mattress and bed linen had been shredded. Forensics had already been through, and numbers had been placed on various items to denote them as evidence. Dunnigan noted that the door had to be opened using a key card, and the windows were barred.

'Mister Finnegan, who shared the room with Doctor O'Connor, is in one of our secure wards,' the manager said. 'Superintendent Tormey is with him.'

'Did he and O'Connor get on?'

'Very well. The poor man is deeply traumatised by what he saw.'

'Could you bring me to him, please?'

'Of course.'

The 'secure ward' was, in fact, a padded cell. Gary Finnegan was a morbidly obese man who, in another life, had been an accountant. He was sitting on the floor dressed in blood-spattered pyjamas with pictures of Jim Henson's Muppets on them when Dunnigan entered. Tormey was leaning against the wall, his hands deep in his pockets.

'Mister Finnegan, my name is David Dunnigan, I am a civilian consultant with the National Bureau of Criminal Investigation.'

'She came,' the fat man said in a tiny, high-pitched voice. 'She came out of the shadows and made him bleed.'

Dunnigan noted that there were fine spider-web patterns of blood crusted onto Finnegan's cheeks. He glanced at the chief. 'Do we have the murder weapon?'

Tormey shook his head. 'I've called Forensics, and they'll be here shortly. As of right now, no blade has been found.'

'Could his room-mate have thrown it out the window?'

'The night manager says it's sealed.'

'Please beware of Mother Joan,' Finnegan said. 'She helped him to die.'

'I've got nothing,' Tormey said, and left Dunnigan to it.

3

THE MEDICAL EXAMINER DECREED THAT LIAM O'Connor had died when a large blade (seemingly the same knife that had inflicted the cut to his forehead during the attack in the car park) had severed the inferior vena cava in the right atrium of his heart, causing him to bleed out within approximately two minutes – a fact that had not stopped the attacker continuing to stab the man repeatedly and with great force.

An entire team of police officers from three different units combed Coolmine Priory from top to bottom but, the kitchen aside (where no knife fit the shape or profile of the murder weapon), no blade was found. The facility was noticeably short on security cameras, but there was one on the corridor outside the room O'Connor had shared with Finnegan. It suffered an inconvenient malfunction, and had stopped recording for fifteen minutes around the time of the attack.

Finnegan was resolute in his statement about what had happened: the two men had watched a DVD early in the evening (*Mamma Mia!* apparently). An orderly brought them tea and biscuits at approximately nine o'clock, after which they both read for a brief period before going to sleep.

Finnegan said he had been awakened some time later by a scuffle and sat up to find a black-clad figure standing in the room, which was now drenched with blood. So terrified was the corpulent man of this apparition, he had become insensible for a few moments, and when he had next regained his faculties the figure was gone. He had immediately rung for a nurse.

*

'It pains me to say it, but Finnegan's story checks out,' Tormey said, when he and Dunnigan met to look at the evidence the following day. 'If he'd done it, he would have been absolutely drenched in blood. You saw him – he was spattered but hardly soaked.'

'It couldn't have been him,' Dunnigan agreed. 'But if it was this Mother Joan killer, how did she do it?'

'The night manager doesn't know how she got in or how she got out, and Finnegan was dead to the world during most of it.'

'Which leaves us nowhere,' Dunnigan said.

'It leaves us with the conclusion that O'Connor was murdered by the vengeful spirit of a dead French nun who has some kind of axe to grind against abusive men,' Tormey groaned. 'Which is worse than nowhere.'

'Do you think the commissioner will accept that as our report?'

'Do you have any other suggestions?'

'I finally found out that he and the other five met at an anger management support group.' Dunnigan said. 'They had all been sent there due to anti-social behaviour at their respective places of work. It's why they didn't want to divulge how they met.'

'Anyone else in the group receive a book?'

'None say they have.'

'Who ran the sessions?'

'A corporate training company – they're a subsidiary of a British firm that does a lot of leadership mentoring. They work for some pretty high-profile clients, and there hasn't been a single complaint against them.'

'Doesn't mean they're not involved somehow.'

'It doesn't, but I just don't see how it connects. I think our best bet is to go back to the Mother Joan myth. What we're clearly dealing with is a killer who has, for some reason or other, fixated on this particular character. Maybe that's something I can work with.'

'Well, I need some solid leads fast.' Tormey was leafing through the evidence report again. 'The doc was related to the wife of the minister for agriculture and fisheries or tourism and the Gaeltacht or one of those hyphenated departments. All joking aside, the commish is breathing down my neck. We have a dead college lecturer and now a dead surgeon. If it was a truck driver and a petrol pump attendant no one would give a shite, but when the corpses have letters after their names, people start to get nervous.'

'Respectfully, boss, that's not right.'

'Respectfully, I don't give a fuck. Use that big brain of yours and find out what the hell is going on. If it was the Ghost of Evils Past, I want her booked before she can get up to any more mischief, alright?'

'I'll see what I can do.'

'Whatever it is, do it quickly.'

4

ROSS MCSWAIN PICKED UP THE PHONE AT HIS FIRST ring. 'How goes the case?' he asked conversationally.

'Badly,' Dunnigan admitted.

'How can I help you?'

'You mentioned the whole ... um ... role-play aspect of fandom.'

'It's called cosplay.'

'Yes, that.'

'What about it?'

'You talked about it in relation to *Star Trek* and *Star Wars*. Do creepypasta fans do it?'

'To be sure, but it's probably not as popular in this genre as it is for, say, fans of movies or comic books.'

'How do people actively participate, then, beyond publishing stories online?'

'Well, probably the main outlet would be through creepycons.'

'Explain, please.'

'It's where groups of writers and fans get together and share stories and ideas in a real-world setting. Like a convention, but for creepypasta.'

'And are these as well-known as something like Comic-Con?'

'I think they had a creepypasta event at one of the official Comic-Cons a few years back, but it didn't take off, and I heard that a few of the organisers were a bit freaked out by some of the content. No, most are quite small.'

'Are there any that focus on Mother Joan specifically?'

'I'm going to be honest and say that I don't know the answer to that for certain.'

'Could you find out for me, please?'

'Let me make some calls.'

*

McSwain rang back later that evening as Dunnigan was packing up to go home.

'There is one group that meets regularly in a college in London,' he said. 'They call themselves The Watchers, and their website says they are dedicated to Mother Joan creepypastas and to her – and I think you'll like this – her *appearances*.'

'Can you send me a link to that site and any other details you've got?'

'I already have.'

'Thank you.'

'Glad to be of service.'

*

The website was an amateurish affair – it consisted of a library of Mother Joan stories, many of which Dunnigan had already read, notices of future meetings of the group, and a page that consisted only of names and dates.

Damien Goldsmith, 2-3-1984
Frederick Forrest, 4-6-1984

The last entry was for the previous week:

Ron Webster, 22-5-2018

He googled Webster's name, and found an obituary. The way the death was written about suggested either a suicide or something suspicious. He continued to run down the list and came across one he thought he recognised (after some thought, he recalled it had been widely reported in the media):

Doctor Mark Murphy, 1-12-2017

A quick internet search told him that Murphy, a physicist from Bligh University in Cork, had been found tied to a table in a storage container on the Cork docks. He had been tortured to death. The authorities suspected gang involvement (the area where his body was discovered had been the location of one or two meth labs in the past).

Dunnigan picked up the phone and called Bligh to arrange a visit.

5

GINA WAS THERE WHEN HE GOT HOME. 'WORKING late?'

'A lead came up in a case. I wanted to follow it for a bit.'

'Was it worth it?'

'Time will tell.'

He sat down on the old couch. She was perched on one of the two wooden kitchen chairs he kept in the living room. Diane had talked to him about getting more furniture when they were together, but when they split up, he had left the place as it was.

Beth was in the bedroom, trying on some new clothes she and her mother had bought that afternoon.

'I want to talk to you about something,' Gina said.

'I'm listening.'

'I'd like to bring my daughter home.'

He nodded. He knew it was coming – it had to sooner or later – but he wasn't ready for it yet. Delaying tactics were called for. 'Do you feel up to it?'

'I never meant for this to be a permanent thing.'

'She's doing so well, in a lot of ways, and not so well in others.'

'I know, and I appreciate it. But she is my daughter and I want her with me.'

'You're here most days. You see her all the time.'

'That's not the same, and you know it.'

'She's near her therapy here. She can walk to it in five minutes.'

'I'd drive her. Why are you so against it, Davey?'

He fell silent and looked up at the poster of the Doctor. His oldest friend. The only person he could tell his deepest, darkest thoughts to. Except he hadn't, lately, because Beth had been there.

If he and the Doctor had been having their usual conversations, he might have told him about how having Beth living with him like this was as much about healing him as it was taking care of her. How he felt like he was somehow making amends for having lost her in the first place, the guilt of which still ate at him like a cancer. About how having her there took away the loneliness he often could not admit he felt.

That's what he would have said to the Doctor. And perhaps what he knew he should have said to Gina. But the words wouldn't come. Not the right words, anyway. 'What if she freaks out again? It could really mess her up if you don't handle things the right way. I've been talking to her therapist, and I know what the triggers are.'

Gina's eyes narrowed. 'I can see that Beth isn't the only one who's jealous,' she said. 'I want my daughter back. I've been patient – now get your head together and sort this out.'

And she walked out, leaving him and the Doctor to their private deliberations.

6

HE TOOK BETH WITH HIM ON THE DRIVE TO CORK – he knew their time as flat-mates was coming to an end, and he wanted to have her close. She seemed happy to go on a road trip, and they listened to a *Doctor Who* audio drama on the BMW's stereo as they travelled.

Dunnigan had an ulterior motive for bringing her along, one he was anxious to hide from Gina: he was becoming increasingly concerned about his niece. The sleep disturbances that had been so dramatic while they lived with his twin had become less ambulatory over time (she had only sleepwalked twice since the move), but he heard her crying out and talking in her sleep most nights, and her anger seemed to be constantly bubbling in the background.

The most alarming thing, though, was that his niece was becoming more frightened daily. He knew memories of her captivity and the abuses she had suffered were slowly returning (she rarely mentioned it, but he could tell from the haunted look in her eyes), and this fact was the source of constant anxiety – it was as if her very consciousness was conspiring to drive her to a breakdown.

Clive was still putting pressure on Gina to have the girl committed, and Dunnigan was genuinely worried that, if things continued as they were, his twin would have no choice but to comply. He knew Beth was barely keeping her more violent outbursts under control, and his greatest fear was that she might snap and really hurt someone.

The day before he went to Cork he met Diane for lunch in the Starbucks near the homeless project where she and Father Bill worked. 'I don't know how to help her with this irrational fear she has,' he said, as they took seats by the window. 'She believes that remembering a particular event – something that happened while she was away – will cause me, you, her parents, basically everyone she cares about, to get hurt. I told her that's not possible, but the stress of it is eating her up. I'm not sure how much longer she can take it.'

'This is standard stuff, Davey,' Diane said gently. 'An awful lot of survivors of abuse are warned that, if they tell anyone about what happened, the abuser will come and kill their families. It's sick and it's evil, but it's a very common story. It's how a lot of predators maintain secrecy.'

'How do I make her believe it's all a big lie?'

'How's the therapy going?'

'All Harriet will say is that we have to give Beth time.'

'Sounds like a plan to me.'

'The problem is, time is something we don't have. Gina wants her to move home and Clive wants to send her to a secure facility for psychotics and I think that if something doesn't give really soon, Beth will seriously harm herself or someone else. And I couldn't live with that.'

'I'm going to say something, Davey, and you aren't going to like it.'

Dunnigan laughed bitterly. 'You don't usually warn me in advance.'

'I'm trying to go easy on you today, seeing as how you're obviously tired and stressed out.'

'Thanks. I think.'

'You can't fix this for her.'

'I know that!'

'You know in your head, but in your heart you want to take all her pain away. I've been part of your life for a couple of years now, and I know a little about your guilt and sadness. Davey, when I met you first those two emotions defined you. They *were* you, in a lot of ways. Getting Beth back is like someone has waved a magic wand and offered you the chance to make everything right. Only you can't. All the fucking sick shit Beth has been through can't be taken back, no matter how much you might want that. She'll either remember or she won't, and if she does, she'll see the world hasn't ended and you and Gina and Clive are just fine. I know I advised you to take a stronger stance on her violent outbursts, but this is different. You have to step back and let her work through it.'

'I don't think I can step back.'

'Here comes another tough comment.'

'Go on.'

'It's not about you. If you love her, let her be.'

'I thought you were going easy on me.'

'Tough love.'

He laughed dryly again and watched people bustling past on the quays outside. 'Why does love have to be so hard?'

'Sometimes the best things are,' Diane said sadly.

7

BETH BOUGHT SOME MAGAZINES IN A PETROL
station on the journey south, and when they arrived at Bligh
she went to the canteen while Dunnigan spoke to the head of
the Science Department.

'Doctor Murphy was a nice man,' Professor Turner told
him. He was willowy with white hair and pale green eyes, and
was dressed in a tweed suit.

'Did anything out of the ordinary occur during his
time here?'

Turner looked uncomfortable.

'This is completely confidential,' Dunnigan said.

'Unless it finds its way into the courts.'

'I'm just making a routine inquiry. Doctor Murphy's case
may not be linked to my investigation at all.'

Turner fiddled with his watch-strap awkwardly. 'Perhaps
you should speak to our Equality Officer, Mister Byrne.'

'I'd be happy to.'

*

Byrne was a tall, gangly, long-haired young man wearing a
suede jacket and sporting a bow-tie. His office had posters for

Greenpeace and The Smiths' *Meat is Murder* album on the wall. 'Mark Murphy had one complaint made against him,' he said, once Dunnigan had assured him that everything he said would be kept private. 'He made some improper advances to one of the ancillary staff.'

'An administrator?'

'One of the domestic engineers.'

Dunnigan chewed on that one. 'A worker in the canteen?'

'She was more in the hygiene field than culinary.'

'Are you telling me she was a cleaner, Mister Byrne?'

'I don't like labels.'

'No, but they have their uses,' the criminologist said. 'Is the lady in question working today?'

'Yes. She'll be coming on shift in three quarters of an hour.'

Dunnigan noted that Byrne knew the details without having to check. 'Would you tell her I'd appreciate five minutes of her time?'

'Of course. I'll give Martha a ring right away.'

Yuri Chechnik

He did not recognise the girl in the picture Frobisher had given him.

All the women he had seen in the house in Galway had been half-starved and three-quarters of them were addicted to smack. The name, however, he remembered: Beth – or Carla as she had been known in the house – had been one of the ones with complaints logged against them, making her one of the reasons he was in that shithole of a place to begin with.

Once he got back to Ireland it was easy to track down the girl through her uncle – the fact the man worked for the police did not bother Yuri at all. He was not in a hurry to end this dance – he would take his time, watch them for a while, and make his move when the opportunity presented itself. Which it would – it always did.

The pair shared a flat near Dublin's city centre. Yuri found that a building right across the street had an empty room, and it was easy to break in. He brought in a folding chair and some food, and began his vigil.

Since his near-death experience, he slept little – he suffered from recurring headaches, which disturbed his rest and gave him bad dreams. It did not matter. All it meant was that he would not miss any of his prey's comings and goings.

He followed the criminologist's car out of Dublin city early one morning. Yuri had stolen a Volkswagen Golf GTi, and he kept three cars back to ensure the man did not notice his tail (although the Romanian did not for a moment believe he would – police or not, the man was lazy and seemed unconcerned for their safety).

After the long drive to the university, he parked in the row just behind them, and watched as they went into a building with the words Science and Technology *written in large letters above the door. Through binoculars, he saw the uncle go one way, the girl the other.*

He found her in the canteen, sipping a cup of something, a magazine called SFX *open in front of her.*

He looked so different after his ordeal he was not really worried she would know him, but he put a baseball cap on his head and pulled his hoody up too, just to be certain, and after getting some tea he took a chair at the other end of the room and pretended to look at his phone.

He had not had a woman since he was shot.

He was going to enjoy ending his dry spell.

And he would make her uncle watch.

8

MARTHA WINGARDEN REMINDED DUNNIGAN OF Diane.

She was in her thirties and had long blonde hair loosely tied back and strong, pretty features. She was not tall, but gave the sense of energy and determination. The criminologist liked her immediately.

'I did not care for Doctor Murphy,' she told him. They were sitting on a bench outside the library.

'Do you mind telling me why?'

'He just ... he just wasn't a very nice person.'

'The head of his department told me he *was* a nice person – in fact, that was all he would say about him.'

'He was a creep, alright?'

Dunnigan nodded. 'I'm not here to judge you,' he said. 'If you tell me this man behaved improperly, I believe you. I'm just curious about how he died.'

'Why would I know anything about that?'

'I'm not saying you do ... but was there anything odd about Murphy's behaviour?'

'Everything about him was odd.'

'Did he mention a book?'

Martha turned sharply to look at him. 'Why do you ask about a book?'

'You know about it, don't you?'

She nodded, and he saw that her lower lip was trembling and she was close to tears. 'I have it,' she whispered, and then the tears came in a surge.

Dunnigan looked around to see if they were drawing attention, and fumbled in one of the pockets of his jacket for a tissue. 'His book?' he asked, handing her the crumpled offering.

She nodded, wiping her nose. 'I put it in a box in my attic and I haven't looked at it since that night.'

'How did you get it?'

She shook her head. 'I don't want to talk about it. Please don't make me.'

'People are dying, Ms Wingarden.'

'If they're like him, they deserve it.'

'Is it up to us to decide that?'

She sighed a long, shuddering sigh. 'I hoped it had all been a bad dream.'

'I wish it was.'

And as the sun shone and students studied on the well-tended lawn, she told him of the night she had been saved from a horrible death by Mother Joan. When she was finished, she looked at him with eyes bloodshot from crying. 'I wanted it not to have been real,' she said, 'but I couldn't stop thinking about her. I ... I went online, and found some forums where people actually *talked* about things like this happening, and I learned she was called Mother Joan. I was able to ask some questions and find out some things. There's a group called The Watchers – I sent them an anonymous email, and told them to add what happened to Murphy to the list.'

'Why?'

'So people will know he was a monster, and died because of it.'

'I see.'

'I learned a lot of things from those forums.'

'What kind of things?' Dunnigan asked.

'That even though I still see her in my dreams and she scares me half to death, Mother Joan is not a force for evil. She's good. If she hadn't been there, Murphy would have cut me to pieces.'

Dunnigan shrugged. 'Thanks for your time,' he said. 'I'm sorry if it was painful.'

'Are you going to keep looking for her?'

'It's my job.'

'Say you've looked and you can't find her.'

Dunnigan stood up and offered his hand to Martha, who held it for a second rather than shook it.

'I think the world is better for her being in it,' she said.

'I'll keep that in mind,' the criminologist said gently, and left her, tear-stained and trembling.

9

THE MAIN GARDA STATION IN CORK CITY WAS ON Anglesea Street.

The sergeant, a big friendly man with a large belly and a thick head of grey hair, was pleasant enough. 'I'd love to be able to tell you there was more to it than there appeared, but I can't,' he said, sipping coffee from a chunky mug with the Garda insignia emblazoned on the side.

'You sound very certain.'

'Murphy was found by a bunch of kids who had gone to a deserted part of the docks to drink cider and smoke dope. They found an open storage container and went in but could smell something was off. They were right – it was what was left of Doctor Murphy. He'd been tied to a carpenter's table using gaffer tape and then someone had gone to work on him with every tool in the box. Most of his extremities were missing, and not a small amount of his interior parts too. The killer went hard, there's no doubt about that.'

'And you're sure it was one of the gangs?'

'We're an hour and a half from Limerick. Last year we got a call because one of those very containers, a five-minute stroll from where Murphy was carved up, was on fire. It turned out someone was cooking crystal meth in it, and the kit had exploded.'

'What makes you believe a physics lecturer was involved in something like that?'

'Haven't you seen *Breaking Bad*?'

'I'm more of a sci-fi fan.'

'The gang link wasn't our first theory, but then we had a look at his computer, and we changed our minds.'

'Why?'

'He was into some nasty stuff.'

'For instance?'

'Things you need to go to very bad people for. Pursuits that are highly illegal and cost a lot of money. Believe me, Mark Murphy was linked to some unsavoury individuals. It looks like one of them caught up with him – could have been for any number of reasons – and had a very sharp conversation with him.'

'But there are no witnesses, and no forensic evidence?'

'The implements used were all still there. As were all the parts that had been removed. But other than that, nothing.'

'Could you give me the location of the storage container?'

'Why?'

'I'd like to have a look.'

'There's nothing there anymore. The place has been cleaned out by the Forensics lads.'

'Humour me.'

The sergeant scribbled the directions on a slip of paper.

10

BETH WANTED TO HAVE DINNER IN THE ENGLISH Market, so they went to Farmgate, where they managed to get a seat at the railing overlooking the busy shopping area below. Dunnigan had chowder and she consumed a huge serving of sausage, mash and beans, with gravy on the side.

'I don't know where you put it,' he said as she tucked in. 'You're still so skinny.'

'I've got a lot of years to make up for.'

They applied themselves to their food.

'Your mum and I had a talk last night.'

'What about?'

'She'd like you to move home.'

Beth gave him a rapid glance, then returned her gaze to her plate. 'What do you think I should do?'

He had some soup. It was excellent. 'I would love you to stay with me forever, but I don't think it's really my decision to make.'

'If you're asking me, I don't know what I want.'

He didn't want to put her under any pressure, but didn't want the decision to be made without involving her, either.

So much had been decided for her throughout her childhood. 'I love your mother.'

'I know that.'

'I don't want to hurt her – even though I know I have, in the past.'

'I don't want to either – and I went for her with a knife.'

He laughed at her candour despite himself. 'You did indeed.'

She cut off a piece of sausage and dipped it in the gravy. 'I was still operating from the old rule book, where if you didn't want to do something, you took a chunk out of the person who was trying to force you.'

'You don't have to do that anymore.'

She grinned, a sad, winsome smile. 'It's nice to know I can if I need to, though.'

11

EVENING HAD SETTLED OVER THE CITY AND DUSK was coming down as Dunnigan parked outside a long red and blue metal container situated at the eastern end of the Cork docks, on the northern side of the Lee. Across the river he could see the shape of Blackrock Castle, and on the water a freighter moved slowly into the shipping lanes. 'Want to come for the wander?' he asked Beth.

'No, thanks. I'll just read my magazine.'

'Okay. Won't be long.'

The container stood on its own beside a derelict shed made from boards of plywood and corrugated iron that was leaning drunkenly to one side. There was nothing else along this stretch of the waterway for quite a distance in either direction: a haulage company had its yard a quarter kilometre to the east, and one of the various shipping offices was based to the west. The burned-out skeleton of the meth lab that had combusted sat desolately about 1,500 yards to Dunnigan's left like some long-dead creature the water had given up.

The doors on the container were warped, twisted and burned – whoever had taken Murphy had obviously used considerable force to gain entry. There was a spot near the ground where the safety bar would have locked shut that was blackened much more than the rest. It looked as if an explosive charge had been detonated there.

'And I suppose ghosts use Semtex now,' he said to himself and, standing up, took out his phone and switched on the torch app.

The sergeant had been right – the first thing that struck him as he stepped into the container proper was the powerful smell of industrial-strength bleach. The place had been cleaned thoroughly. He continued in, regardless. The structure had been wired for electricity (a fuse box protruded from the ceiling over the door) and a bare bulb had been centrally hung. He flicked the light switch, but nothing happened – clearly, the power had been disconnected following the demise of the person who paid the bills. Cheap tongue and groove flooring had been put down, and four indentations denoted where the table had been.

He squatted down and examined the corners and cracks between the laminate boards, but the place was clean as a whistle.

Sitting on the floor, he closed his eyes. Sometimes being in a crime scene and mentally replaying the events that took place there helped him to visualise, but this evening he was getting nothing.

He stood up.

As he did so, he heard another car pull up outside.

12

BETH WAS ENGROSSED IN HER MAGAZINE, READING an article about the movie *The Sword and the Sorcerer*, from the 1980s. It sounded like the kind of dumb fun she and Davey enjoyed, and she thought she might ask him if he'd like to watch it with her.

So focussed was she on her film research, she almost didn't notice the car's slow approach. The engine sound eventually roused her from her reveries and she spotted the vehicle when it was about a hundred yards away – a small black hatchback.

Instinctively she slid low in her seat, hiding from view.

She heard the car pull up a little away from the BMW. Reaching up, she angled the rear-view mirror so she could see the driver. He was a tall, heavily muscled man, wearing fitted jeans and a grey hoodie. There was something about the way he moved she didn't like – it had a reptilian quality to it that was eerily familiar.

She didn't know how and she didn't know where, but she was certain she had encountered this man before. He wasn't Frank Tormey and he wasn't Father Bill, and he certainly wasn't her dad. Which meant there was only one way she could have come in contact with him.

He was one of them.

For several long seconds Beth was literally paralysed with terror.

Somehow, she had known this was going to happen – they knew the memory had returned. It didn't matter that she hadn't told anyone, the details of what had happened being in her head was enough. She felt as if an electric current was pulsing through her, locking her joints rigidly in place and making it hard for her to breathe.

The man began moving towards the driver's side of the BMW, and some kind of survival instinct kicked in. Gently Beth opened the passenger door and slid out, rolling under the car and lying flat. She could see the black work boots of the stranger. He stopped, obviously looking to see if anyone was inside. Then there was a pause, followed by the sharp sound of a bullet being jacked into the chamber of a handgun.

And the man's boots vanished from view as he walked into the container Davey had just entered.

13

DUNNIGAN HELD OUT HIS ID CARD AS THE MAN entered the container. 'Sir, my name is …'

The stranger didn't pause, but walked right up and pistol-whipped him across the jaw, knocking him backwards. 'Where is the girl?'

Dunnigan staggered two or three steps, dazed and confused. 'I … What? Who are you?'

'I ask you where is the girl?' He lashed out with a kick that connected with Dunnigan's gut and lifted him off the ground, taking the wind entirely out of his lungs. The criminologist landed hard, gasping for oxygen, his stomach heaving. He could not have spoken even if he had wanted to, so just lay there, waiting for his chest to start pumping again, trying to work out what was going on.

The man with the gun was not inclined to give him a chance to recuperate. Bending down, he grasped Dunnigan by the hair. 'You and she were together when you leave the city. I not see you stop, but she is not in car and she is not in here. Did she go for walk?'

'I came here alone.' Dunnigan managed to force the words out. His mind had caught up with current events: they had come for Beth. Despite all the safeguards and precautions, the bastards had bided their time and now they had come for her. He felt a rush of righteous anger. He would die before giving her up – in fact, he would be glad to. He struggled to his knees and stared the man down. 'No one was with me. You've made a mistake.'

'You funny man. Stupid, but funny.' He hit him with the gun at the base of his skull this time, and stars exploded across his vision. 'I can hit you all night.'

'Be my guest.'

The disfigured man chuckled. 'I watch you, police man. I see you with her. Very warm. Very tender. She is like your daughter, yes?'

Dunnigan spat blood and tried to stand. His head swam and his limbs wouldn't work properly.

The man reached down and hauled him up. 'We get off to bad start. I am Yuri. Your friends, they give me this face.' He removed his hood and hat, and even in the gloom of the container Dunnigan could see the striations of flesh and bone.

'My friends?'

'You come to our place in Galway. I hit you with hurl, woman punch me in the throat, man shoot me in the face.'

Dunnigan shrugged. 'They did not act on my authority.'

'You were angry when you found little Beth?'

'No.'

'Did you chastise Mister Murtaugh and his men for killing and maiming to find this girl you had lost?'

'No.'

'Did you go to confession and say, "Father, I am an ungodly man for allying with evil, violent people"?'

'I'm an atheist.'

'You were happy, I bet. You had a party, yes?'

'What do you want, Yuri?'

'I have a party planned too,' the man answered good-humouredly. 'We are going to have much fun. But I cannot start without your niece. So ...', he dragged Dunnigan over to the wall and sat down, '... we wait.'

14

BETH CRAWLED FROM UNDER THE CAR AND CREPT to the doorway. She could hear shouting and scuffling inside, but it was too dark to see what was going on. Not that she needed to.

The man was there for her.

She realised she was hyperventilating, as she had when she thought she saw Frobisher in Dundrum, and tried to fight the overwhelming rush of abject fear. She could not go back – she *would* not go back. Her heart pounded in her chest and she thought she might collapse.

That fucker has your Uncle Davey! A voice somewhere deep inside her spoke up. *Davey never gave up on you – are you going to give up on him?*

She leaned against the wall of the container and sobbed, biting her hand to quell the sounds. She knew what she had to do, and prayed she had the strength to do it.

Drying her eyes on her sleeve, she walked quickly and quietly back to the BMW, opened the driver's door and released the boot. The only thing inside with any potential was the wheel brace. She picked it up and hefted it, feeling its weight and getting a sense of how it balanced in her hand.

As a weapon it wasn't ideal – it was short, which meant she would have to get up close and personal with the shithead. But then, beggars couldn't be choosers. If that was how it was going to go, then she would play the cards she'd been dealt.

She took a deep breath, walked over to the container and rapped as hard as she could three times on its metal wall.

Use the anger, she told herself. *Harriet has been talking about healthy ways of dealing with it. Well, this is going to have to do.*

'Hey, fuckface,' she shouted, surprised at how strong her voice sounded. 'Are you going to stay in there or are you coming out to play?'

From inside she heard a shuffling movement, followed by heavy footsteps.

And then she ran as hard and as fast as she could.

15

YURI LEAPT TO HIS FEET AT THE SOUND OF BETH'S voice. Grabbing Dunnigan by the arm, he rushed to the door, dragging the battered man after him. By the time they got outside, the girl was nowhere to be seen.

'Beth!' Yuri screamed, holding the gun to Dunnigan's head. 'Come here now, or I will shoot him dead where he stands.'

There was no response, just the sound of the wind blowing up the river from Lough Mahon.

'She does not care so much for you,' Yuri said. 'Maybe she too scared.'

'I hope she runs and doesn't look back,' Dunnigan hissed.

'Let's see,' Yuri said. 'Beth,' he called again, walking further out into the pathway, pushing Dunnigan in front as he went, 'I have need of you to come with me. I do not want to harm your uncle, but I will do so if you do not comply with my wishes. I am going to count to five, and if you do not make yourself visible, I will do something bad. It is your choice.'

He paused, scanning the area. Dunnigan was doing the same – he could not see where Beth might be. There was a clear view in both directions and nothing to hide behind.

'One,' Yuri shouted.

Somewhere in the distance a klaxon sounded. Dunnigan was aware of traffic noise very far off.

'Two.'

Herring gulls bickered atop a lamppost. Water lapped.

'Three,' Yuri said, and shot Dunnigan in the arm.

Dunnigan saw the flash, and his brain told him to jump out of the way, but as the thought entered his mind, he felt what seemed like someone punching him and he fell over onto his side – only then did he hear the loud blast of the report.

He tried to get up, but his right arm was numb and unresponsive. Awkwardly, he fumbled with his left.

That was when the singing started.

16

BETH RAN WITH NO PLAN OR FORETHOUGHT –
she just wanted to put as much distance as she could between
herself and the gunman. She realised after covering about a
hundred metres that the nearest building was very far away,
and she was still within easy range if he decided to shoot her.

The dockside was in darkness now – across the river lights
twinkled.

Looking about her, she saw that her only hope of escape
was to scale the dock wall and jump into the River Lee. She
sprinted over and, looking down, saw a narrow gangway made
of steel, probably used by maintenance workers to access the
hulls of boats. She tucked the wheel brace into the waistband
of her jeans, then gingerly lowered herself.

The platform was fastened to a series of stone columns
that sat atop huge concrete blocks and seemed steady enough.
She tested it once by jumping, then started to edge back the
way she had come – maybe a sneak attack would be possible.

Beth knew their only hope rested on her getting the drop on
the thug who had her uncle, but exactly how that resolution
might play out, she still had no clue, especially if she ended
up in the water. It suddenly occurred to her that if the bad

man looked over the railing, she would be seen – she had to get onto one of those blocks and out of sight, if she could.

She peered into the space between the struts, water lapping below her. It was dark in there and smelt of boat fuel and rotting seaweed. To her left, something flapped – she assumed it was a seagull.

Beth heard the gangster shout her name. She desperately tried to assess the distance between the gangway and the columns. She didn't think she could make the jump. She *had* to make the jump

He threatened to shoot Davey.

She *must* help her uncle. There was that movement again – closer this time. She looked quickly in the direction, but whatever it was had gone.

The man screamed for her to come.

She began to run up the gangway, oblivious to the risk of falling into the water.

He began to count.

Whatever was in the shadows seemed to be following her as she ran. She still could not get a good look at it – she had a sense of it being vast and dark and flowing. Above her, the man had reached two in his count. Her whole world was caught up in the sound of his voice.

She came to a ladder that led back up to ground level. He reached the number three. She placed a foot on the first rung and something black and huge landed on the gangway beside her.

Then she heard the gunshot, and the strangest music she had ever heard began to drift across the river on the wind.

17

DUNNIGAN HALF-KNELT/HALF-CROUCHED, FEELING weak and dizzy as the world filled with the sound of what seemed to be a hymn or a plainchant – he wasn't a music fan, so didn't feel qualified to judge. At first Dunnigan thought the melody was being played on a stringed instrument, a viola, perhaps, but the more he listened, the more he thought it was a human voice – it was quite unlike anything he had ever heard before.

'What is this?' Yuri asked, the gun hanging loosely by his side.

'You wouldn't believe me if I told you,' Dunnigan said faintly. The world felt like it was getting smaller and smaller, and his arm was beginning to throb as if it had its own heartbeat. He realised he was going to lose consciousness, and bit his lip as hard as he could. The additional burst of pain brought the world back into focus.

From the corner of his eye, he saw something land on top of the storage container. The singing became louder, almost deafening.

'Beth, you stop this and come to me,' Yuri bellowed. 'I will shoot him again!'

'You don't have the guts,' Dunnigan said, and began to laugh. Once he started, he couldn't stop – this was as bizarre a situation as he'd ever been in, after all.

Yuri looked at him as if he had grown a second head, and kicked him in the face. Dunnigan felt something pop in his nose, followed by a sort of gushing sensation, but there wasn't much pain.

Staying upright was too difficult, and he keeled over again. Yuri pushed the criminologist onto his back. The song had reached a shrill, screeching pitch. It hurt to listen to it.

'I have no guts?' Yuri shouted over the din.

'You're a coward,' Dunnigan hissed.

'Well, this coward is going to put your guts all over the tarmac.' He levelled the barrel at Dunnigan's mid-section.

Over his shoulder, Dunnigan saw the nightmarish figure of Mother Joan slowly, in juddering, shuddering starts, rise to her full height atop the storage container. As he watched, she spread her cloak, like wings.

Before the ghoul had a chance to spring, Beth Carlton, adding her own scream to the cacophony, charged at Yuri, smashing the wheel brace into the side of his head with an audible crunch. Before he had a chance to fall, she hit him a second time, breaking his jaw and knocking out even more teeth.

As if someone had hit a switch, the music stopped.

Insensible, Yuri Chechnik crumpled to the ground.

'I didn't tell! I didn't tell! I didn't tell!' Beth shouted, kicking him as hard as she could manage in the head, the back, the stomach, the balls.

Yuri's gun landed right beside Dunnigan, who scooped it

up and pointed it unsteadily at the prone figure, now lying in an ever-widening pool of blood.

'Don't move,' Dunnigan said, and passed out.

Had he been conscious, he would have noticed that Mother Joan was gone.

'Daddy, I had a bad dream.'

You blink your eyes and sit up. The fluorescent hands on your clock tell you it is late – 3.33 a.m.

'Do you want to hop into bed and tell me about it?'

'No, Daddy.'

It seems unnaturally dark. You can barely make out your daughter's pale form in the darkness of your room.

'Why not, sweetie?'

'Because in my dream, when I told you about the dream, the thing wearing Mommy's skin sat up.'

For a moment, you feel paralysed; you cannot take your eyes off your daughter. The duvet behind you begins to shift.

'She told me her name is Mother Joan.'

Posted by hacker_red
www.wickedwords.com

Part Five

INTERLUDE

1

DUNNIGAN CAME AROUND IN HOSPITAL. TORMEY was asleep on a chair, Diane perched on the end of the bed fiddling with her phone, while Beth sat cross-legged on the floor reading a graphic-novel edition of *The Midwich Cuckoos*.

'Look who's awake,' Diane said, when Dunnigan opened his eyes.

'This is getting to be a bit of a habit,' the chief said, stretching and yawning.

Beth said nothing, just looked up, gave a meek smile, and returned to her book.

*

'Do you want to tell me what happened?' Tormey asked an hour later, once Dunnigan had been brought toast and tea, and Diane and Beth had gone back to the hotel they'd booked into, to change their clothes and shower.

He did, leaving nothing out.

'Beth gave me an edited version,' the chief said, when Dunnigan was finished.

'What did she leave out?'

'The arrival of Witchipoo.'

'She might not have seen her.'

'You just told me the music was so loud it hurt your ears.'

'I'd been shot. I could have been hallucinating.'

'I don't think a bullet to the arm affects you like that.'

Dunnigan tried to shrug, but it hurt, so he stopped. 'How's Yuri?'

'Not doing too good. Beth managed to hit him in a weak spot in his skull – he'd recently been shot there, so the wheel brace went in like a knife through butter.'

'Ouch.'

'Quite. Doctors don't know if he's going to regain consciousness, and even if he does, there's no telling if he'll ever be right again.'

'He was going to kill me.'

Tormey reached over and put a hand on Dunnigan's arm. 'It seems likely he was going to kill you both. Beth was acting in self-defence. Quite frankly, I think the girl deserves a fucking medal. I might even see if I can organise one for her.'

Dunnigan lay back and felt sleep reaching for him again. 'Have you spoken to Gina?' he asked.

'She's been in.'

'How mad is she?'

'If there was a Beaufort scale for women's tempers, and I think there should be, she'd be clocking in at about a force ten.'

'That's bad, is it?'

'I believe it's the worst you can get.'

'Maybe it would have been better if Yuri had killed me.'

'You could be right.'

2

WHEN HE WOKE AGAIN THE ROOM WAS IN darkness but for a dim light from the hallway by which Gina was reading the paper. 'Hello,' he said.

She closed the paper and folded it carefully. 'How's your arm?'

'It feels as if someone shot me in it.'

'I don't blame them.'

He smiled, but she did not respond in kind.

'I have some things I need to say.'

'Can they wait until I regain my strength?'

'No, they can't.'

'I thought as much.'

'You and Beth always had something the rest of us couldn't be a part of, even when she was little,' Gina said, ignoring him. 'And I was okay with that. You were the whole world to me when we were kids, so it made sense you would be to her too.'

'We don't have to do this,' Dunnigan said.

'Yes, we do. You know I never blamed you when she was taken, don't you?'

He nodded.

'When Clive wanted to kill you, when our parents disowned you, I always had your back. You were … you *are* … a part of me, and even in the face of the greatest loss a mother can experience, I defended you.'

Dunnigan said nothing. He had learned that silence sometimes worked better for him than speaking, which so often resulted in him saying things that offended people, even when he hadn't meant to.

'You went to the ends of creation looking for her, and when you drew the anger of wicked men, I begged you to stop. I didn't want to lose you, but you didn't care. It was like she had a homing beacon only you could perceive and you had no choice but to follow it – it was hard-wired into you to keep going until you zeroed in.'

'It was kind of like that,' he said, the words coming out in spite of his resolution.

'I know. I get it.'

'Do you?'

She hugged him. She smelt very faintly of perfume and soap. 'It's why you were mad at Father Bill when he went on his solo run to track her down,' Gina said, after a time.

'I always thought it was going to be me that found her,' he said. 'I couldn't understand why he waited until I was on the other side of the globe.'

'Have you asked him?'

Dunnigan thought about that. 'Not in so many words.'

'Because you don't talk to people, even the ones who care about you.'

'I'm trying to work on that.'

'I know you care deeply for Beth. And I know she loves you. You have been a complete dickhead to me, but to her you have been a sweetheart.' She hugged him again. 'And having said all of that, I do not want my daughter around you.'

He pushed her away from him. 'What? Come on, Gina, that's ridiculous!'

'I'm not trying to hurt you, Davey.'

'Well, you are failing dismally, then.'

'I'm sorry, but I don't think you're safe with her. Because of you she now has to live with the knowledge that she has more or less killed someone, on top of all the other nightmare crap she had floating about in her head. You knowingly put her in harm's way and I am not going to allow that to happen again.'

'What about what she wants?'

'I am not going to let you play that card, Davey. Right now, I don't want you seeing Beth. I'm not saying it's a permanent arrangement, but I think you two need some space.'

She leaned over, kissed him on the forehead, and walked out before he could say another word.

3

HE WAS DEEMED FIT TO LEAVE THE HOSPITAL THE
following day. Gina had already left with Beth, so Diane drove
the BMW home, with him pushing imaginary brakes all the
way back to Dublin.

'Want to tell me what's wrong?'

'You can't drive, is what's wrong.'

'You know damn well that I did both advanced and defensive
driving when I was in the army, so I am, in fact, a better driver
than you.'

'You hide it well.'

'Did the bullet dent your personality too? Oh, no, I forgot,
you were a complete moron before you got shot.'

They drove on in silence.

'Gina doesn't want me seeing Beth anymore.'

'Well, you did take her on a live murder inquiry where she
came in contact with not one, but two killers, one of whom
she had to bludgeon to a pulp with an iron bar. Maybe I'm
off-beam, but I have a feeling a lot of mothers would struggle
with that.'

'There was no way I could have known she was going to
encounter a criminal.'

'No, because that never happens during a *criminal investigation*!'

'I don't think she's being fair.'

'David Dunnigan, do you know how much leeway you're given by your friends and family on a daily basis?'

'How do you mean *leeway*?'

'I am referring to the fact that almost everyone you deal with turns a blind eye to rudeness, unreasonable and annoying character traits, bizarre eccentricities and general pissiness. We do this because, underneath all of that bullshit, there beats the heart of a good and decent man.'

'Thank you?' Dunnigan said.

'Shut up. I'm not finished. Every now and again, you push someone beyond breaking point, and they have to cut you loose for a bit. It happened to me in Greenland. I'm pretty sure it happened to Miley too – let's face it, he stayed to get away from you. It has now happened to Gina.'

He looked sulkily out the window. 'Why are you here if you hate me so much?'

'You drove me to the point I wanted to strangle you. I mean, I *knew* I couldn't be in a romantic relationship with you anymore – if you could call what we had a romantic relationship to begin with. But I got over it. I still love you, you weird asshole. Gina does too. Give her some time and she'll remember that.'

'But what about Beth?'

'From what I know of that girl, she will drive her mother to distraction asking to see you. I give it a week.'

'You failed to signal when you changed lanes just then,' Dunnigan said.

'I will stop the car and let you walk,' Diane said, in complete seriousness.

4

DUNNIGAN MADE TEA AND A CHEESE SANDWICH when he got home, which was about all he was able to do one-handed. (His arm hurt like hell but he did not want to dull his faculties with painkillers, so he put them in the bin.) He sat on the couch to watch Tom Baker as the Fourth Doctor in *City of Death*, one of Beth's favourites. Baker's eccentric performance and the daftness of it all lifted his mood somewhat, although he missed his niece terribly. Maybe Diane was right and Gina would get over it.

She had to, didn't she?

When the series ended he sat in the silent flat and gazed up at his poster. 'Just me tonight, Doctor,' he said. 'Beth's gone. I managed to almost get both of us killed – you wouldn't believe it, but they were literally queuing up to do the job.'

He paused. 'If Mother Joan came to kill me, I wonder why she changed her mind.'

He stood up and went to the window, which was his favourite spot to think. 'Was she afraid of Beth? I suppose watching her beat the living daylights out of a mobster might have been off-putting, but that doesn't seem likely.'

He chewed the problem over for a bit. 'And aren't there meant to be rules about how she works? Rituals?'

There were: the subtle hints, the stalking, the delivery of the book – why had none of these things happened? Why had she circumvented her usual patterns and then not even bothered to complete the task?

'Of course,' he said, 'maybe she wasn't after me at all. Perhaps it was Yuri.'

He discounted that – Mother Joan's victims were men who hid their sins and led double lives. Yuri was cut from a very different cloth.

'Which means our fairytale monster has broken her pattern,' he said, grinning at the Doctor. 'Something, by all accounts, she isn't supposed to be able to do.'

He made more tea and went back to the window. The street was quiet outside. Peaceful.

'Normal, run-of-the-mill human serial killers have rituals too,' he said. 'Places they like to hunt, victim profiles they favour, even times of year they prefer to work. It is unusual for them to change their methodologies, but not unheard of.'

Stress might cause such a breakdown. Or surprise. Some kind of crisis.

'Over-identification with a potential victim,' he said. 'That tends to be a big one, doesn't it? Serial murderers abort their plans when they find themselves *liking* a potential kill.'

How do you begin to like someone? Familiarity.

'How does Mother Joan choose her subjects? How does she know the things she does about them?'

All the people she had killed were professionals: doctors, lawyers, academics. Why choose that demographic? The obvious answer was availability and easy access.

She had to be staking them out – getting to know them, observing, gathering evidence.

'From that website, it looks as if she travels – we have deaths here and in the UK.'

She had been forced to abandon the kill in Cork – what was she likely to do?

'She's going to run. She'll want to return to base, lick her wounds.'

Where was base, though? Where was the monster's lair?

An urban myth would want to dwell somewhere densely populated.

'I think I'm going to London,' he said to the Doctor.

He was due a trip, and it might help to get his mind off the problems with Gina. He pulled over his laptop and booked a ticket for the following morning.

Ernest Frobisher

'Yuri Chechnik is in a coma from which he is not so likely to recover,' the psychiatrist Ressler said as he hung a fresh drip and checked the blood pressure monitor.

'How?'

'It seems little Beth Carlton has claws like the she-wolf.'

Frobisher wanted to scream, but the act would have used more oxygen than he could spare. There was a time when he had people at his immediate disposal to deal with irritating problems like David Dunnigan, but the criminologist had, in the space of a year, compromised his operations to an alarming degree. He had been forced to lay low, to find a hole to crawl into. Any moves he made against the man had to be careful and deliberate, nothing that could be traced back to him or his people.

Now the girl, that cheap little bitch, was at large again with knowledge that could bring all the fires of hell down on the After Dark Campaign, and she was proving equally difficult to neutralise.

Why hadn't he killed her while she was still in his clutches? He had to begrudgingly admit to himself that her continued existence was down to two reasons: firstly, he never in a million years thought she would be rescued from the grip of his organisation, which was vast and complex; and secondly, she had, even at the lower end of the sex trade, continued to make money, and one thing Ernest Frobisher knew was that you never cast aside a steady earner – his father had taught him that much.

Through lidded eyes he watched Ressler adjust the feed on his respirator.

He was still uncertain about the psychiatrist. There was about him a quality that made Frobisher nervous – like a wild dog that had never been fully tamed. Everything the man did seemed to be for his own amusement – Frobisher had come to believe that the only reason he allied himself to the After Dark Campaign was because it suited him to do so. Maybe it was time to finish the training process. Was it not true that all a dog wanted was to be told what to do?

'Why do I keep you around, Ressler?'

'I would not wish to guess your motives, Mister Frobisher.'

'Your job is to make my problems go away.'

'A noble task indeed.'

'The next time I see you, bring me a fucking solution.'

Ressler bowed and left the room. Even the wildest beast wanted a master.

Frobisher slept. These days, he spent more time sleeping than doing anything else. His food came through tubes, air was blown right up what was left of his nose, and his shit and piss were pumped out of holes in his abdomen into plastic bags.

At some stage (day or night meant nothing to him anymore – it was all the same) Ressler returned.

'I bring a solution.'

'Tell me.'

The psychiatrist placed an iPad where Frobisher could see it. The video of Mother Joan attacking O'Connor was playing on the screen.

'Our eyes and ears in the Irish Department of Justice brought this to my attention,' Ressler said.

'What the fuck am I watching?'

'Death. Your friend and mine Mister David Dunnigan is investigating her.'

'And how is this going to help us?'

'You asked me earlier why it is that you keep me around. My role, before Mister Dunnigan caused us such problems, was the psychological conditioning of the children you abducted, so they become compliant and could be used for whichever purpose we saw fit.'

'Yes …' Frobisher responded, but he was already beginning to guess Ressler's plan.

'I am going to introduce myself to Death, and use my old skill set to bend her to our will.'

'What, pray tell, might that be?'

'I think she could be a very effective weapon.'

And Frobisher smiled. It was not a pleasant sight.

Part Six

THE WATCHERS

Mother Joan

The voices quieted only rarely.

Over the years she had learned not to listen to them, but sometimes the noise in her head got so great she thought her skull would fracture from the force.

The only thing that quelled the din was the hunt.

It had become what she lived for, all that gave her purpose. The streets of cities were jungle tracks, the towering buildings the looming shapes of mountains and hills, and she made the shadows her cloak – the men she chased were so fat and lazy and stupid, she could just as well have been invisible.

Each death brought her a small, temporary peace, and for a while she felt as if the world was settling into a kind of normality. But then the voices would begin their shouting all over again, and she knew she could never rest.

Worse still, the voices had started to bring with them physical pain.

It came in waves that crashed over her with terrible ferocity and left her insensible, drenched in sweat, begging for release. Nothing seemed to quell it, and there were days now when she could not move, when all she was able to do was lie in the darkness, sobbing, praying for an end to this suffering.

Experience had taught her not to trust her mind, but she believed she had mastered her body's frailties. That it was letting her down so badly was a source of terrible anguish.

The only way to find comfort was to begin a new hunt.

Hacker_red had told her of a fresh target – a psychiatrist who had been responsible for abducting children for the sex trade. He would soon be in London, according to her source. Perhaps it was time she made herself known to him.

Once he knew her name, he would belong to her.

And she to him.

1

THE CITY OF LONDON UNIVERSITY (OR *CITY*, AS
its students fondly called it) had been established as a law
school in the 1850s. Its beautiful red-bricked façade overlooked
Northampton Square and the campus (a series of framed
photographs just inside its atrium informed Dunnigan)
boasted past-pupils as diverse as Mahatma Gandhi and
Margaret Thatcher.

A new academic year had just begun and students loaded
with books and bags milled about as the criminologist
scoured the noticeboards in an attempt to find out where The
Watchers, the group of Mother Joan fans with their curious,
amateurish website, would be meeting that evening.

A young woman in a pink and blue hijab directed him to
the office of the Students' Union.

'Ah, yes, the pasta nerds,' the pretty blonde girl behind the
desk said. 'They've booked A15 – you're three hours early,
they're not supposed to be there until 7.30. And when you
see Josh, would you tell him he still hasn't paid the group's
society registration fee?'

Dunnigan thanked her, and went to look for the
A corridor.

When he located the room it was occupied by a class in full swing, so he went to get tea and something to eat.

Returning fifteen minutes before the allotted time, Dunnigan found that someone had pushed the tables aside and placed the chairs in a circle, in which (so far) three people were sitting. On the whiteboard was a huge poster of Mother Joan and below it, in the same style of Garamond script used in the Black Bibles, were the words *The Watchers*.

'This is a private meeting,' an overweight, ponytailed kid with a scraggly beard warned when Dunnigan came in.

'It didn't say that on your website,' the criminologist shot back.

'It's a closed group, dude,' a thin, acned youth with a Flock of Seagulls haircut piped up. 'We're not taking new members.'

'What's the criteria for joining?'

'The man just told you – we're not open for business.'

The third person was a little older than the other two, and wore a sports coat over an REM t-shirt.

'Even if I told you I'd seen her?'

Ponytail scoffed. 'Every pasta fan says they've seen her. You know the way out.'

Dunnigan opened the buckle on his tote bag and pulled out O'Connor's Black Bible.

'Do they all have one of these?'

The trio froze.

'Dude, was that made for you?' Flock of Seagulls asked, his voice barely above a whisper.

'No. But I knew the previous owner: he features in the photographs.'

'Is he … is he still breathing?'

Dunnigan shook his head.

'You'd better come in,' REM said. 'The others are going to want to hear your story.'

*

Seven more arrived over the next fifteen minutes, all young men. The kid in the REM t-shirt was the oldest, and he didn't look a day over twenty-four. As each of them came in and took a seat in the circle, Dunnigan began to think he had made a mistake – The Watchers looked more like an encounter group for disenfranchised teens than the first line of defence against a serial killer.

He was about to make his excuses when REM, who told Dunnigan his name was Josh, stood up.

'This man has travelled here from Ireland.' He put on a deeper, more dramatic voice than his conversational style from earlier. 'He has seen the Mother's work first hand.'

'So she does cross the water,' a Goth in a ripped black shirt said, clearly awe-struck by this news.

'Mister Dunnigan says he is researching the Mother for a book,' Josh continued. (Dunnigan had thought the evening might go more smoothly if he drew a veil over his police connections.) 'Maybe we can answer some of his questions.'

All eyes settled on the criminologist, who suddenly found that all the questions he had seemed vaguely ridiculous. 'Why are you all here?' he finally blurted. 'Are you fans, or geeks, or emos or … I'm not sure I understand.'

A litany of scowls greeted this line of questioning.

'If you'd really seen Mother Joan you'd get it,' a kid with ginger hair said. 'You shouldn't have let him in here, Josh.'

'It's a valid question.' The group's leader raised a

conciliatory hand. 'Let's try to enlighten Mister Dunnigan on what we do.'

There was a glum silence for a moment, then Flock of Seagulls (the group referred to him simply as 'Flock') said, 'Most of us are, y'know, interested observers. I mean, obviously we're fans of creepypasta, but you must understand that a lot of those writings are real – it's a way of getting the word out about how messed up the world has gotten.'

'We are living through the end of days,' a skinny kid whose hair was dyed in the rainbow colours interjected. He wore a kimono-style dress over ripped jeans 'If you've seen her, you already know that.'

'I believe she killed my dad.' Ponytail looked as if he were about to burst into tears.

'Why?' Dunnigan asked.

'Because he was an asshole.'

Dunnigan surveyed the group and didn't know whether to stay or just make a dash for the airport. Finally, deciding he had nothing to lose, he held up the book. 'My research has revealed that at least nine Black Bibles have been found in Ireland. I believe there have been two deaths linked to this person you call Mother Joan so far, and one incident where she was seen by witnesses but did not commit the crime.'

'She was hunting, but not ready to strike.' Flock was almost bouncing up and down with excitement.

'How can you be sure of that?' Dunnigan tried to keep the incredulity from his voice. 'I mean, couldn't there be any number of reasons?'

'She's bound by the rules,' Rainbow said, as if this was the most obvious thing in the world. 'It's how it works.'

'She has to atone and by so doing make others atone.' Josh spoke the words with real seriousness.

'It's hard to see the light when you're dead,' Dunnigan deadpanned.

'Mother Joan is doomed to wander the earth until the end of days, making men see the evil of their ways or die.' Ponytail chanted the words like a mantra, finishing in a whisper: 'She is the Ghost of Vengeance, dude.'

'I don't believe in ghosts,' the criminologist said wearily. 'Look, I'm researching a series of murders. Admittedly the killer seems to have adopted the identity and dress of a supernatural figure, but that doesn't mean she actually is supernatural. If we're even dealing with a "she" to begin with.'

'Do you know the story of Mother Joan?' Josh asked him.

'I know all about the genesis of the character on the web and I've read the stuff about the seventeenth-century French nun.'

'That's only part of it.'

'It's inconsequential,' Dunnigan said. 'Do any of you know how to stop her?'

'You came here looking for answers,' Josh pointed out. 'Let us give you some.'

'I don't want more ghost stories.'

'Just listen.'

Mother Joan

She had been aware of the psychiatrist as soon as he arrived in the city, which occurred the day after she returned from her hunting trip in Ireland. She tracked him from the airport and watched as he walked up the street to his hotel.

He moved with the natural grace of a gymnast or a dancer, and despite the fact that she had revealed herself to him twice now, looming out of the shadows of an alleyway the first time and actually stepping across his path the second, he had behaved as if she were not there and continued on his way, oblivious.

Never before had she encountered a man who did not quake in her presence.

This one was different. She did not like it.

She perched on a roof by his window and peered inside. He had his back to her, working on something on the table. Gently, she got her clawed fingers under the rim of the frame and pulled the panel open. In a single movement she was inside, and drew herself up so she loomed over him, her arms raised in a posture of dominance and aggression.

Ressler moved so fast she barely saw him, and the syringe he had been filling was pressed into her thigh before she could reach the leuku knife. As she plummeted towards unconsciousness she heard him say, 'Do not worry, my dear. This is just morphine – enough to put you to sleep until I have you somewhere secure. It will not be harmful.'

She fought it all the way, but even the seven screaming voices were drowned out by the darkness.

2

'THIS PART OF THE MOTHER JOAN LEGEND BEGINS not far from here, in a place that was called *Cuneburna* by the Celts,' Josh began. 'We know it as Kilburn. The earliest reference to that name dates back to the twelfth century, and refers to a priory – a convent – built on the site of a hermitage established by a wise man named Godwyn – allegedly a member of the Knights Templar who fled here to find solitude after the horrors of the Second Crusade. The first residents at the priory were a small group of Augustinians, but after they left, the land was gifted to the Ursulines, and they flourished.'

'Henry VIII dissolved the convent as part of the purges in the sixteenth century,' Ponytail continued, 'but legend has it the nuns returned and continued to work in secret, serving the community despite the risks. It was seen as an act of penance – living the religious life in a land where the threat of arrest, torture and execution was very real.

'It's believed that during the Civil War Mother Jeanne des Anges, the historic Mother Joan, came to the abbey and worked as an *almist*, collecting food, clothing and money to alleviate the suffering of the poor in an attempt to repent for her role in the Loudun witch trials. While she lived on what

269

is now Abbey Road, legend has it that she arrived home to the priory one evening to find that a local commissioner had forced his way in and was violently beating the abbess. Joan drew a knife and cut his throat.'

The group fell into reverential silence – except for Dunnigan, whose silence was more of the bored variety.

'Don't you get it, dude? That is the first record of the Mother taking a life,' Rainbow said.

Dunnigan looked about the collection of awed faces, utterly unmoved.

'Don't you see?' the youth continued. 'It all started here! This is where her mission began, where her fate was, like, sealed!'

'Is there more to the story or are you finished?' Dunnigan had decided it was definitely time to leave these kids to their ghosts and conspiracy theories.

'The nuns fled, fearing the murder would bring more soldiers, and Joan returned to France,' Josh said.

'Or so it was thought,' Rainbow added.

All eyes were on Dunnigan. 'Why are you staring at me like that?' he snapped.

'Will we bring him?' Flock looked about the group, grinning.

'I could do with a drink,' Josh agreed.

'What are you talking about?' Dunnigan was really exasperated now.

'Let's go to the pub,' Ponytail laughed, slapping him on the back.

Harriet Grantham

Beth Carlton had been experiencing anxiety around large groups of people, so it seemed reasonable to ease her back into the normal life of the city by holding some sessions outside the therapy room and taking a few trips to the city centre.

Harriet Grantham saw these excursions as explorations of Beth's personality. One of the problems faced by people who have experienced long-term servitude is that all their decisions have been made for them – they have never been given the opportunity to express their particular tastes and interests, having been forced to adopt those of their oppressors.

Beth's profound tea addiction stemmed from only being offered that drink by the people who held her. She had no personal style as she'd had no option but to wear whatever clothes her captors gave her, without question. Her preferences in television, films and books were based on whatever she could remember watching and reading as a small child, and her reactions to any kind of stress were those of a pre-schooler – she lashed out physically or had a temper tantrum if backed into a corner.

Harriet wanted to help the girl develop a sense of identity based upon things she herself enjoyed rather than the tastes of others, so their trips into Dublin were as much about learning what the world had to offer (away from the selective filter of her rather eccentric uncle or her overly protective mother) as about acclimatising her to the hustle and bustle of a normal weekday in town.

'What's your favourite colour?' Harriet asked her,

271

stopping in front of a shop window. They were on Parnell Street strolling slowly arm in arm. 'If I were to tell you we were going to a fancy dinner and there would be dancing afterwards, what colour dress would you pick?'

'Pink,' Beth said, without pause for thought.

'Pink is nice. Which shade?'

'That one.'

The girl pointed at a long sequinned dress adorning one of the mannequins.

'Are you choosing that because the dress is right there in front of you? I've told you you can have any one you want.'

'Maybe I'm not interested in going to a dance,' Beth replied sulkily.

'Don't you like dancing?'

'No.'

'When did you last give it a try?'

The girl slipped her arm out of Harriet's and moved further along the street. 'A while ago. I didn't enjoy it.'

'Why not?'

She stopped in front of a large window that had a variety of flat-screen TVs of multiple sizes on display, from miniature tablets to 80-inch widescreen models. They were all playing Sky News, which was focusing on the big story of the month: the US business magnate Wilfred Hubert was visiting Ireland to negotiate the setting up of an outpost of his empire with members of the government. If it happened, the deal would generate hundreds of jobs and billions of euro in revenue. Hubert was big news – he was loud, brash, perma-tanned and richer than God. As Beth watched, his visage was magnified unpleasantly on the huge screens.

'I asked why you didn't like the dance you attended.'

'Because of him,' the girl said, motioning at the screens, her voice barely above a whisper.

'I don't follow,' Harriet said, puzzled, but before she could get another word out, Beth grabbed her by the hair and slammed her face into the glass pane, stunning her.

The girl was already long gone through the crowds by the time the therapist regained her senses enough to try and staunch the blood that was flowing freely from her nose.

3

THE PILGRIM'S REST WAS A TRADITIONAL PUBLIC house that sat between a newsagent's and an Indian takeaway on the ancient thoroughfare of Kilburn Lane, in north-west London, which was one of the quaintest streets Dunnigan had ever seen: its houses looked right out of a 1950s Ealing comedy.

The Pilgrim's was quiet when they arrived, and the landlord, a smiling elderly man in a starched white shirt, red tie and braces, seemed not at all put out to see a large group of oddly dressed students with multi-coloured hair descend upon his establishment; in fact, he greeted them with a warm grin. 'Why, Justin, how are you, my lad?'

Rainbow lost his usual scowling countenance, and grinned at the barman. 'Hullo, Claude. We were wondering if you might give this gent the guided tour?'

'I'll just ask Mabel to step in and then I'd be glad to.' The old man pulled an expensive-looking smartphone from under the bar, and, putting a pair of glasses on his nose, began to stab at the screen with his forefinger.

'Why do I want a tour of an old pub?' Dunnigan asked Ponytail, his patience growing exceedingly thin.

'You know how we mentioned the priory? The place Mother Joan made her first killing?'

'Yes.'

'That's here, dude. At least, this pub is built on the site where it used to be. There's a plaque on the wall over there, if you don't believe me.'

Dunnigan looked in the direction indicated and, sure enough, a brass sign declared that the site had been a resting place for weary travellers since the year 1134.

'My good lady wife will be here in a jiffy,' Claude said, taking off his apron and coming from behind the bar. 'Shall we go upstairs?'

A door at the rear of the room opened onto a narrow stairwell, dark wooden beams crossing its ceiling. As they filed up, the old man used a wooden match to light a candle set in an old-fashioned candlestick, and followed them.

'In 1895 this house was no longer a priory,' he began, closing the door behind them so the passageway was plunged into a darkness illuminated only by the candle's flickering flame. 'And hadn't been for 200 years. The building was owned by Ben Carruthers, a wine merchant and inveterate drunkard.'

The Watchers, with Dunnigan bringing up the rear, clustered into the hallway at the top of the stairs.

'He was a terrible man,' Claude said, shaking his head at the memory, 'and terrorised his wife and children; it is recorded that he often beat them publicly on the street when he had liquor taken.'

'And we all know who can't abide wife-beaters,' Ginger said, elbowing Dunnigan and winking.

'Sshh!' Goth said from the back of the crowd. 'I love this bit!'

The space was a little cold, and slightly claustrophobic with such a large group squashed in, and the flame threw long shadows on the walls.

'Now this house had, over the years, developed a reputation for being haunted,' Claude continued. 'It is said that the youngest Carruthers child, Beatrice, told her governess she often saw a tall lady, dressed in black, passing by her room at night. The child, at first, thought her mother had employed a new maid, but when she inquired, no such servant had been recruited.'

He paused for effect.

'Beatrice slept in this room, right here.'

He pushed open a wooden door, revealing a small chamber, complete with trestle bed.

'That means Mother Joan walked right along this passageway!' Flock whispered to Dunnigan.

'I have managed to grasp that implication, thank you,' the criminologist retorted.

'On the night of the 12th of December, 1895 the neighbours heard a terrible row coming from this building. Ben had been in his cups all day and had lost extravagantly at cards at his club. As was the norm, his family were suffering for it.'

'Bastard,' Ginger spat – he was clearly enjoying himself tremendously.

'By ten o'clock that night the house had fallen into an uneasy silence, and by eleven, the whole family was in bed,' Claude continued, his voice a hushed whisper now. 'But somebody was not asleep.'

'We know who that was,' Ponytail said, gleefully.

Virtually running to the end of the passageway, Claude flung open the last door.

'The next morning, Ben Carruthers' manservant found him lying on the floor of this room, his throat opened, a black book clutched to his chest. Beatrice later said the ghostly woman had passed her door just after her father came upstairs. The child never reported seeing the spectre again.'

Dunnigan peered into the room – it had also been preserved as a bedroom, and he noted that a red stain – obviously gloss paint – had been artfully placed on the floor.

'Now, who's for drinks?' Claude asked, beaming.

4

'IS THIS WHAT YOUR GROUP DOES?' DUNNIGAN asked Josh when they were seated at some low tables in the small bar downstairs.

'Have a meeting and then go to the pub?' the young man grinned. 'Yeah, sometimes. One or two of us might share some creepypastas we've written, or talk about new ones we've found, but this is a really important social outlet for a lot of us. For some, like Giles over there,' he was talking about Goth, 'it's their *only* social outlet.'

'There's a page on your site – names and dates ...'

'Ah,' Josh nodded in affirmation. 'That's the *real* work of The Watchers.'

'We scour the web for news stories that look like they might be her.' Flock was sitting beside Josh. 'When we identify one, we put it into a search engine that Monty there wrote,' he nodded at a chubby, nervous-looking youngster with a shock of curly hair who had not said a word all evening, 'and it trawls the net for references on message boards, web forums, pasta sites – the whole deal – and then collates them. If all the details add up – abuse of women or children, stalking, the appearance of a book, a suspicious-sounding death – we add it to the list on our page.'

'How often do you find one that you feel is genuine?'

'It used to be one or two every twelve months. Over the past couple of years, though, she's accelerated.'

'Why do you think that is?'

'Hacker_red has a theory,' Josh said.

'Do you know who hacker_red is?'

'No, but we all follow him on social media.'

'What does he or she think is going on?'

'*He* thinks Mother Joan is about to go into a sleeper state.'

'I don't know what that means.'

'She's on the verge of going dormant,' Josh explained. 'Basically, Mother Joan is dying.'

Bradislav Vaslav Chechnik

'Your brother is dead.'

The call came in the middle of the night. Only his closest friends and associates had his personal number, yet here he was, speaking to a stranger who was delivering bad news to him in fluent Romanian, although spoken in a strange accent.

'I talked to Yuri four days ago,' Bradislav said. 'He told me he is coming home soon. You are a liar.'

The phone beeped and buzzed in his hand.

'Open the message I have just sent you.'

It was a picture of his brother, his face stove in, lying in a hospital bed. Bradislav wanted to scream, but he gritted his teeth and let the anger ferment inside him. There would be screaming, yet.

'Would you like to know who did this?'

'Yes.'

'Go to Ireland and arrange for your brother's body to be brought to your homeland. The girl you seek is in Dublin. You can give her the death she deserves.'

'How do I know you are not setting me up? Maybe you want to kill both brothers.'

'The girl who made such a mess of your brother's face has become a nuisance to my employer. She needs to be taken out of circulation. By doing this, you will avenge Yuri, but you will also be doing my superior a favour. He will owe you one in return.'

'Who are you and who is this employer?'

'You can call me Phillipe,' the voice said. 'You do not need to know who I work for. Suffice it to say he is very

wealthy and very powerful and he needs this girl silenced permanently.'

'*I will silence her,*' Bradislav said through his rage. '*Eventually.*'

5

THE KIDS STARTED TO DRIFT OFF AROUND TEN, BY which time Dunnigan was too tired to continue being angry with himself over the wasted effort of going on such a wild-goose chase.

He was putting on his coat when the group's programmer approached him.

'I'm Monty,' he said, his voice soft, almost feminine.

'Yes, Flock told me. I'm going back to my B&B now.'

'It's her name.'

Dunnigan looked puzzled. 'What are you talking about?'

'You asked how to stop her. It's her name that does it – the secret is in her name. You have to tell it to her.'

The criminologist sighed and picked up his tote. 'That doesn't make any sense. She lets every person she's going to kill know what her name is – it's in the first verse of the poem in the book she sends them: *When the bitter night is dark and cold it's then you might see Mother Joan.* If all you have to do is speak her name to drive her off, why would she give all her victims the ammunition to do it?'

'Maybe Mother Joan *isn't* her name,' Monty said, and the ghost of a smile played across his chubby features.

'Of course it is.'

'Think about it,' Monty said, and, turning, walked rapidly away.

Dunnigan was about to do the same when Claude, the old landlord, called him over. 'You're writing a book about the black lady, I hear?'

'Well, I'm doing some research on her, yes.'

'You should have a chat with Merle Ely. He might have a story to tell you.'

'I'll be travelling back to Ireland tomorrow, Claude, but thank you.'

'I'm sure he'd talk to you tonight,' the landlord said. 'He lives on his own, just a few doors from the pub, and he don't sleep much. Will I give him a ring and see if he's still up and about?'

'Okay,' Dunnigan said, reckoning he had come this far.

*

Merle Ely was about the same age as Claude and dressed in a similar style: slacks with a razor-sharp crease ironed into them, a very crisp white shirt, blue braces and a matching tie.

'Claude and I were in the army together,' he told Dunnigan as they sat opposite one another in his living room, which was decorated in a masculine style – leather furniture, walls painted in brown and cream hues, a picture of a wooden sailing ship over the fireplace. 'I was injured and got an honourable discharge – he served his twenty and bought the pub.'

'Did you move here to be near him?'

'Were you ever in the military?'

'No, but I have a close friend who was.'

'When you see action with a person, it creates a bond that's like family, but possibly closer. Claude knew I was having some trouble – depression, addiction. He contacted me when this house came on the market, and he's been a huge support since I came to Kilburn. I owe him a great deal.'

'He said you may be able to give me some information regarding the Mother Joan legend,' Dunnigan said, uncomfortable with the direction the conversation was taking.

'She's not a legend,' Ely said stiffly.

'All I've heard since coming here are local ghost stories,' Dunnigan said.

'I have a Black Bible.'

The criminologist blinked. 'I'm sorry,' he said, not sure how to respond.

'There's no need to be,' the man said, calmly. 'I am at peace with the fact.'

'How long have you had it?'

'Ten years.'

'But ...'

'I changed my life,' the older man explained. 'I got help. I lost my wife and my job in the process, but I turned things around.'

'You repented,' Dunnigan suggested.

'I did. My life was a mess when she visited me. I was a drug addict – not the kind you see begging for coins in the street: I was very functional and respectable and my dealer wore a white coat and worked in a chemist. But I was still a junkie.'

'We've all got our ghosts,' Dunnigan said, recalling his conversation with Diane before going to Cork.

'One evening I was driving home from the city when I ran over a homeless woman. I was six sheets to the wind, travelling way too fast, and suddenly there she was going over the bonnet. I can still hear the thud as she hit the ground.'

'But you kept driving,' Dunnigan guessed.

'I didn't even slow down. The terrible thing is, there were no reports in the newspapers, and no policeman ever knocked on my door – it might as well never have happened. But a week later, Mother Joan came into my life. And changed it.'

'Are you grateful to her?' the criminologist asked incredulously.

'She forced me to be a better man.'

'It's amazing how the threat of a bloody death focuses the mind.'

Ely smiled without humour. 'Once I got off the drugs, I couldn't live with what I'd done, so I handed myself in. Would you believe, the police wouldn't arrest me? No one had ever found a body, so no harm, no foul. I got a stern talking to, but that was the extent of it.'

'And now you have to live with the guilt.'

'That is my sentence. My penance. Some time later, though, I was contacted by this man.' He handed Dunnigan a crumpled business card. On it were the contact details for Detective Inspector Alfie Jones.

hacker_red

He liked to think he was the agent of his own destiny, but as the years went on, he started to understand she was steering him, guiding his hand in subtle and wonderful ways.

Before Mother Joan stepped out of the shadows he had been a nobody with a mediocre degree in programming, posters of Sonic the Hedgehog fixed with Blu-tack to the bedroom wall of the house he still shared with his mother.

He had tried everything to make his mark – his pitches to various gaming companies had been politely rejected. The app he designed to control all the tech devices in the house through your smartphone was completed a week after the cunts in Apple released exactly the same idea (without any of the bugs and glitches his version retained). His outline for a lengthy series of sword and sorcery novels turned out to be alarmingly similar to George RR Martin's A Song of Ice and Fire *series – far too close for any publisher to even consider it.*

He was left with no choice but to try and put his work out online.

The only problem was, thousands of other writers were doing the same thing, and no matter what he posted, he was lucky to get more than five or six likes and a couple of comments. It was incredibly frustrating.

Then the poem arrived, and everything changed.

The online community loved it, copying and pasting Mother Joan into legend within the space of a few weeks. More stories and information followed, and his online persona was forged from the eerie fictions she sent and he posted.

The fact that he was authoring none of it did not bother him at all.

He had a role: get the message out – let the world know Mother Joan is watching. Hacker_red had millions of followers, people hanging on his every word, and for the first time in his life, he had respect.

It was an anonymous kind of respect – his real name was a closely guarded secret, but that suited him, as it left him free to pursue some other, more financially lucrative (and highly illegal), hacking projects.

So it came as a surprise when a zip file was sent to his personal email address, with the subject line Mother Joan.

It contained information concerning a Belgian psychiatrist who had been involved in some unpleasant dealings for a group called the After Dark Campaign, which seemed to be a multinational criminal syndicate, from what he could gather. The shrink who was the subject of the files had once been highly respected in the medical community, but had apparently developed a series of dangerous and unethical procedures involving drugs and violent therapies which he used upon women and children the organisation had abducted, to make them fearful, compliant, and therefore far less troublesome when sold into whichever industry they were destined for.

A brief message accompanying the file stated he should pass this information on to Mother Joan, as the psychiatrist, whose name was Doctor Phillipe Ressler, was going to be in London that week. She would surely be interested in meeting such a monster.

Hacker_red had never given the Mother a victim before.

The idea of doing so gave him a hard-on.

6

DUNNIGAN WAS STAYING AT A B&B ON BELSIZE
Road.

He was almost at the guesthouse when his phone rang – it
was Gina.

'Where is my daughter?'

'You don't know?'

'Stop messing with me, Davey, or I swear to God I will kick
your ass, and you know I can!'

'Hold on for a moment – you're telling me she's run away?'

'She is a twenty-two-year-old woman, she can't run away.
I'm saying she's gone. She was with Harriet Grantham when
she freaked out. Beth hasn't been right since coming back
from Cork, if I'm honest. She sent me a text to say she was on
her way to see you.'

'But I'm in London.'

'Yes. The thought had occurred to me.'

'I got a missed call from her this morning, but when I
tried to ring her back the phone was switched off. I thought
nothing of it.'

'Maybe that was because she was on a plane.'

Dunnigan arrived at the gate to his lodging and sat down

on the wall outside. 'She couldn't have got on a plane,' he said. 'She doesn't have a passport.'

'If you fly Aer Lingus you can get into the UK from Ireland with a driver's licence.'

'She doesn't have a driver's licence.'

'Actually, she does. I thought it might do her confidence good if she learned. We got her a provisional one yesterday.'

Dunnigan shook his head in wonderment. 'I'll call you back.'

Beth picked up on the first ring. 'Guess where I am!'

7

HE MET HER AT CHARING CROSS STATION.

He was torn between being overjoyed to see her and upset at the thought that this was likely to put him at even greater loggerheads with his sister, but he pushed such thoughts out of his head and hugged her and told her she was an eejit and that her mother would kill them both.

He couldn't get another room at the B&B, so he gave her his bed and slept on the floor.

'Beth, why are you here?'

'I was worried about you.'

'Your mum said you got a bit upset with Harriet.'

'I don't want to talk about that.'

'You came all the way to London, but you don't want to talk to me?'

'I don't want to talk about *that*.'

'Okay. Let's try this one: why didn't you tell Frank about Mother Joan being at the docks in Cork?'

'I didn't think it was important.'

'She has hurt lots of people. She was probably there to hurt you or me.'

'No. She wasn't.'

'How do you know that?'

'I just do. I don't know why she was there, but I think she was trying to protect us.'

He propped himself up on an elbow. 'What makes you say that?'

'She's lonely. I know something about that. I saw her when I was hiding below the docks, and she seemed so sad. She wasn't trying to hurt us, Davey. When she started to sing, she wanted to help.'

And that was all she would say on the subject.

8

DI ALFIE JONES SAID HE WOULD DRIVE OUT TO Kilburn and they met in some tea rooms not far from where Dunnigan was staying. Beth was still asleep when he left the room, so Dunnigan reckoned she wouldn't get up to much mischief until he returned.

The policeman was in his early fifties with a head full of hair that had once been blond but was now well mixed with grey. He sported an impressive paunch, was dressed in a leather jacket and jeans, and looked tired and shop-worn. 'You've come to ground zero,' he said. 'This is where it all began.'

'I met The Watchers last night.'

'Fucking bunch of headcases,' Jones said. 'They haven't a clue what they're messing with.'

'And I talked to Merle Ely.'

'Interesting bloke, if a bit misguided. So – she's causing mayhem in your neck of the woods, then?'

Dunnigan told him.

'You've actually seen her?'

He nodded.

'You're a lucky bastard, d'ye know that? Very few clap eyes on her and walk away.'

Jones had a mild Welsh tinge to his speech.

'Have you been as lucky?'

'No. My involvement with Mother Joan has not been blessed with good fortune.'

'But you're still after her?'

'Don't know how to stop. I've been chasing her since I joined the force.'

'You must have learned quite a bit about her over the years.'

'You'd think. In 1984 five people were killed over the course of a month, right here in Kilburn. They were all successful men with good jobs – one was a local politician, an MP. Each vic was found in their home, all stabbed to death, and their families reported they had become agitated and paranoid prior to their deaths. Two of the deceased told their wives that they'd been followed by a hooded woman, and three mentioned hearing strange music.'

'Suggestive.'

'And there's this.'

He passed a scrapbook to Dunnigan, opening it to a page containing a photograph of a crowd gathered around a podium where a man was speaking. 'This was taken during the miners' strike,' Jones said. 'The bloke speaking is Grant Noble, a Conservative MP. The rally pictured here took place three weeks before he was found dead.'

He turned the page to one where a section of the photo had been enlarged.

There, among the crowd just behind the politician, was a hooded figure: Mother Joan.

'I was in uniform when the murders happened in '84. We were sure it was politically linked – England was a mess at the time, the strikes had torn communities apart, and no one was surprised when an MP turned up dead. The old git had been speaking out against the unions and cheered on the employment of scab workers, so he was a prime target. But then the other deaths happened – a GP, a bloke who ran an insurance company, a music promoter and an accountant – and there was nothing to connect them. I was put on a door-to-door canvas after the promoter was killed, and this lady who lived across the road from him – a real curtain-twitcher, she was – she told me a woman had been calling at his house late at night, but not waiting for him to answer the door. She was knockin' and runnin' away, like a kid making a nuisance of themselves. Didn't make sense. I wrote it up and forgot about it. Didn't think of it again until five years later. I'd made detective and was working on the murder of a retired soldier – he'd been involved in some anti-terrorist business, and again, the brass reckoned it was open and shut, probably Provos. Except his missus told me they'd been bothered by someone waking them up during the night, knocking on their door. And not just the front door – she said someone banged on their bedroom door too, and they didn't have no kids. And then there was the book. The Black bloody Bible.'

'Mother Joan,' Dunnigan said.

Jones nodded and drained his tea in a single gulp, as if talking about it had made him thirsty. 'Mother fucking Joan,' he said, deliberately pronouncing each word. 'I thought she'd packed it in, for a while. It went quiet, like. But the bitch is back.'

Bradislav Vaslav Chechnik

He arrived in Dublin with only one bodyguard, and collected his brother's body from the hospital morgue. It took a day to organise the paperwork, and every painful minute became another indignity he was determined to visit on the person who had left him the sole surviving member of a once great dynasty.

When the shipping had been arranged and his people in Romania prepped to receive Yuri's remains, he called Phillipe.

'I regret she is not in Ireland anymore,' the voice at the end of the phone informed him.

'You are fucking with me.'

'I wish I was. The girl is now in London. She is staying in a guesthouse in Kilburn. I suspect she will not be there for long, so you had better hurry.'

'I am losing patience with you, Phillipe. If I arrive in England and find you have lied, I will be paying you a visit and I will take my debt out of your hide.'

'You Romanians have such a colourful turn of phrase. Call me when you land. I will give you the address.'

'You will not be there to meet me?'

'Sadly, no. I will be entertaining a very special lady of my own.'

9

JONES SCRATCHED THE DENSE STUBBLE ON HIS jaw. 'You should go home,' he said to Dunnigan. 'I've been at this my whole bloody career, and it has cost me everything. They think I'm off me trolley down the nick, and I'm starting to agree with them.'

'Why do you say that?'

'I became sort of obsessed. There's been ghost stories and old wives' tales about her in these parts for years, but I always thought it was just fables to scare kids and keep 'em in line. Even when I started to find links between these myths and the murders, it took me yonks to really accept Mother Joan was real. But it started to add up, see? I began to join the dots, and it got so I thought it *had* to be real. And then, well ... I had me encounter.'

'Your encounter?'

'Last year we got some security footage of a person in a black cloak enterin' an old warehouse complex in Clapham. I went out there for a gander. Place was completely derelict – no fucking reason for anyone to go in or out.'

'Why do you think she was there?'

'To draw me to her. I'd been all over the building and was

about to pack up and go home, when that bloody singing started. I thought someone was playing a trick – piping the sound through speakers or something. It kept getting louder and louder until the fucking windows were rattling. Really put the wind up me. I got out of there. And this is the bit that really scared me – the song came on through the radio of me bloody car when I switched on the engine.'

'I've heard the music, and it is unnerving. Are you certain it wasn't just … I don't know … just stuck in your head so you thought you heard it in your car?'

'It stopped when I switched off the radio. All that was left was the ringing in me ears.'

'I've heard other people say the same thing happened to them.'

'Don't make it less scary. Do you know what the song is?'

'You've been able to identify it?'

'I couldn't get the fucking thing out of me head for weeks.'

'So what is it?'

'It's the Gregorian Act of Contrition.'

'You're telling me she asks God to forgive her sins as she prepares to kill someone?'

'We are dealing with one very confused and fucked-up ghost.'

'Ghosts don't show up on CCTV footage, detective.'

'Ain't you seen the shows with all those weird videos? Derek Acorah and that?'

Dunnigan looked at the man with pity. 'Derek Acorah? Are you serious?'

'There's strange stuff out there.'

'In all the time you've worked this, have you come across anything concrete?'

'Nothing that led anywhere useful.'

'One of the things I specialise in is going back over case files to find patterns others have missed. Maybe if I looked through your paperwork, I could shed some light. A fresh set of eyes?'

'Can't hurt, I suppose.'

'Will I travel with you to HQ?' Dunnigan asked, motioning for the bill.

'No need, mate,' Jones replied. 'I've got the files in the boot of me car.'

10

DUNNIGAN WAS USED TO WORKING HIS WAY
methodically through mounds of paperwork when examining
cold cases, so he was shocked to see the material relating to
Mother Joan could all be contained in one moderately sized
cardboard box (which had once contained Fig Rolls, according
to the logo on the side).

'This is all you have?'

'Sixteen cases, excluding the ones in '84 – I was only
peripherally involved, like I said, but I'm sure your people
can have them sent over, interdepartmental cooperation and
all that.'

'But where's all the interview notes? The crime scene
photos? Telephone records? Bank statements?'

'In the box. The thing with the Mother Joan cases is that
there's always so little to go on – the deaths happen in the
victim's home or place of work, almost always in a room with
one way in and out. In half the cases the killer had to pass
someone to get to the victim, yet that person saw nothing.'

'Yes, but still …'

'Don't think we didn't do our jobs, lad. We looked at these
every which fucking way.'

Dunnigan sighed and took the box from the detective. 'Give me twenty-four hours.'

'Take as much time as you need.'

'I'll call you tomorrow.'

Jones nodded sadly. 'Don't get your hopes up. There's nothing in that box that'll bring you much more than sleepless nights.'

'I don't sleep much anyway,' Dunnigan said.

'Me neither,' Jones said, and closed his boot.

11

BETH WAS UP WHEN HE GOT BACK TO THE ROOM
and was sitting on the bed, freshly showered, watching Phillip
Schofield and Holly Willoughby on TV.

'I have the complete first season of *Captain Scarlet* on my
laptop,' Dunnigan said. 'The original 1960s series.'

'That's okay. I like Phillip and Holly.'

'Yes, but it's Captain Scarlet. You know: Gerry Anderson,
Supermarionation …'

'This is good, though! Come and watch with me for a bit.
I like it when they start giggling and can't stop.'

'I don't know what to say to that.'

She got up, gave him a kiss and a hug.

'I think you should think about going home,' Dunnigan
said. 'We agreed we weren't going to hurt Gina, and this is
going to upset her a lot.'

'I'm not ready to go yet, okay?'

'Why not?'

'Look – I promise I'll tell you about it. Just not now.'

She turned up the volume on the TV, but he walked over
and switched it off. 'Beth, I have to work.'

Scowling, she walked to the door. 'I'm going to get some breakfast.'

He said 'okay' but she was already gone. Later, when things fell asunder completely, he would look back on this moment and realise that Gina had been right – he should have called after her, shouldn't have permitted her to go off alone. But the task at hand, the mystery, was calling to him, and a tantrum from his niece was the last thing he wanted to deal with (as much as he truly loved her), and as the door closed, he pushed her from his mind until it was already too late.

12

HE SPREAD THE SIXTEEN CASE FILES OUT ON THE bed and opened his laptop. Using Google Maps, he marked out where each of the murders had taken place, including Kilburn to denote the 1984 killings. The trajectory articulated a rough circle about the city. He looked at the locations – they were all loosely linked to finance, but nothing else suggested itself.

He made some tea, pulled over the small table and chair his landlords had been kind enough to provide, and opened the earliest file, dated 3 October 1989.

David Dunnigan was not a brilliant investigator. He did not make tremendous leaps of logic, nor did he have a capacious memory, recalling insignificant details others had missed. His gift was an uncanny ability to see patterns in human behaviour – to make links and see similarities, often subtle ones, that had not appeared obvious to others.

He did this by going painstakingly through each piece of documentation, word for word, line by line, and making copious notes in his tiny, spidery handwriting on endless sheets of paper, which he had the habit of folding into a pattern of squares that helped him access the information quickly (and acted as a kind of reference system), and that no one else could make head nor tail of.

He could do this hour after hour without losing concentration, something his colleagues in Harcourt Street often marvelled at – Dunnigan was usually the first one in in the morning, and the last to leave at night.

His superpower (as he liked to think of it, although he had never used the term when discussing his technique with anyone else) was his ability to maintain focus for extended periods.

Three hours later he had made his first sweep through the files, and had spread a chronology of events out on the floor – it made no more sense than anything else relating to Mother Joan and appeared to be completely, wilfully random.

Beth hadn't come back yet, so he texted her: *Are you okay?*

About three minutes later a sad face emoji was texted back.

His niece was sulking. Well, she would just have to get over her funk – he didn't have time to pander to her.

He went out for a sandwich and sat in a Starbucks watching the crowds go past through the window.

People are what make or break a case, Tormey had always told him. *The devil is not in the detail, it's in the soul of your suspects.*

Dunnigan went back to the room, stopping at a shop to pick up some Blu-tack and a pair of scissors en route.

He cut sheets of paper into small uniform squares and used them to make identity cards for everyone still alive that had been involved in the UK cases, then did the same for the seven in Ireland. The squares listed name, age, occupation, place of employment and any other identifying details.

There was still no link – no strand he could grasp at and

weave into something meaningful. He lay on the bed and allowed his mind to go blank. He was looking too closely – perhaps he should step back.

He spent an hour working up a profile of Mother Joan – everything he had been told by all the people he had spoken to, all the stories and articles he had read, all the podcasts and videos and paranoid conspiracy theories. Taking a lead from what Monty had told him, he wrote a list of all the names by which he had heard people refer to her: Mother Joan; the Mother; Mère Jeanne des Anges; the Dark Lady; the Caped Woman. The character sketch took up the entire wall above his bed, and when it was done he stood on the mattress and allowed his mind to linger over the information.

Religion; abuse; blame; guilt; exploitation; penance; revenge; contrition; myth; fear; female power; male corruption.

McSwain had said that Mother Joan was unlike Slender Man because he was without motive, while she was defined by it – yet there was no clear pattern to the killings save that the men (so far he could find no female victims) were in some way callous or cruel in their treatment of women – even down to Merle Ely, who had mowed down a woman in a hit-and-run.

He slid off the bed and stretched out on the floor.

Jones said the police had initially believed the murder of the MP Grant Noble had been politically motivated, and the same had been believed of the former soldier Christopher Wayne. He went to the wall of names and examined the details of both men.

Noble had been a soldier in his youth, but he had been in a different regiment to Wayne, who was SAS. At the time of his death Wayne had been the assistant manager of a private security company, Maylor Consulting.

Dunnigan pulled over his laptop and entered the name – the company was now a huge concern providing everything from bodyguarding services for royalty, to support for government forces in conflicts all over the world. Maylor was, more or less, a private army.

Idly, he punched Noble's name in alongside Maylor's.

The MP had been on the board of the company for a brief time before becoming an MP, after which he had stepped down to focus fully on politics.

He had been going through the files for almost eight hours, and he had found a link. It wasn't much, but it was the first similarity he had found, and experience had taught him such things were often the first threads of a larger tapestry.

And as he was about to begin pulling at those threads, it suddenly occurred to him that Beth had still not returned.

Beth Carlton

She understood as she stormed up Belsize Road that she was not really angry with Davey – she was frightened. She had come to London because she needed the kind of advice only he could give, but there was a part of her that was too scared to begin the conversation.

They had said bad things would happen if she ever told. She was to forget about what she had seen, forget what she knew.

And it had been easy at first, because she didn't really know anything.

It had happened three days after her fourteenth birthday.

The men at the party she and three other girls had been driven to were the usual wrinkled, walnut-skinned faces in suits. They drank and they sniffed white powder and they wanted to have their fun. Beth had no access to a television or a computer, and anyway, names were never a feature of such meetings.

She and another girl whom she thought had been called Dova (the girls were always coming and going, and she rarely got to know them well) were told to go to a bedroom with one man in particular. He was very high from the white powder, and he wanted Beth to pull his hand-painted silk neck-tie tight around his neck while he fucked her friend. Halfway through, he started to choke Dova, wrapping both his hands around her throat. Maybe he was really strong, or maybe it was the effects of the drug, but Beth remembered hearing the crunch of bones in the girl's neck. She had clawed his face in an attempt to stop him, making him bleed quite badly, but it made no difference. By the time the man was

307

finished, Dova was an unusual shade of purple, and there was thick black blood pumping from her ears. Beth pulled the tie off the awful man's neck and used it to wipe the stuff away, speaking gently to the girl and shaking her softly, but somewhere deep inside, she knew it was pointless.

There wasn't a lot of fuss made about it – men dressed in white plastic bodysuits came and the body was taken away, Beth was put in a car and sent back to the apartment.

She was back in her room before she realised she was still clutching the bunched-up tie, which was stuck to her hand now by the dried blood: a combination of Dova's and the man who had killed her, almost obscuring the letters 'W' and 'H', emblazoned in the tie's underside.

The fact that she still had it terrified her. But she knew what to do.

There was a small back garden to the apartment block – the girls used it as a smoking area. She had put the tie in a plastic bag and shoved it down the back of her tracksuit pants, then waited until Louis, one of the men she knew was lazy and tended to doze when on overnight shifts, came on duty at midnight. As soon as his head touched his chest, she had taken the bundle downstairs and buried it in the flowerbed, under a bush where no one would see the disturbed earth. She whispered a short prayer for the dead girl, and then crept back upstairs, passing the still-snoring Louis in his chair in the hallway.

She went to bed, and in the morning Uncle Ernie was there. If she ever breathed a word about what had happened to anyone – any of the other girls, any clients, anyone at all – he, Uncle Ernie, would find everyone she had ever loved, and kill them slowly. To make sure she understood what he meant, he had shown her a DVD of him visiting this kind of attention on a woman.

She still dreamed of what he made her watch, of the woman's screams and imprecations. Despite everything Beth had endured, she had not imagined such cruelty existed.

By the time Frobisher left her that day, she wanted to forget all about it. She didn't know who the vile man who had killed Dova was, and reckoned she would never see him again. As he was leaving her, Frobisher turned. 'The gentleman you entertained last night mentioned he had a tie. He left it behind, and the cleaners didn't find it.'

She blinked. She had almost thought she'd got away with it. Luckily, she was prepared. 'I didn't notice a tie,' she said.

'He claims it was part of the game you three played.'

'No. He had me put his belt around his neck. If he had a tie, he'd taken it off before I came into the room.'

Frobisher had looked at her with that cold, reptilian stare of his. 'Really? He was certain you used a tie.'

'It was a belt. Brown leather. A thin silver buckle.'

He nodded slowly. 'Yes. One of those was found.'

She thought she would pass out from fear. She took a deep breath and said, 'Well, then.'

He made the face that passed for a smile, and was gone.

She had remained true to her word and had not thought of the man again, until Davey had found her – in the years between her encounter with him and her rescue, he had become famous and his face was now everywhere.

Beth took out her phone and plugged in earphones. Her mother had introduced her to the music of Bruce Springsteen, and she had discovered that Diane liked him too. There was a greatest hits album on her phone, which had a basic MP3 player, and she switched it on as she walked.

She turned into Queen's Park, found a bench and sat down.

It was a pleasant September day. On the lawn in front of her a mother and a little boy were playing. The kid had a fluorescent pink and green plastic ball and they were tossing it back and forth. Beth watched them as the opening salvo to 'Badlands' blasted through her earphones.

She had buried the memory of what had happened so deeply that the first few times she saw photos or film footage of the man, she hadn't even realised it was him – there had just been a sense of unease and discomfort at the sight of him, the ugly sound of his voice. But then, a lot of people seemed to not like him – from what Beth had heard, he was generally held to be a lout and an oaf, albeit an oaf with enough money to buy Mars.

She had seen a poster of him in Dundrum on the day her mother and Davey had taken her shopping that first time, and she now realised it was that which had probably caused her to hallucinate Ernest Frobisher.

But it wasn't until she came face to face with his image that day on Parnell Street, with her therapist talking about parties and dances, that it all came flooding back.

This was her truth: Wilfred Hubert, whom the entire world seemed in thrall to and who was meeting with the heads of Ireland's government that very day, had choked an adolescent girl to death while he had sex with her. He had murdered a child, and very bad people had made the problem go away.

She knew she should tell. Someone like that should not be walking around as if he owned the whole world. But she was very, very afraid.

Davey would understand.

As that thought occurred, a shadow fell across her and, looking up, she saw a tall, middle-aged, sharp-faced man in a well-tailored suit smiling down at her. Another, slightly younger man, similarly dressed, appeared to be waiting for him by the entrance to the park.

'You are Beth Carlton?' the man asked, and he had an Eastern European accent. 'I think you knew my brother.'

She stood, but it was too late to run.

13

DUNNIGAN TEXTED HER AGAIN: *WHERE ARE YOU?*
Almost immediately a skull emoji appeared on his phone in
response. He pulled on his jacket, rapidly texting back: *Beth,
please call me. I'm worried.*

The street on which the B&B resided was a mixture of
shops and flats. He pulled up a map of the area on his phone.
Google informed him that he was standing on an ancient
Celtic pathway leading all the way to the Cathedral City. It
had been popular with pilgrims, who would often stop to take
holy water from a well that once existed nearby. *Interesting*,
Dunnigan thought, *but hardly useful to me right now.*

He was about to try ringing his niece when something
caused him to look up. Standing across the street, dressed in
a light summer suit, smiling beatifically, was Doctor Phillipe
Ressler.

It took Dunnigan a moment to register what he was seeing,
and, as if locked by an invisible force, the two enemies gazed
at one another across the busy road.

The psychiatrist (a known associate of Ernest Frobisher
and a confirmed people-trafficker, not to mention a man with
a questionable grasp of medical ethics) was currently on the

run from Interpol. The last time Dunnigan met him, Ressler had tried to kill him.

From his position across the street, the Belgian actually waved at Dunnigan, and at that moment a truck rolled past. By the time it was gone, he was nowhere to be seen. Searching up and down the road yielded no sign.

Wondering if he was going mad, Dunnigan was about to call Jones when his phone flashed again: a message from Beth. The criminologist read it, and had to sit down on the pavement. The text read: *Please beware of Mother Joan. The countdown has begun.*

14

'WHAT DO YOU THINK IT MEANS?' THE DETECTIVE asked him.

They were sitting in an all-night café. Jones had called in some favours and the patrol cars in the area all had photos of Dunnigan's niece and were keeping an eye out for her, but a further nine hours would have to pass before she could officially be treated as missing. The criminologist had called Gina, in the hope that Beth had made contact with her, but the answer was negative.

His twin, frantic with worry, was also furious with him. He wondered if there could be any hope of repairing their relationship now, and thought it unlikely.

Dunnigan was using every bit of restraint he could muster to stop himself falling apart. His greatest fear since finding Beth was that the men who had abducted her would snatch her back and, this time, make sure he never found her again. That nightmare had now become a reality, even if her captor was not who he had expected it to be. Blind panic and raw, gibbering insanity tore at the edges of his being, but he refused to pander to them. *It's not too late*, he told himself.

'I think it means Mother Joan has Beth and we are on a deadline.'

Jones was eating a bacon sandwich. 'Or this Ressler bloke *wants* you to think the Mother has her,' he said, around a mouthful.

'But why?'

'Put you off the scent.'

'Why show himself to me, then?'

The Welshman took another bite of his food – melted butter and HP sauce ran down his fingers. 'You'd been working on the files ever since I left you, yeah?'

'Yes. I took a break to get a sandwich, but—'

'Never mind that. You were at it for hours on the trot. Your head must have been addled. Are you positive you saw this psychiatrist bloke?'

'I'd know him anywhere.'

'How long did you see him for, would you say?'

'I don't know – ten, fifteen seconds.'

'And you're dead positive it was him?'

'Yes.'

'And he's in league with Mother Joan now, is he?'

'I know it doesn't make sense, but—'

'I think you have to be prepared to consider you got it wrong.'

'I don't make mistakes.'

'Alright, let's agree to disagree. If Mother Joan *does* have her,' Jones placed the last piece of sandwich delicately in his mouth and wiped his hands with a napkin, 'it presents us with a problem. It doesn't fit her MO.'

'She doesn't kill women,' Dunnigan agreed.

'So why take her?'

The criminologist rubbed his eyes. 'There's only one reason I can think of.'

'Go on.'

'To get to me,' Dunnigan said. 'She's trying to lure me to her.'

'Why? Are you a child molester or a wife-beater?'

'I'm hunting her. I think I'm close. Just like she drew you to the warehouse to warn you off, she's taken Beth as a way to send me a message.'

'So what are you going to do?'

15

THERE WAS NOTHING ELSE EITHER OF THEM *could* do. Dunnigan, reasoning that the quickest way to find Beth was to find Mother Joan, spent the rest of the night making connections between each of the murders and Maylor Consulting: some, like Noble, were obvious and immediate; others, like the music promoter, were more difficult – it turned out he had sourced the bands at a fundraising event Maylor held for famine relief in Ethiopia. By the time he was finished, he still wasn't 100 per cent certain of the link to the Irish cases – Mark Murphy had travelled to South America regularly, and Maylor did a lot of business there, but it seemed tenuous, and he found a document that suggested O'Connor had volunteered as a field surgeon one summer when he was a student, and the agency he had signed up with provided medics for the firm.

Then he found it: Maylor ran a subsidiary wing that provided team-building and conflict management courses for professionals – which included an anger management programme.

That left Merle Ely.

He called him at 6.30 a.m., and to his surprise the man answered.

'Have you ever had any dealings with a company named Maylor Consulting?'

'I did some training for them,' he said without pause, 'many, many years ago.'

'What can you tell me about them?'

'My guess would be that their money has not been accrued through the most honourable of means, but then, whose has?'

'I'll be in touch,' Dunnigan said, and hung up.

He lay down on the bed to rest his eyes for a moment, and opened them again to find it was 11 a.m. An attempt to ring Jones only yielded a recital of his voicemail message: 'It's Bob. Leave a message if you'd like to. If you wouldn't, then sod off – I don't know why you bothered ringing in the first place!'

He sent an email to Maylor Consulting requesting a meeting, and then called Tormey.

'I heard about Beth. Is there anything I can do at this end?'

'What's our relationship like with the tech boys at present?'

'Shit. Why?'

'I need an anonymous internet poster tracked down.'

'Has he been peddling in kiddie porn?'

'No.'

'Racist shit, then – incitement to hatred and all that?'

'No. He writes horror stories.'

'And this is illegal why, exactly?'

'He's the guy who posted the poem about Mother Joan – the one that's in all the Black Bibles.'

'Is he in our jurisdiction?'

'Doubtful. My guess is he's in the UK.'

'I'm sorry, but they won't do it, Davey. You know how dodgy all the online privacy stuff is just now.'

'Thanks anyway, boss'

And he called Father Bill and asked him to find Toddy.

Part Seven

IN THE DEEP WOODS

1

FATHER BILL CALLED HIM BACK AT THREE O'CLOCK.

'Sorry about the delay – it took me a little time to persuade Toddy to help. He isn't having a good day.'

'Did he do it?'

'He's with me now. Would you mind explaining to him what it is you need?'

'I already explained it to you, Father.'

'Yes, and I gleaned from what you said that you are looking for someone, but that is where I lost the thread. Tell him.'

Dunnigan heard the phone being handed to someone.

'Toddy is here.'

'Hello. This is Davey Dunnigan.'

'Toddy doesn't know anybody with that name.'

'Yes, you do, Toddy. I need you to help me get a postal address for someone from an anonymous post on a web forum.'

'Why do you want Toddy to do this?'

'It will stop some people getting hurt. Hopefully.'

'What is the website address for the forum?'

'It's www.wickedwords.com.'

*

Twenty minutes later Father Bill called him back.

'You owe Toddy dinner and drinks.'

'He's done it?'

'He has an address, this poor fellow's national insurance number, his credit rating – which is terrible, by the way – and his mother's maiden name. Do you want me to go on?'

'I probably don't need all that.'

'I'll email you the edited highlights.'

'Thank you, Father.'

'Your niece is missing again. Please tell me you know where she is.'

'I hope to soon.'

'Good. Isn't it an amazing coincidence that when you hit the first speed bump with Gina you shag off on a monster hunt? Did you really think Beth wouldn't go scarpering after you?'

'I don't have time for this, Father.'

'You never do.'

'That's not fair.'

'Please wrap up your quest, find that child and get your arse back so we can fix this mess you've created. Gina and Beth are worth it, don't you think?'

'Goodbye, Father.'

'See you soon, I hope. Be careful!'

And he hung up.

Mother Joan

When she came back to herself, she had the sense she had been unconscious for a long time. She was secured to a bed with thick leather straps, and she was naked, her cowl and blade gone.

She could see trees through the window of the room, but that was all.

Ressler came. He fiddled with something below the bed, and it swung around so she was suspended upright, looking the psychiatrist in the face. He took blood, measured her height, the circumference of her skull, the thickness of her waist. He said nothing and took copious notes. Finally, he left her, the bed still in its vertical position.

She slept some more and was awakened by the sound of the door being unlocked as he came back, this time in his shirtsleeves, carrying what she first thought was a club or truncheon. He stood before her, holding the tip of the stick at eye level so she could see the twin prongs protruding from it. 'I regret we must pass through the flames before we reach the promised land,' he said, pushing a button in the base of the cattle prod, causing electricity to dance between the appendages.

She began to pray the Rosary aloud. He laughed and it began.

She lost count of how often he came and hurt her. Soon she was covered in burns from the shocks and bruises where his blows fell. Sometimes he injected her with a drug first, which seemed to make every nerve ending sing, and his attentions became a symphony of agony.

She could not understand what he wanted. There were no

questions, no demands, just his presence and his desire to hurt her, from which he seemed to derive no pleasure.

It mattered little, though. Physical pain was inconsequential to her. She continued her prayers, and the voices bellowed curses and foul ululations, and chaos reigned.

Finally, he arrived without the prod. 'I hope we have reached an understanding, my dear,' he said, stroking her cheek. 'You planned to kill me, so I had to punish you. That is reasonable, is it not?'

She spat at him, tried to bite his hand.

He laughed, and injected her, but instead of more anguish, she was bathed in bliss. The physical pleasure was delectable, but even more euphoric was the silence – the voices dwindled to a murmur, then ceased completely.

She felt her body sag, and sleep – a beautiful restfulness – sweetly enveloped her.

It did not last – what felt like moments later she shuddered awake. The seven demons in her head were even angrier than before, screeching for sodomy and human flesh and demanding satisfaction. She tore at the straps and wrenched her frame back and forth until she thought she would break bones. Just as she reached crisis point Ressler was back and the needle stung her and peace was restored.

Again the maelstrom returned, much, much worse now. This time she became so distressed she dug her teeth into her shoulder and tore off a huge wad of flesh. Her head pounded and she felt that her skull must sunder.

And then it stopped, and a gentle hand was stroking her hair. 'I want us to be friends,' Ressler said softly.

'Thank you,' she mumbled, sobbing with relief. It was as

if all her pain and grief had been lifted after so long. How had he made the demons go away?

'You are welcome, my sweet girl. I only wish to be of assistance. You seem so lonely.'

He was right. She had been for a long time. She wanted to rest, for this to end. She wanted it so badly.

'Friends help each other, do they not?' Ressler continued. She tried to focus on his voice.

'Allow me to tell you a story,' he said. 'Would you like that?'

Once, he began, there was a terrible, evil man who had a beautiful young niece. It turned out Mother Joan had met this monster – it was on the docks in Ireland and she had seen the girl fight to protect him, but Phillipe told her the child's affections were misplaced; in fact, they were based on fear and loathing. This devil, David Dunnigan, had abused and harassed the poor child when she was only a babe, beaten and tortured her as one might a dog to make it savage, and she cleaved to him because she knew no better.

Mother Joan saw all this in her mind's eye, like a vision, and it filled her with righteous anger.

'Outside this building is a great forest,' Phillipe told her. 'He has used demonic arts to track you here, my dear. Do not falter. Do not stay your hand, as you did before. Strike him down.'

She nodded, eager that he understand that she was ready to do the Lord's work.

'He will bring other bad men in his wake,' Phillipe continued. 'Destroy Dunnigan, and then flee and bury yourself deep inside the earth. Rest until I return for you.'

He reached over then and – she still trembled to think of it – kissed her cold forehead. She permitted a whimper to escape, and he smiled.

'If you do this, dear lady, I will make it so the voices never trouble you again.'

She would be ready when the monster came.

There would be blood. Of that she was certain.

2

'ARE YOU QUINN ALDEN?'

The man stood at the door of his council house in Streatham. Dunnigan knew (from Toddy's tenacity) that he was forty-three years old, but he looked a good ten years more than that.

'Yes.'

He was wearing cargo shorts and a t-shirt with an image of a Sega Mega Drive on it that struggled to contain his girth. His hair had been teased into a style that might have looked appropriate on a member of One Direction but seemed ludicrous on a middle-aged man.

'Also known as hacker_red?'

The oddly coiffured person blanched, looked up and down the street to see if anyone was watching them, and pulled Dunnigan inside. 'Who sent you?' he hissed. 'Was it Tharg?'

'The alien editor of the comic *2000 AD*?' Dunnigan asked, surprised. 'I don't think he's a real person. Back when I read that book regularly it was edited by a guy named Steve McManus, but he retired years ago.'

'Tharg is the handle of a hacker I work with, bitch!' Alden

said impatiently. 'Look, man, state your business or blow. I have shit to do, know what I mean?'

Dunnigan showed him his ID. 'I want to speak to you about Mother Joan.'

'I gots nothing to say about that,' Alden said, walking down the hallway to a kitchen that could have done with an urgent clean three months previously. 'I post my words, my fans pass them on, that's all there is, babe.'

Alden was whiter than Dunnigan (who was pasty even with a suntan), a fact that made his ghetto patois seem rather misplaced.

'Where did you come across the poem?' Dunnigan asked, choosing to ignore that he had just been called 'babe'.

'I composed that thing. It's art, man.'

'I have reason to believe your "art" appeared in a book given to a murder victim in 1984,' Dunnigan said, 'when you were nine years old. Which calls your authorship into some question.'

'Who tole you that crap?'

'It's in a file held by the London Metropolitan Police. I can bring you down to the station and show you, if you'd like. I expect they'd also be interested in how you have been able to manipulate welfare records so a weekly payment is still made to a Muriel Alden – who died in 2005 but remarkably seems to still be collecting her pension. Isn't it amazing what a little computer know-how can achieve in the right hands?'

'You talkin' whack, bro! And keep it down – my mum is upstairs, and I don' want her hearin' shit about my nana's pension!'

'Alden, I am not your bro or your babe or your bitch. I am here representing the Irish police, and I am collaborating with the London Detective Squad. A young woman has been abducted, and I need to find her. Please stop wasting my time and tell me where you got the poem.'

'It was PMed to me.'

'You received it via a personal message – on social media?'

'Yeah, I was rockin' a MySpace page back then. You remember MySpace?'

'What did the message say?'

'Nuthin' else, man. Profile was for Mother Joan, had the photo an' all. I just thought it was a cool creepypasta, so I posted it – 's what you is meant to do! No one else claimed it, so I got all the credit. Over the years, more an' more stuff come my way, and it too good not to share.'

'You're a hacker – do you know where the messages are coming from?'

'Shit like that, you don't go lookin'. It rude.'

'Can you find out?'

Alden looked uncomfortable.

'Well?'

'I don't know where the mos' recent stuff is from, but I traced the first few messages I got.'

'What was the source?'

'A laptop.'

'That's not much help.'

'Do you think I'm a fuckin' idiot? It was a company laptop, dude.'

'Which company?'

'Outfit called Maylor Consulting.'

'Do you have the details of that computer?'

'I'll write them down,' the hacker said.

3

ALDEN WALKED HIM TO THE DOOR.

'This person has been in contact with you, off and on, for ten years now.'

'So? Ain't nuthin'.'

'You've acted as her voice, you've pretty much managed her publicity. Through you, this whole mythology has sprung up.'

'That's how the pasta thing works. You send it out an' the peeps either loves it or hates it – they fuckin' down with Mother Joan. It ain't me, dude, it's her.'

'The Watchers told me you think she's about to go into some kind of hibernation.'

'Says she's dyin', man. Sent me a message this mornin', says one of her demons is back and she gots to kill it or it take her to hell once an' for all. She gots one last job to do, then she gone.'

'Did she say any more than that?'

'Nope. 'S all she wrote.'

'If she contacts you again, could you call me at this number?' Dunnigan handed over his card.

'Okay, but I don' think she will. Says she's gone to the forest to rest before the last battle.'

'The forest?'

'Yeah.'

'Any idea where it is?'

'She says it in the north.'

'Okay. Thanks.'

They paused in the open doorway.

'How do I stop her?' Dunnigan asked. 'You know her better than anyone. What's her weakness?'

'She ain't got one, man. I was you, I'd get my ass as far away from her as you can.'

Dunnigan left with more questions than he'd had before he arrived.

4

MAYLOR CONSULTING HAD OFFICES JUST OFF THE
Strand. A secretary who looked like she had stepped off the
set of a Bond movie told him he was expected, then made him
wait for twenty minutes. The magazines on the table in the
reception area (which was decorated to look like a gentleman's
club from the Victorian era) were a mix of *Men's Health*, *The
Economist* and *Guns & Ammo*. He left them where they were
and read some more creepypastas on his phone.

'Mister Dunnigan. My sincere apologies.' The man who
stood before him was tall and trim, dressed in a three-piece
suit. His steel-grey hair was gelled tight back on his head and
a gold pin in the shape of a spear was in his lapel. 'My name
is Lorne Tanner. Please come to my office. Can I have Glenda
bring you anything to drink?'

Dunnigan declined, and followed his host.

'How can I help the Irish police this morning?'

'What do you do, Mister Tanner?'

'Me personally?'

'Your company website suggests you are a security firm,
but some of your services could be construed as the provision
of mercenaries.'

'Which would be illegal under British law. As our name suggests, we provide a consulting service.'

'What do you consult on?'

'Personal security for political leaders and celebrities; the management of large-scale events – we offered guidance on the safe running of the London Olympics, for example; specialist training for military personnel; tactical guidance for entrenched forces; corporate team-building – would you like me to go on?'

'Where do you recruit your staff?'

'Most are ex-military.'

'Like Merle Ely?'

Tanner looked puzzled for a moment.

'And Christopher Wayne?'

'Those are names I haven't heard in a long time.'

'And Grant Noble?'

'What is this about, please?'

'Does the name Mother Joan mean anything to you?'

'Not a thing. I am a very busy man, Mister Dunnigan. Will you please get to the point or leave me to my duties.'

'Someone is killing people linked to Maylor Consulting, and it's been going on for more than thirty years.'

Dunnigan told him the story, and to his credit, Tanner listened without interruption.

'You think this may be an employee?'

'The poem and a number of other posts were emailed from a laptop registered to your company.'

'That doesn't mean your Mother Joan is one of my people. Maylor staff members are entitled to pursue their own interests outside of work, and there is nothing in our codes of conduct that would prohibit one of them using a company laptop to post fiction to the web.'

'The text they posted has been used as the calling card of a serial killer,' Dunnigan said curtly. 'That's enough to at least arouse suspicion.'

Tanner pursed his lips. 'Alright. I won't argue with that. If you can give me the identification number for the laptop, I can get our tech boys to find out who it was assigned to.'

Dunnigan handed him a sheet of paper with the details Alden had given him printed on it. Tanner dialled a number on his phone. 'Moe, I have something I need you to do for me as a matter of urgency.'

*

'Her name is Hester Kitt,' he said ten minutes later. 'She worked for us from the mid-1970s until 2009.'

'Did you know her?'

'Yes, but not well. She retired, as far as I know.'

'What kind of work did she do for you?'

'She was a lecturer – military history, operational procedures, that kind of thing. I can get HR to send me the file.'

'I'd appreciate that.'

'She'd be somewhere in her late sixties now.'

'So?'

'A bit old to be running about stabbing people.'

'How old are you, Mister Tanner?'

'I'm sixty-seven.'

'Do you think you could overwhelm me physically if you had to?'

Tanner smiled coldly. 'Before you could get up from your chair.'

'I think you've just made my point for me,' Dunnigan said.

5

JONES RETURNED HIS CALL WHEN HE WAS IN THE Tube station.

'Hester Kitt has degrees in European History and Theology, and get this: before joining the British Army she was an Ursuline novice,' Dunnigan said, looking at the photo on the file Tanner had given him, which showed a hard-faced, angular woman with ash-grey hair. The personal details section of the document said she was six feet two inches in height.

There was the sound of keys clacking.

'Last known address is in Bloomsbury.'

'I'll meet you there.'

*

The house was on its own at the end of Montague Street near the British Museum. There was a small garden that had run to weeds and the mail slot was clogged with fliers and bills.

'Doesn't look like there's anyone home,' Dunnigan said.

'Famous last words,' Jones muttered. He took a Glock 26 pistol from inside his jacket. 'I go in first. You *only* enter when I give the all-clear.'

Dunnigan nodded.

Jones banged loudly on the door. They waited. He banged again. Still no response. After a third knock, the detective used the butt of his handgun to break one of the panes of glass in the door, and reaching in, released the lock and turned the handle.

Inside all was dust and silence. Dunnigan did as his companion asked and waited at the door while the detective passed inside. Cars moved on the busy thoroughfare. A feral pigeon settled on the low garden wall and eyed him in a bored manner. A van pulled up across the street and a man got out, pressed the automatic door lock, and walked briskly towards Russell Square.

'All clear,' Jones called from within.

The house had been decorated in a spartan manner. Everything was tidy and placed just so. The living room contained a couch, armchair, a small television and a bookshelf, most of the volumes relating either to religious or military history. The kitchen was scrupulously clean. Upstairs contained two bedrooms and a bathroom.

'What's Zyprexa?' Jones asked, looking through the contents of the medicine cabinet.

'I don't know.'

'Or Haldol?'

'Haven't a clue.'

The detective put them in his pocket.

Under the bed in what they took to be the spare bedroom they found a polished wooden box. It was padlocked.

'Alfie – did you get a warrant before coming out here?'

'No, but we both thought we heard someone in distress and had to affect an entry to investigate.'

'So it's like that, is it?'

'It is very like that. Do you give a fuck?'

'I don't have time to. I need to find Beth.'

'Exactly.'

Using the butt of the gun as a hammer, Jones broke the lock and opened the box. Inside was a collection of ornate knives, some of which looked to be antique.

'Interesting,' the detective said.

Dunnigan's attention had been caught by a picture on the wall of the bedroom. It was a painting of a nun dressed in full clerical garb, flowers clutched to her breast, her eyes seemingly rolled upwards so only the whites could be seen. In the right corner, the words 'Mère Jeanne des Anges' had been written.

There was a small garden in the back, about half of which was taken up by a shed. It, too, was secured by a padlock, which Jones easily circumvented. Reaching in, he found a light switch. Stepping inside, he stopped dead.

'Have a look at this, Davey me boy.'

Peering over the detective's shoulder, Dunnigan saw a long wooden table, laden down with pens and ink, pieces of card and swatches of black leather, various scalpels for trimming and bottles of paste and glue. The walls were lined with filing cabinets both men knew would be filled with photographs.

'I do believe this is where the Black Bibles are born,' Jones said.

'It's definitely her, then,' Dunnigan agreed, although the knowledge gave him little comfort.

6

DUNNIGAN GOOGLED THE MEDICATION JONES had found as the policeman drove them back to the police station.

'They're antipsychotics,' he said. 'Usually used to treat schizophrenia.'

'The fact both bottles are full and in her bathroom, and she's obviously been gone for a while, probably means she's not taking them as regularly as she should,' Jones retorted.

*

At the offices of the London Met, Jones checked that no news had come in about Beth (it hadn't), then pointed at an empty desk beside his. 'You can work from there for a bit – the owner's out on training today.'

Dunnigan began to make his way through the file Tanner had given him on Hester Kitt – he had only been able to give it a cursory glance so far. While he did that, the Welsh detective took the bottles of pills out of his pocket, and picked up the phone. 'Yeah, I want to find out who prescribed these meds, please. I'm gonna send you over a photo of the labels. Can you follow them up from that? Great. Here they come, brace yourself.'

Five minutes later: 'Thank you very much. Do you have a number? Fabulous.' He hung up and called across to Dunnigan, 'Those meds were prescribed by a Doctor Eamonn Marsden. I'm going to give him a buzz now.'

'Good. I have the name of the convent where she did her novitiate. It's right here in London.'

'I'll follow up on the GP if you want to call the nuns.'

'I'm going over there,' Dunnigan said, standing up. 'She might still be in touch with them, and if I don't keep busy I'm going to go crazy.'

'Fair enough. Call me if you learn anything.'

Dunnigan nodded and left.

7

THE URSULINE ORDER RAN A SCHOOL IN Wimbledon that had a small convent attached. Dunnigan met Sister Bonaventure, the Mother Superior, and they talked in the gardens.

'I always love this time of year, now the children have returned to us from their holidays,' the nun said as they walked down a gravel path between raised beds bedecked with an explosion of flowers. 'Only us old women left. The children make us happy – they remind us of the beauty the world still holds, even in these uncertain times.' She was tiny and hunched over with twinkly eyes, dressed in a dark blue cardigan over a simple white blouse and pleated grey skirt.

'Do you remember Hester Kitt, sister?'

'Oh, I do, I do,' Sister Bonaventure said. 'She came to us in 1966. She was a pretty thing. Full of life and passion.'

'How long was she here?'

'Until she was nineteen. Three years.'

'What happened to her vocation?'

'The Lord had other plans.'

'Didn't she join the army after leaving? That seems quite a dramatic turn-about.'

The little nun tutted and placed a hand on his arm. 'That depends on your perspective, doesn't it? There have been many orders that had feet in both worlds. Wasn't Saint Joan of Arc a soldier as well as a saint?'

'What happened to Hester Kitt, sister?'

'Sit here with me,' she said, leading him to a bench that overlooked the school playing field, on which a class of school children were engaged in a soccer match.

'I had high hopes for Hester – Sister Jean was the name she chose for herself.'

'After Jeanne des Anges?'

'Yes. The child was absolutely dedicated to the work of the Ursuline order, and knew our history upside down. She had read all about the awful things that passed in that town in France, and she believed Mother Jeanne had been treated poorly by history. She'd done all this research that showed it had been a plot to kill the poor priest they burned at the stake, and Mother Jeanne and the rest of the sisters were just collateral damage. She told me she believed Jeanne should be put forward for canonisation.'

'A noble aim.'

'It was, but poor Sister Jean became obsessed. For a person to be made a saint, there must be a number of proven miracles attributed to them. Hester began praying to Mother Jeanne, which would have been fine, but for the fact that it became pathological – she wasn't sleeping, she would stay up all night performing rosaries and novenas and repeated incantations to her. Finally, Matilda, who was Mother Superior at the time, ordered her to stop, for the good of her health.'

'It seems odd for a nun to be told she's praying too much,' Dunnigan observed.

'I would imagine that, if she had done it one hundred years earlier, she would have been considered a saint herself. However, even as long ago as the 1960s we were a little bit more enlightened – it was clear the poor girl was having some kind of breakdown.'

'Did she stop?'

'That was the problem – she said Mother Jeanne wouldn't allow her to stop.'

'I see.'

'Matilda had her sedated, but it didn't seem to have much of an impact. We took turns sitting with her, to try and keep her mind on other things. I helped, along with everyone else.'

'What was that like?'

'There were times, during the night, when it seemed she believed Mother Jeanne was speaking to her, answering her back as if she was having a real conversation. She began to talk in French, a language we had no idea she knew, although she appeared quite fluent.'

'Most kids have a few words,' Dunnigan suggested.

'This was more than a few.'

'Did things improve?'

'We finally sent her to an abbey in Germany where some of the sisters had medical training. There had been talk of having her committed, but it met with resistance.'

'Why? She was mentally ill.'

'I agree,' Sister Bonaventure said, patting the back of his hand. 'But you must remember, David – we are a religious order, which means we are all predisposed to a belief in the supernatural.'

'I suppose you would be.'

'As I have already told you, there were times Hester believed she was talking to Mother Jeanne. But there were other times she believed she *was* Mother Jeanne. And that was the stumbling block for some of the sisters here.'

'Why?'

'They came to believe – and quite resolutely – that Hester Kitt was being tormented.'

'She was – by schizophrenia,' Dunnigan said.

'No, David. Some of the older sisters thought she was possessed.'

8

THE NUNS INSISTED ON FEEDING HIM, AND HE
rang Jones from the refectory. 'She was sent to a convent
near Munich, according to some gossip I picked up over tea.
They sent her there because a couple of the sisters had some
psychiatric training, but it seems pretty clear they also tried to
perform an exorcism on her.'

'They still do that?'

'Not so much now, but this was the late sixties.'

'No wonder she went mental.'

'She was already halfway there. The fact that she was never
sent to a psychiatric hospital meant there was no barrier to
her joining the military – she wouldn't have set any alarm
bells ringing.'

'Doctor Marsden tells me that as well as treating Hester
Kitt for what he classified as *mild* schizophrenia, the old girl
has cancer.'

Dunnigan remembered what Alden had said about Mother
Joan dying. 'It doesn't seem to be slowing her down.'

'It doesn't, does it?' Jones agreed.

'How long has Marsden been seeing her?'

'Since the mid-eighties.'

'So right through her active killing period.'

'He says she's been experiencing bouts of paranoia and insomnia. He also told me she suffers from something called … hold on a sec.'

Dunnigan heard paper rattling.

'Here we go. Tardive dyskinesia. It's a side-effect of some of the drugs she's been on.'

'What are the symptoms?'

'Random muscle movement, facial spasms, involuntary eye flutters, jerky and exaggerated actions of the limbs ….'

Dunnigan remembered the strange dance he had seen Mother Joan perform on the CCTV footage. Could that have been a result of this condition?

'Doctor Marsden also spoke about a traumatic event Kitt experienced when she was working for Maylor in Uganda. She was caught up in some kind of attack – barely got out in one piece.'

'There's wasn't any mention of it on the file Tanner gave me,' Dunnigan observed. 'But then, traumatic events are part of the job if you're a soldier.'

'Yeah, but the timing fits – this would have been 1981, maybe as late as '82.'

'Can we get more details?'

'I've had the commish ring Maylor and ask them to send over everything. If they don't, we'll set the Ministry for Defence on their arses.'

'Bravo.'

'We've got the uniforms doing a door-to-door around Montague Street, but so far we've turned up nothing. No one has seen her in about three weeks. Looks like she's found a bolthole.'

'The bloke she was talking to online – Alden – seemed to think she had gone to a wooded area. She described it as a forest.'

'Nearest one from here is Epping. It's a bit built-up though – a lot of tourists and dog walkers and what d'ya call 'em … twitchers.'

'That's probably not it, then.'

'Look, mate, she's fucking off her trolley. It doesn't have to be a real forest – there are copses and the like in Hyde Park.'

'Where's she originally from?'

'Somewhere in Surrey.'

'Alden spoke about her being in the north.'

'Lancashire? Tyneside?'

'Are there any forests there?'

'You'll have to ask Mister Google.'

'I'll check it out. I'm going to call my sister and then head back to the station.'

He hung up and was about to dial Gina's number when his phone beeped and buzzed. It was a message from Beth's phone: *Please beware of Mother Joan*, and a geotag from somewhere called Kielder Forest, which was in Northumberland. *58 hours and counting.*

9

DUNNIGAN RENTED A VAUXHALL ASTRA FROM
Hertz, arranging to return it in a week. Then he got on the
M1 and drove for six hours without stopping.

It was four thirty when he pulled into the carpark of a
Travelodge just on the edge of the 250 square miles of Kielder
Forest, which seemed to stretch like a vast green ocean as far
as the eye could see. He booked a single room, and when he
got there checked his phone, hoping for another message
from Beth. To his chagrin he saw there was virtually no
coverage – one bar flashed onto his phone intermittently, so
he assumed that if a text had been sent, it had simply not
made it through. He placed the handset on the windowsill,
where coverage looked to be the strongest, and hoped
for the best.

He got a ham and cheese sandwich and brought it to his
room, then began researching the area on his laptop. Fifteen
minutes later the phone buzzed.

It wasn't from his niece, but from Diane, asking him to call
her. He thought about responding, but decided he wanted to
leave the line free in case Beth managed to ring or Jones had
any news.

He put the phone back where it had been and paused to gaze once again at the breathtaking vista of the forest.

He had never seen anything like it, and was a bit daunted at the idea that he was proposing to walk in there (cars were only permitted in specially designated areas, which he doubted a fugitive would choose as their hideout) to rescue his niece from a deranged killer. He watched as the sun dipped below the treeline and night took the woods in its grasp.

He fancied he could feel Mother Joan looking back at him from the shadows between the trunks.

*

In the middle of the night his phone buzzed again. He checked the time: it was 3.33 a.m. The message was from Beth's phone and read: *48 hours and counting*.

10

HE KNEW WITHIN AN HOUR OF WALKING INTO
the trees the next morning that he was hopelessly out of his
depth. He had hoped the Google Maps app on his phone would
guide him, or at least give him a sense of where he was and how
far he'd gone from the road, but the lack of coverage made his
phone useless, and the landscape, once he left the path, always
looked exactly the same and seemed devoid of landmarks.

The trees formed a never-ending parade of brown trunks
and sinuous branches. He was surprised at how silent it seemed
once the path disappeared from view, and the only birds that
seemed to call were wood pigeons, who would explode from
cover with a clatter of wings and disappear almost as quickly.
And the darkness once he passed more than ten or fifteen
yards into the trees was shocking – he tripped on roots and
brambles twice, then resorted to using his torch to ensure he
didn't stumble.

He blundered here and there, feeling hopelessly lost and a
little panicky, until he spotted daylight through the branches,
and pushed his way out onto the pathway, almost at the exact
spot he had gone in. Angry with himself, he walked back
to the viewing point where he had left his car, and drove to
Kielder village, where he stopped at the convenience store.

He bought the two ordnance survey maps that covered the forest and a pair of hiking boots. He had one of the maps spread out across the bonnet of the Astra when a battered-looking white Ford Transit van pulled up beside him.

He ignored it, took his phone out and began taking photographs of the map, trying to capture each grid – he reasoned it would be easier to have all the information stored on his phone than carry both maps, and it would eradicate the need to constantly fold and unfold them, particularly if it started to rain.

'You're wastin' your time at that, pal.'

He looked up to see a tall, dark-haired, dark-eyed man standing over him, looking amused. His hair was cut short and he was dressed in green waterproof trousers and a light olive-coloured jacket. 'Am I?'

'The whole point of the map is so you can follow the trails, and see where you are in reference to the whole thing. Breakin' it up into bitty pieces like that will just confuse you. And if you're plannin' on heading into Kielder, you don't need to be confused.'

Dunnigan realised as the man spoke that he was Irish.

'I'm Davey Dunnigan.'

'Joe Keenan. And this is Finbar.'

A small boy, perhaps ten years of age, arrived beside the man. The lad had a tiny, fuzzy, white and brown dog in his arms. The dog appeared, for all the world, to be smiling.

'And that's Rufus.'

'Hello,' Dunnigan said.

The boy said nothing, just looked at him with wide eyes.

'If you want to go into the woods, I can show you,' Joe Keenan said. 'Act as your guide, like.'

'You know the area?'

'You could say that. We're livin' out there.'

'In the forest?'

'That's right. We've set up camp right in the middle of it, haven't we, lad?'

The boy nodded.

Dunnigan looked at them. He had already picked up from the man's speech patterns that they were Travellers – members of one of the nomadic clans that had long since lived on the peripheries of Irish society. Many Irish people viewed them with a degree of distrust, but Dunnigan had no such issues. He'd rarely had any dealings with Travellers, and tended to reserve judgement until he had a reason to make one. 'I'd be very grateful,' he said, after pondering for a moment.

'I don't mean for free, like,' Joe Keenan said quickly. 'I'll need payin'.'

'Of course. Will fifty pounds a day cover it?'

'Fifty for me and a tenner for Finbar. You can have Rufus for free.'

'Why would I want either Finbar or the dog?'

'You'll see.'

'Alright. It's a deal.'

'Twenty up front.'

Dunnigan reached into his pocket and handed him the money. 'I need to go now.'

'Why the hurry? You a birder? Looking for the boar?'

'I'll tell you once we're underway.'

The man shrugged. 'No skin off my knuckles.'

The criminologist would thank fate for putting the Keenan family in his path.

11

THE TRANSIT WAS A REMARKABLE VEHICLE. Dunnigan couldn't believe so much space could have been created out of so little. Finbar's bed was set into the roof, and Joe explained that his was created by flattening down the table, which locked into the seats to create an area big enough for him to lie down. The mattress, duvet, etc. were all stored in cupboards at their feet. A small cooking stove and sink were set into the wall, and windows with orange curtains provided plenty of light. It was clean, comfortable, and perfect for the little family.

'I did all the work meself,' Keenan told him. 'It does for me and Finbar, doesn't it, lad? We have a tent we can pitch outside too, when the weather is good, but if it isn't – and that's often enough – we can just bunk up in here and we're safe as houses.'

'Is there a Mrs Keenan?'

'Died five years back.'

'I'm sorry to hear that.'

'Me too. She was as fine a woman as anyone could ask for. But we do alright. Me da was of real old Traveller stock. Taught me how to live off the land. That's why we like places like Kielder. Everything we need is right there. All you have to do is take it.'

'Aren't a large portion of the woods National Park?'

'So?'

'Well, doesn't that mean the wildlife is protected?'

'Now, you don't think we go bothering the animals – even the tasty ones – in places where it would be illegal to do so, do you, Davey?'

'I suppose not,' Dunnigan said.

'Now, if we were to accidentally wander into one of them places, and my shotgun should go off without my intending it to, and a roe deer or a pheasant or a bunny was in the way – well, I'd be sorry that happened, but it would be a damned waste not to take the poor craythur for the pot. Anyone could see that!'

Dunnigan had to laugh, in spite of his anxiety. The man's approach to life was simple and practical and Dunnigan knew they would get on.

'We're almost at our camp now,' Joe said, and turned the van off the road and onto a track that was little more than a groove between the trees. 'Do you want to tell me what we're looking for now, or would you like me to guess?'

'Like I said – when we're underway.'

Keenan drove on in silence, weaving the van in and out of the trees. At last he said, 'You're payin', so we'll play it your way.'

And the trees closed in like a green mist.

Part Eight

BADLANDS

Ernest Frobisher

He had houses and bolt-holes bought under assumed names by shell corporations all over the world, and to prevent detection and the possibility of arrest he was forced to move regularly between them.

He had grown up on the estate in Northumberland, the windows of which overlooked the huge verdancy of the forest of Kielder, and even now as the disease hungrily devoured him, this was where he preferred to be. Ressler had set up a medical facility in the basement for him, and friends of the After Dark Campaign rented the upstairs area and made a point of living there six months out of every year, so no suspicion was aroused.

One of the servants had wheeled him out onto the veranda when he saw a dark figure suddenly alight on the wall that adjoined the woods. It paused for a moment, weaving like a moray eel in the current, and then was gone into the trees.

'She is impressive, is she not?'

He hadn't noticed Ressler arriving at his side.

'You've returned her to the wild, I see. You had your fun?'

'She is quite the creature. I could write a paper on her psychiatric issues that would win awards, but she is a remarkable physical specimen, also. She has some unique qualities.'

'How'd you break her?'

'I applied the usual methods and brought a few new ones into play also.'

'I'm fascinated.'

'You flatter me, sir. Our dark friend is suffering from profound delusional paranoid schizophrenia – she hears a

chorus of voices that leave her not so much as a moment of peace. I applied a liberal dose of sodium thiopentone, which quieted these auditory hallucinations, but amplified them on their return. She was both relieved and grateful when I informed her I had the capacity to silence them permanently.'

'She's your pal now?'

'*I would not go that far. The drug I used makes an individual susceptible to suggestion. I led her to believe that our mutual friend Dunnigan is the type of bad man she likes to kill. And I told her that my removing the voices from her head is conditional on her removing Dunnigan from the world.'*

'You're a scary guy, Ressler.'

'From you, sir, I take that as a compliment.'

'It wasn't meant as one. Anything else I should know?'

'She's dying.'

'How's that?'

'*Her blood tests show she has metastasised cancer of the ovaries. I've given her enough painkiller to keep the worst of it at bay for twenty-four hours, but she'll need more. To get all these drugs, she must do our will. I have made sure the criminologist is coming here to find her, just as she goes out to find him. Mother Joan works for us now. For you. But in a most ironic way, so does David Dunnigan.'*

'And the girl?'

'Our friends from Romania are bringing her here to kill while her uncle watches.'

Frobisher made the choking, coughing noise that indicated he was laughing. 'Bravo, Ressler. You've set up all the dominoes. Now all we have to do is knock the first one over.'

'Patience, sir. The game has just begun.'

'You'd better make sure it's a good one, because patience is a virtue I do not possess,' Frobisher growled. 'And if that bitch talks, we're all finished. Wilfred is a fucking Great White Shark in the pond we're all swimming in. If he goes down, he will take each and every one of us with him, and the fallout will be catastrophic.'

'I understand your concerns, sir, but even if she did tell someone, it is surely her word – this crazy, disturbed, abused girl – against a captain of industry. Who would take her seriously?'

'I don't know. Something at the back of my skull itches when I think about it. Like there's an important task I forgot to deal with. It rankles at me.'

'I see.'

'I don't really care if you do or you don't. Just make sure it's done. I need that girl dead.'

'Between a deranged serial killer and the Romanian Mob, I think we can rest assured.'

1

JOE KEENAN PARKED THE TRANSIT IN A WIDE, FLAT area about half a kilometre from the path. As soon as they stopped, Finbar hopped out and scuttled back the way they had come, Rufus hot on his trail.

'Where's he going?' Dunnigan asked.

'He's covering over the tyre tracks.'

'Why?'

'Don't hurt to be careful.'

While they waited for the boy to return, Keenan packed a rucksack. 'What's in your man-bag?' he asked, nodding at Dunnigan's tote.

'The maps I bought.'

'What else?'

Dunnigan unbuckled it. Inside he had his phone; a smaller bag that contained a set of earphones, a charger and a 30 gigabyte flash drive; the file on Hester Kitt; Volume 3 of Garth Ennis's graphic novel *The Boys*; a tube of Polo Mints; a bar of Cadbury's Fruit and Nut and a bottle of Nestea (lemon flavoured).

'You can leave all of that here – take the chocolate and the sweets if you like, but the rest of it will only weigh you down.'

'What about my tea?'

'I'm bringing bags and a kettle. You can carry the cups.'

'Okay.'

'We'll be gone for most of the day and it's a long hike. You're goin' to feel the ground – walkin' through woods isn't like walkin' down the street. It's soft underfoot and you have to work harder to move. Carryin' comic books and a phone you won't be able to use and … I don't even know what them things are – it's just stupid.'

'I think you've made your point.'

'I'm not tryin' to be a bollix, Davey. You're payin' me to get you where you wants to go, and that means you need to listen when I talk. Alright?'

'I understand.'

'Good man. Now that your bag's empty, you can take these.' He tossed over the cups, three tins of beans and one of peaches.

'This is all the food we're bringing?'

'Most of what we need we'll find as we go along,' Keenan said.

'If you say so.'

'I do.'

He took a long double-barrelled shotgun from a brace fitted just inside the sliding door of the Transit. 'Here comes Finbar. You ready to head out?'

2

KEENAN HAD BEEN RIGHT ABOUT THE TERRAIN. The forest floor was not flat, but undulating. Rocks and fallen branches dotted their path, and at times the land dropped into dips and gullies which had to be climbed out of. Within the space of an hour Dunnigan was soaked in sweat and gasping for breath.

'You want to stop?' Keenan asked. He seemed completely unaffected by the journey, and Finbar and Rufus had run on ahead chasing butterflies.

'How much further?'

'Another two hours to get to the first spot you showed me on the map. If that's where you're sure you want to go.'

'I am.'

'I know a better one.'

Dunnigan stopped and leaned against an ash. 'You do?'

'You're lookin' for the lady in the black cape.'

Dunnigan gazed at his dark-eyed companion. 'How did you know?'

'You're not a birdwatcher or a rambler. No binoculars, your clothes are all wrong, and you don't know how to read a map. You don't belong here. Neither does she.'

'You've seen her, then?'

'I have.'

'Do you know where's she hiding?'

'I know where she goes. I've no interest in followin' her. So far she has left us alone, so we've left her alone. She's not been here long – bit less than a week – but she's done no ill from what I can see. No reason to think she will, either.'

'Yet you're bringing me to her.'

Keenan hefted his gun and watched his son and the dog jumping over a stump after a Painted Lady. 'You can't do her any harm. Once you get a look at her, you'll see for yourself.'

'Really?'

'The lady isn't alive,' Keenan said. 'You can't hurt a spirit.'

'Just show me,' Dunnigan said.

'We need to go that way, then.' Keenan nodded towards the north-west.

3

'WHY ARE YOU IN KIELDER?' DUNNIGAN ASKED him as they trudged on. As a rule he hated small talk, but he felt it might keep his mind off the burgeoning panic he was experiencing. 'I thought Travellers valued the clan. With your wife having passed, I would have thought you'd want your family around.'

Keenan used his boot to crush a patch of bramble so the criminologist could pass through, then followed him. 'You know the Travellers well, do you, Davey?'

'I've lived in Ireland for most of my life.'

'Lots of friends in the Travelling Community?'

'I wouldn't say that.'

'I didn't think you would. When the missus died, I ran. Didn't want to be around people too much. Kept meself to meself.'

'I understand that.'

'All Travellers like space, and in a place like this, you've got miles and miles of it.'

'Do you ever see yourself going back to Ireland?'

'Not in the near future, no.'

'Are your parents still alive?'

'You ask a lot of questions for a man barely able to stand up.'

They came to a point where the track they had been following ended in a rocky outcrop. Below them the forest fell away in a slope covered in bracken and heather. About a kilometre distant, Dunnigan thought he could see a shimmer of water through the trees.

'That's Kielder Burn,' Keenan told him. 'River gets quite wide at that spot. It's where we're headed.'

They began to descend the escarpment.

'Finbar, it's gettin' to be lunchtime,' Keenan called to the lad.

The boy looked back, nodded, and whistled at the small dog. 'Bird, Rufus,' he said. 'Catch us a bird, boy.'

The dog paused, it's tailed wagging merrily, and then bolted off into the undergrowth.

'Why don't you run ahead and test the waters, lad?' Keenan asked his son.

'Okay, Dad.' And the boy bounded off too.

'Only a wee bit further,' Keenan said, slapping the exhausted Dunnigan on the back. They plodded on for a bit in silence, until he broke it with, 'Did it ever occur to you that my family don't want me hangin' around?'

'Why ever not?' Dunnigan said, surprised.

'It's a long story, Davey. I'll tell you another time.'

'Fair enough.'

'Listen,' Keenan said. A bird was singing a beautiful, chattering, melodic song somewhere to Dunnigan's right. 'That's a blackcap,' Keenan said. 'Isn't it the sweetest thing you've ever heard? It'll be heading to Spain any day now, so you have to enjoy that song while you still can.'

Dunnigan paused. The sun was on his back, the wind whispered through the trees, and the wood smelled of dog rose and pine needles.

'There are worse places to be, eh, lad?' Keenan said, noticing his reveries.

'There are,' the criminologist agreed, the fact Beth wasn't there to experience it almost causing him physical pain.

'Let's see what Finbar and Rufus have for lunch,' Keenan said, and they walked on towards the glistening burn.

4

THEY REACHED THE RIVER AND KEENAN LED HIM to a shallow spot at a horseshoe bend. 'We'll cross here.'

Dunnigan looked about. 'I don't see any stepping stones or a log or ... '

'It's maybe six inches deep.'

The criminologist walked down to the edge and peered into the slowly moving brown water. 'My boots will get wet.'

'Oh, for God's sake, come here, will you?' Keenan took off his backpack, putting it on so it hung over his chest. 'Put your arms around me neck.'

'Why?'

'I'm going to give you a jockeyback. That way your lovely new boots will stay nice and dry.'

Dunnigan looked at the man, trying to work out if he was joking. Seeing nothing but mild irritation in the brown eyes, he shrugged and did as he was bid, and Keenan splashed across.

Rufus, his tongue hanging out and his tail ablur, was waiting at the other side.

'Hello, fella,' Keenan said, bending down to rub the dog's head. 'Have you got us something good to eat?' A rabbit path led along the bank for five hundred yards. The smell of smoke drifted on the breeze. 'Here we are. The best restaurant in the forest, and I have reserved us the finest seats in the house.'

Finbar had lit a small fire in the hollow left when a tree had been blown over – the upturned roots provided shelter and the trunk a place for them to sit. Two brown trout were roasting on sticks over the flame, and a pigeon hung, already plucked, from a branch above the lad's head. Dunnigan was loathe to stop, but he had to acknowledge that he was physically exhausted and ravenously hungry. If he was to continue, a short rest and some food were luxuries he was going to have to indulge in.

'Take out them tins and I'll start them heating,' Keenan said, 'and you can get us some water from the river for tea.'

Finbar reached into his bag and tossed the criminologist a small kettle.

When Dunnigan got back, the beans, the tops of their cans partially removed, were sitting in the embers bubbling. 'Will I put a bit o' spice in yours?' Keenan asked.

'Please,' Dunnigan replied, and the man applied a pinch of cayenne pepper.

'Now stick that kettle on to boil and we'll have some tea in hand in a jiffy. Then all will be right with the world.'

Dunnigan didn't know if it was the fact that he was starving from the exercise, or whether it was the freshness of the protein (Finbar had also picked some fresh sorrel, which was cooked by stuffing it inside the fish and pigeon) or the savoury quality the woodsmoke added to everything, but the criminologist thought it might be the finest meal he'd ever had. If he hadn't been so over-wrought, it would have been a memory he would have looked back on with great pleasure.

When the main course was finished, Keenan opened the tin of peaches and they passed it between them.

'When we're finished here we'll make for a patch about a mile downstream,' he said. 'We need to make sure we're downwind, 'cause she has a nose like a feckin' bloodhound. I've seen her test the air, and the slightest thing sends her off through the woods like a deer.'

'And you're sure she'll visit that place?'

'We've seen her there a few times, haven't we, Finbar?' The boy nodded, peach juice running down his chin.

'Probably goes there to get water,' Dunnigan observed, dreading a further trudge on so full a stomach.

'I've never seen her eat or drink,' Keenan said. 'I don't think she does. A spirit wouldn't have no need of such things.'

'Why would she go there, then?' Dunnigan asked.

'I think she just likes it,' Keenan mused.

And that was all he would say on the subject.

5

AT 3.35 P.M. THEY REACHED THE PLACE KEENAN said Mother Joan frequented.

'There's a kind of a hillock right through that grove of sycamore,' Keenan said, 'and we'll be able to see the river but not *be* seen.'

Dunnigan still wasn't happy. 'You say she's skittish,' he said. 'I'm not convinced she won't spot us.'

'Make us a hide, Finbar,' Keenan said. 'Davey Crockett here says we're still too much in the open.'

Without any further instruction the boy busied himself collecting branches and scrub and he and his father constructed a shelter under which the three of them and the little dog crawled.

'Happy now, Mister Frontier Man?'

'I think this will do nicely,' Dunnigan said.

'Y'hear that, Finbar? We done good.'

*

An hour passed.

'What are you gonna do when she shows?' Keenan asked. He was lying on his back, chewing on a pigeon bone he had saved from lunch.

'My plan is to follow her back to wherever she's hiding. I think she has taken my niece.'

'Seriously?'

'Yes.'

'We ain't seen no one else, have we, Finbar?'

The lad shook his head.

'I don't think she's a bad spirit. She's not done us any harm, and I'm sure she knows we're livin' nearby.'

'I believe she's killed quite a lot of people.'

Keenan made a 'you don't say' expression. 'Well, I ain't goin' after The Caped Lady,' he said. 'You do that, you're on your own. I don't reckon she's got no girl with her, and I'm damn sure she won't want you findin' where she sleeps.'

'That's up to you. Will you wait for me here?'

'I will, but I'm tellin' you this: you take off into those woods, you probably won't be comin' back.'

'I'll be very careful.'

'Don't matter.'

Dunnigan sighed and shifted his weight. It was approaching five o'clock, and the ground under them was starting to get damp. 'It doesn't look to me like she's going to show her face this evening anyway.'

'She'll be here.'

'If you say so.'

*

Another hour passed.

Dunnigan began to get drowsy. His head had fallen forward onto his chest and his breath had become regular, when Keenan shook him.

'Look sharp. One o'clock.'

He pulled himself onto his elbows and peered through the branches. Below them the river made a furrow through the woods. He had to blink a couple of times to focus on what he was seeing, but there, bent low over the stream as if it was looking at its reflection, was a cloaked and hooded figure.

Dunnigan had only ever seen Mother Joan in person once (the term 'in the flesh' didn't seem appropriate) and he was daunted by what he was witnessing. She seemed huge: the folds of the cloak were spread about the ground, making her seem like a huge bird or perhaps a bat. From what he took to be the sleeves of the garment, two claw-like hands were dug into the earth, as if seeking purchase, and the hood, which was long and ended in a point, showed only darkness beneath.

As he watched, her entire form seemed to sway and undulate. Suddenly, as if she had received an electric shock from the ground, her entire form jerked, then settled. It was eerie and unsettling to observe.

'There she is,' Keenan whispered directly into his ear. 'So, what do you think – you fancy followin' that into the deepest part of the woods at night?'

Dunnigan shushed him. The criminologist understood on a visceral level that he was terrified, and he tried to vanquish the emotion: he would not permit it to handicap him, not when he had come so far. The only thing that mattered was Beth, and there was precious little time left. 'I'm going to try and get a little closer,' he said.

'You're a feckin' idiot, is what you are,' Keenan retorted.

Dunnigan was about to move when the creature below them froze. It was like someone had hit a pause button – even the flapping of her cloak in the wind seemed to cease. Instantaneously the hood shot up, as if tasting the very air, and then, supernaturally quickly, Mother Joan shot up the nearest tree and disappeared into the branches. Dunnigan was aware of a slight swaying in the canopy as she moved through the treetops, but in seconds, even that was gone.

'Did she catch our scent?' Dunnigan asked, unsure what had just happened.

'Not possible,' Keenan said, standing up and stretching. 'Wind is blowing towards us.'

'What happened, then?'

'I don't know. Something else must have spooked her.' Keenan looked uneasy for a moment, and almost seemed to be sniffing the air himself.

'I have to go after her.'

'You wouldn't get more than a mile. The land gets boggy that way – you'd fall in a sinkhole and drown.'

'I have to!'

Keenan grabbed him by the shoulder and spoke sternly. 'You're no good to her dead. Nothin' and nobody, not even that ghost, is goin' to be traipsin' about Kielder in the dark, 'cause that's just plain stupid. Ain't nothin' more we can do here tonight. If we follow the river we'll hit the path in a coupla miles, and that'll take us close to the Transit. We can start fresh in the morning.'

'Why didn't we go that route to get here, then?' Dunnigan asked in vexation.

''Cause this ain't where you said you wanted to go,' Keenan retorted. 'Come on. It'd be nice to get home before tomorrow.'

6

IT WAS ALMOST TEN WHEN THEY GOT BACK TO the van.

'And we'll try again tomorrow?' Dunnigan asked.

Keenan nodded. 'It wasn't us she was runnin' from, so I don't see why not. There's another place I've seen her, by the deer park. It's further, though.'

'Let's start earlier, then.'

'You're the boss.'

Dunnigan checked his phone. Another message had come through: *Your time is nearly up*. But with the coverage he wasn't sure when it had been sent, and the usual timestamp was noticeable for its absence. 'I'm staying here tonight.'

'I don't run a boardin' house.'

'You said you've got a tent. Let me sleep there, and we can head out as soon as it gets bright.'

Keenan looked at Finbar, who looked at Rufus, who was licking himself with great determination. 'It'll cost you extra.'

'Done.'

'I haven't told you how much extra.'

'I don't care. Where's the tent?'

*

Keenan pitched the shelter, which was one he had fashioned himself using ash branches, canvas tarpaulin and climbing rope. When it was up he tossed some blankets inside. Finbar was making griddle cakes on a huge skillet pan.

They ate under the stars, the forest about them like a silent, listening throng.

When they were finished, Finbar read the final chapter of *Call of the Wild* aloud to the two men, which told the story of how Buck, a sled dog during the Yukon Gold Rush, eventually left human society to become a member of a wolf pack in Northern Canada after his beloved owner was murdered.

'Do you think Rufus wants to be livin' in the wild with his own kind?' the boy asked when he had finished. It was the first time Dunnigan had heard the boy speak more than a couple of words.

'Don't you think he is?' Keenan asked.

'We ain't dogs, Dad.'

'That little mutt has been with us since he was a pup too small to sit up on his own. He *thinks* we're his kind – he don't know no different. I reckon he'd be fierce lonely if he didn't have you to play with.'

Rufus was curled up on the boy's lap, his eyes bright and aware – clearly, he knew that he was being talked about.

'What kind of a dog is he?' Dunnigan asked.

'Far as I've been able to discern he's part Jack Russell, part bichon frise,' Keenan chuckled. 'A coupla years ago we were parked on the banks of the Yarrow River in Scotland, and Finbar seen a farmer come down to the water with a bag, and dammit, wasn't that bag makin' a awful squealin' sound.

Farmer chucks it in and down it goes right away – he'd put some rocks in to sink it. Finbar here waits for the man to go and then he jumps right on in – didn't even bother to check how deep the water was. Nearly feckin' drowns his own self. When he gets out, he finds the bag full of scruffy little white and brown pups, and only one of 'em is still alive, and that one only just. My lad sat up with that dog day and night until he was sure he was goin' to be alright, and that dog ain't left his side since.'

'A proper rescue dog,' Dunnigan said.

'Time for bed now, lads,' Keenan said.

Without complaint Finbar got up, Rufus held snugly under his arm, and hugged his father.

''Night, Mister Davey.'

'Goodnight, Finbar. Thank you for all your help today.'

The boy blushed and went into the Transit.

'You want another cup of tea before retiring to your boudoir?'

'Please.'

Keenan picked the kettle up from the flames (using a cloth so as not to burn his hand).

'Now that it's just us men,' he said, when their cups were replenished, 'how would ya like to tell me why a educated city chap like you thinks a ghost has stolen his niece?'

Dunnigan gave him an abbreviated version of Beth's story.

Keenan listened intently. 'I am truly sorry for your troubles,' he said. 'But I meant it when I said that Caped Lady don't have her.'

'I have to believe she does,' Dunnigan hoped Keenan wouldn't hear the tears hovering on the edges of his voice.

'Why?'

'Because I don't have anything else to go on.'

They were quiet for a time and drank their tea.

'You said you'd tell me why your family are upset with you,' Dunnigan said eventually, clearing his throat.

Keenan picked up a stick and tossed it onto the fire, which shifted and spat. 'Not much to tell.'

'I thought you said it was a long story.'

'Feck it – I could *make* it long, but it really isn't. My wife died. I took Finbar and we went into the mountains of Donegal for six months. Didn't come out except to get what few provisions we needed. I didn't have a plan, just thought we'd stay there until I didn't feel empty anymore. And that is what I would have done, only the world had other plans. One day Finbar got sick. I thought it was just a cold, reckoned he'd sweat it out by himself. But he fell asleep and he wouldn't wake up. I went kinda mad – drove like a crazy man to Letterkenny and got him into the hospital. Turned out he had meningitis – luckily it was the kind they can treat and they pumped him full of medicine, and told me he was gonna be alright.'

'Thank goodness for that.'

'The doctors said he'd be in the hospital for a few days, and they wouldn't let me sleep in the Transit in their carpark – some shite about insurance. So I had to go to the official Traveller halting site just outside the town, where I could make camp without bothering the locals.'

'I take it you don't approve of sites like that.'

'Look about you – this is what I approve of. Some of those government-sanctioned places have curfews, for feck sake: it's like bein' in prison. No, give me the woods or the hills or moors. But I had no choice, so I pulled in for the few days. And it was there that I met Ken.'

Keenan looked at Dunnigan as if the name should mean something. Dunnigan made a 'go on' motion, and Keenan continued.

'There were eight trailers in the place, and six of them were owned by members of one family – the Cashes. Out of respect I called in on the caravan of Maisie and Fred, the head of the clan, when I first arrived, to explain I was just going to be there a short time while my son was in hospital. They were very nice, wished Finbar well, and that was grand. Later that night, I got a knock on the door, and it was one of their sons – Ken. He was a bit younger than me, but he had a bottle of whiskey and he said he'd heard about my young lad and wanted to see how I was doin'. I thought nothin' of it; he seemed a good kind of a chap and I didn't mind the company, so we had a few drinks. He called the next evenin' too, and I was kind of expectin' him the evenin' after that. Finbar was due to be discharged from the hospital the followin' mornin', so I told Ken we'd soon be on our way. And ...'

Dunnigan waited. Keenan was clearly struggling to find the appropriate words.

'He kissed me.'

Somewhere in the woods behind them an owl screeched. Moments later another called out in reply. A bat flapped lazily after a moth that had been drawn to the light of the fire.

'I was a bit drunk, but not *that* drunk. I pushed him away, and he sort of sat there, lookin' at me, and just like that I knew that I had wanted him to do it. I haven't a clue how *he* knew, but he did. And one thing led to another and he spent the night. We were woke up the next mornin' by a hammerin' on the door of the Transit. His da and his brothers.'

'They knew what had happened?'

'I don't think I was the first,' Keenan said. 'Bein' gay – which I don't know that I am, by the way, I mean, I loved my wife – but, well, while attitudes might be changing in some corners of the Travelling Community, this crowd were having none of it! They beat seven shades of shite out of me, probably would've killed me if Ken hadn't begged for my life. Maisie, the matriarch, told me the next time I came near their part of the country, they'd kill me. I didn't know what to do or where to go after I collected Finbar, so I went home. But the Traveller world is a small one, Davey, and when I got to Dublin, my da was outside the trailer waitin' for me. He told me I had brought shame on the family, and that I should leave and not come back. And I never did.'

'I don't know what to say,' Dunnigan said.

'Nothin' much to say,' Keenan grinned. 'You don't need to worry – I'm not goin' to go all *Brokeback Mountain* on your arse in the tent tonight.'

'I've never seen the film, but I do understand the reference,' Dunnigan said. 'I appreciate your assurance.'

'And I appreciate you not trying to say anything comforting or consoling.'

'I could say "there, there" and pat you on the arm if you like.'

'I don't think I could cope with such an outpouring of emotion.'

'In the morning, we could paint the van in the rainbow colours.'

'Why don't you quit while you're ahead?'

7

DUNNIGAN SLEPT THE SLEEP OF THE DEAD. THE
tent was surprisingly comfortable, and almost as soon as the
flap was closed he drifted off and knew nothing until he was
awakened by someone shaking him.

'You need to wake up, Davey.' It was Keenan.

'What's wrong?'

The door to the tent was open, and he could see that it was
still dark outside. He glanced at his phone and saw that it was
only a little after midnight.

'People are coming.'

'So what?'

'One of them has a gun.'

Dunnigan reached for his boots.

*

By the time he had them on and was out in the open, Keenan
was locking up the Transit and Finbar and Rufus were peering
into the darkness.

'Why don't we just go in the van?' Dunnigan wanted
to know.

'Too slow and too visible. They'd be on top of us before we got anywhere near the road. And we don't know how many there are.'

'Isn't it likely they're just poachers?'

'Finbar says no. Rufus was spooked, and he went out to see what had him rattled. He saw two of them, one up close – he says this guy was dressed a bit like you and fat. Not a woodsman. These fellas aren't hunting anything with feathers or fur.'

'I still don't understand why you think they're after us.'

'Not *us* – me. The Cashes have had a pop at me once or twice before. I don't reckon their decision to let me live sits well with them.'

'If I tell them I'm with the police ....'

'Yeah, that'll really make them like me more, won't it? Hanging out with the Gardaí!'

Rufus's ears suddenly pricked up and he made a kind of skittering movement, as if he wanted to go but knew he shouldn't.

'They're close,' the boy said.

Keenan grabbed Dunnigan by the shoulders. 'Run as fast as you can manage in the direction we went this morning. There's a rock with two points, like horns – you'll find a wee cave under it. Crawl down inside and keep quiet.'

'Why do I have to hide?'

'Because Finbar and me are goin' to lead them away,' Keenan snapped, 'and you'll only slow us down. Now go!'

Running proved too difficult: Dunnigan fell twice, and the second time he came down hard and was worried he had broken his ankle. He ended up walking, taking wide, exaggerated steps, and after what seemed like forever he found the rock Keenan had mentioned and squeezed uncomfortably into the space below it.

He crouched in the shallow hole, trying to make himself as small as he could, hardly daring to breathe. Somewhere in the distance, he heard Keenan shouting and Rufus bark a couple of times. Then the woods fell silent.

He was afraid to move and stayed pressed into the cold stone, breathing slowly through his mouth. (His nose had the habit of whistling sometimes, and he didn't want to be shot due to a malfunctioning nostril.) Straining to hear every sound, he realised someone was approaching through the trees.

With a sure tread, the person got closer and closer. As Dunnigan listened, he heard them take a few steps, then pause, then come forward again. The jerky, staccato movement called to mind only one person.

It's Mother Joan, he thought. *I'm going to be caught like a rat in a hole!*

He tried to get out and discovered he was stuck, wedged into the stone – a terrible, suffocating sense of claustrophobia gripped him, and he struggled to free himself from the trap his hiding place had become. As he did so, the walker in the woods came to the rock just above him and paused.

In a single, desperate burst of movement, Dunnigan flung himself out of the cave and rolled over on the forest floor, coming upright to face the presence that had been stalking him.

'Fancy meeting you here,' a grinning Diane Robinson said.

8

DIANE WAS WEARING A GREEN PARKA, CAMOUFLAGE leggings and military-style boots, her blonde hair wrapped tightly in a bun and fixed on top of her head.

'What are you doing here?' Dunnigan asked, completely taken aback.

'I came with Bob to find you.'

'Bob? Who the hell is Bob?'

'Inspector Jones. Jesus, Davey, he told me you were friends!'

Dunnigan was still struggling to catch up. 'But you were in Ireland!'

'I came when I heard about Beth.'

'Where is Inspector Jones?'

'Last I saw he was chasing that Traveller fella through the trees. They told us at the shop in Kielder village that you'd taken up with him, and some of the forest rangers gave us directions. Not great directions, if I'm honest.'

They made their way back to the Transit and found Jones, red-faced and out of breath, leaning against it, sweating. He had his gun in his hand.

'What are you doing with that?' Dunnigan snapped. 'You could have tripped and shot yourself!'

'Didn't you come here to find Mother fucking Joan?' the detective said between deep breaths. 'Damn right I'm going to have me bloody piece ready!'

Dunnigan scowled. 'She's miles away from here.'

'You found her?'

'I saw her, but she got away.'

'I'm not sure she's really got your niece, mate,' Jones said.

'Why not?'

'We have video footage from a camera in Queen's Park. It shows her being taken by two men.'

'Taken where?'

'They seemed to know where the cameras were placed. We have them heading down a path into the park, but that's where it cuts out.'

'She couldn't have just vanished into thin air.'

'I'm sorry, Davey. The fact you've been brought here must mean something, but I don't like it. You've been out of coverage these past couple of days, so we had no choice but to drive up and look for you.'

'What if they're sending me away from where she is?' Dunnigan asked, his voice becoming shrill with alarm.

'We don't know that, mate.'

Keenan and Finbar stepped out of the trees. 'Am I to believe these are friends and not foes?' Keenan asked.

'I have to go back to London,' Dunnigan replied abruptly.

'Fair enough,' Keenan shrugged. 'Didn't we discuss a fee?'

'Yes, whatever you want. Can you bring me back to the hotel?'

'We're parked a bit up the road,' Jones said. 'Can we hitch a lift that far?'

'All aboard.' Keenan motioned towards the van.

The Transit didn't seem quite so roomy with four adults, as well as the boy and his dog, crammed inside.

'Where do you pee?' Jones wanted to know.

'In the lavatory the Lord provided,' Keenan said serenely. 'The countryside is our toilet.'

'We have a chemical loo in the back,' Finbar whispered to him. 'Dad likes to pretend we rough it more than we do.'

'Spoilsport.' Keenan gave his son a disappointed look in the rear-view mirror.

They were within sight of the road when the woods suddenly came ablaze with light. Keenan jammed on the brakes. 'What the hell is this, now?'

'It looks like three or four cars with their full lamps on,' Diane said.

'David Dunnigan!' A hoarse voice could be heard through the trees.

'You are in demand this morning, aren't you?' Keenan asked sardonically.

'You and me, we have business.'

'Friend of yours?' Diane asked.

'I genuinely have no idea who that is,' Dunnigan said.

'I have someone here wishes to say hello to you. Someone you probably looking for, eh?'

A car door opened and closed, and another voice called out, *'Davey? I'm sorry, Davey.'*

Jones, Diane and Dunnigan all exchanged looks. 'Whoever it is, they have Beth,' Diane observed.

'It looks like time's up,' the criminologist said. 'I'd better go and see what's going on.'

And he pulled open the door of the van.

Bradislav Vaslav Chechnik

He had considered killing the girl as soon as he had her, but what would have been the fun in that? Phillipe suggested her uncle be forced to watch as she was gutted, and the poetry of that idea appealed to the mobster – just as his family had been decimated, so he would destroy the girl's.

The uncle was hunting some kind of escaped lunatic in the woods in the north of England, so the Volatov organisation in the UK sent him five men with experience in the outdoors: two brothers, Klaus and Vern Voors, from Germany; Lev, who was one of his own countrymen and grew up in the Black Forest; a short, blocky Englishman with a bowl haircut and no eyebrows called Zeb, whom he neither liked nor trusted; and a black mixed martial artist from Birmingham who called himself Dwight, and looked as if he spent more time in the gym than he did in the woods: he was obscenely muscled and walked as if the act of doing so hurt.

It seemed, however, that he would not need them – the Irishman was approaching through the trees, and he was unarmed.

'They tell me in the village that he has engaged a gypsy family as guides,' Bradislav said to the Voors brothers. 'Make sure they do not cause any problems.'

The two men peeled off to the left and right and were swallowed by the forest.

Dunnigan had now come to the treeline. He was wearing a long, grey woollen coat, a loose-fitting t-shirt with the words Strontium Dog *emblazoned on it, and blue jeans. He looked thin and nervous. Bradislav gripped the girl by the hair and shook her. To her credit, she did not cry out.*

'Welcome, Mister Dunnigan. We have not had the pleasure. I am Bradislav Vaslav Chechnik. You and your bitch of a niece killed my brother. I wish to have that debt repaid.'

'I keep telling you, you thick fucking asshole, I killed your brother, he had nothing to do with it,' the girl snarled, and he drew back his hand and slapped her so hard she fell to her knees.

The man Dunnigan made to run at him, and three guns cocked loudly in the night air. He stopped.

'You will come with me now,' the Romanian said.

'Let Beth go, and I'll hand myself over without argument.'

Bradislav laughed a long, loud laugh. 'Argument? If you do not move right now, I am going to open up her belly so we can all see what she had for dinner last night. You do not get to argue. That time is passed.'

'Run, Davey,' the girl said through clenched teeth, and he hit her again.

Dunnigan, tears streaming down his cheeks, raised his hands. 'Stop hitting her, for God's sake! I'm coming, Beth. It'll be okay, I promise.'

The girl made a sound that might have been a sob. 'No, it won't,' she said, 'but that's alright.'

In a rapid lunging motion she dropped to her knees and slammed her elbow into Bradislav's groin. He gave a high-pitched whine of surprise, then doubled over and threw up over his shoes. At the same moment someone started screaming hysterically among the trees, and Lev the Romanian hunter's head exploded in a mess of red.

Then all hell broke loose.

9

'I NEED TO USE YOUR SHOTGUN,' DIANE SAID, AS Keenan closed the van door behind him.

'Can you shoot, girl?' he asked, looking at her with an expression she had become used to as a woman in the armed forces.

'I used to be in the Irish Army. I shot guns every day.'

'There's a box of cartridges under the bed.'

Diane loaded both barrels and looked at Jones. 'You any good with that Glock?'

'I've been a copper for thirty-four years, and I have shot me gun in the line of duty five times. I can hit targets on the range, but I'm no gunfighter.'

'You are tonight.'

Jones shrugged and followed her into the dark.

'I'm going to try and sneak up on them,' she said, once they were outside, hefting the gun to get a feel for its weight. 'Can you cover that man and his boy?'

'Serve and protect is what I do,' Jones said. 'Good luck.'

Diane dropped low and jogged off into the woods. Jones marvelled at how little sound she made.

The detective could hear voices from the road, but nothing

else. The trees towered skywards and the wind whispered among them, telling secrets in a language he could not comprehend. A twig broke behind him and he whirled, and Klaus Voors stepped from behind a gnarled oak and shot him in the stomach.

10

THE LANDSCAPE DIANE WAS ACCUSTOMED TO from her military service was primarily mountain and desert, and therefore very different to that which she moved through now, but the rules were the same. She covered the distance from the Transit to the edge of the trees with little difficulty.

Her training had made her adept at remaining silent, and she instinctively took note of which direction the wind was blowing and the patterns of light and dark, keeping herself to the gloom and shunning the spots where the canopy was less dense and moonlight shone through.

She heard Vern Voors, the older of the German brothers (although she would only learn his name, nationality and family circumstances much later), coming towards her and instinctively froze and dropped flat to the ground, allowing the man to go past (and hoping Jones could deal with him) before moving on again. She arrived at the place where the trees met the road and took stock, dropping to one knee and propping her elbow on the other, adopting a traditional hunting stance, the shotgun trained on the line of four men, one of whom had Beth Carlton by the hair, the other three holding handguns.

David Dunnigan, the man she loved in spite of herself (and often, in spite of *him*self), was standing before the armed thugs, his hands in the air.

Diane only partially heard the conversation that passed between Dunnigan and the man who had introduced himself as Bradislav – she was rapidly trying to assess what would be the best plan of attack. She knew she would get one shot off before the strangers opened fire, so she had to make it count. Murtaugh, her old regimental captain, had always told her that, when faced with multiple targets, a good soldier simply plays the odds. There were four men standing in front of three cars: Bradislav was holding Beth, so shooting at him was out of the question – the spray of pellets might hit the girl, and Diane was not prepared to risk that; also, while she had no doubt Beth's captor was armed, the Romanian did not have his gun out, which made him less of a threat, even if only by a narrow margin. The other three were spread in a wide arc, two to Chechnik's left, one to his right.

Always take the easiest shot, was Murtaugh's rule: don't go for anything fancy or grand, aim either for the biggest target or the one directly in your line of vision. The man holding Beth hit her. Diane felt her finger tighten on the triggers. Dunnigan tried to reassure his niece and began to walk forwards. Beth suddenly walloped Bradislav right where it hurt, and Diane, knowing that the moment everyone's eyes would naturally be turned towards their fallen master was just the right time to act, shot the man next to the Romanian in the head.

As she did so, the screaming started in the woods.

11

DETECTIVE INSPECTOR ALFIE JONES HAD NEVER been shot before, and he was surprised by the fact that it did not hurt – not badly, anyway.

Everything seemed to be happening in slow motion. He had watched Diane move into the darkness, then scanned the area about the Transit, one hand on the pistol, the other supporting his wrist to keep the Glock steady. Keenan and his son remained in the van, the engine of which was still idling.

Scan to the left.

Scan to the right.

He moved to the other side of the Transit, executed the same motion. Guarding a stationary vehicle parked in an open area made it impossible to keep every line of vision clear, and he was considering climbing on to the roof, which would offer the best vantage point, when he heard a twig breaking and the biggest bastard he had ever seen stepped from behind a tree.

He felt something hit him squarely in the guts, and he was lifted right off his feet and slammed into the door of the Transit. For several long moments he couldn't breathe, and that panicked him more than anything – he was sure he would suffocate – but then, like a machine turning over, his lungs started pumping again, although he noticed a rattle in his chest that wasn't there before.

He would have to get that checked out.

His lower abdomen felt cold, and, looking down, he saw that where his paunch had been only seconds before there was now a mess of torn flesh with some tubes of pinky white protruding from it. *That*, he thought, *probably isn't good*.

'You are in my way, friend,' the man who had shot him said, still standing at the oak tree behind which he had been hiding. 'Move.'

'Sorry, mate,' Jones said, laughing at the good of it (which *did* hurt, if he was honest). 'I'm afraid I can't do that.'

Pointing the Glock at the man, he squeezed off a shot that went far to the right of its target.

'Could you stay still while I try that again?' Jones said, and then Mother Joan reached out of the branches of the oak with her white, clawed hands, and gripped the man by the throat.

Mother Joan

Something was wrong – it was not as Phillipe had told her it would be.

Bad men had come, probably drawn to Dunnigan's evil. She sensed them as soon as they reached the edge of her world, and right away she hated and feared them. They brought weapons and anger and they had a prisoner.

From her perch in the canopy she saw them beat the girl, Beth, and this monster, Dunnigan, whom she had been told was cruelty itself, wept for her and offered himself in exchange.

Was this a subterfuge? Was he lulling them into a false sense of their own safety so he could tear them to pieces? She was about to fly down and wage war upon them when she became aware of a woman approaching through the undergrowth. Something about her seemed familiar, and Mother Joan realised she was a soldier. She had rarely encountered another warrior woman in her long years, and for a brief moment she was confused and unsure. Peering through the leaves, she saw this peculiar combatant train her weapon on the men who had the girl.

Movement caught her eye to the rear: two of the bad men were making their way back to where the father and son waited in their van, and she would not allow that family to come to harm. Trusting that this new arrival would protect the girl, she moved like a huge black spider through the branches until she reached the boughs of a gnarled and twisted oak. Guns flashed below her.

She drew her blade and crept down the bole of the tree.

12

JOE KEENAN WATCHED IN HORROR THROUGH THE Transit's window as the policeman was blown off his feet. 'Finbar, go below.'

The boy lifted the floor in the rear of the van to reveal a small compartment, and he and Rufus climbed in, dragging the carpeted board back over them. Keenan pulled a metal box from under his seat and took out something wrapped in oiled rags. His eyes still on the events unfolding outside the van, he unwrapped an Enfield No. 2 revolver and quickly loaded six bullets into the chambers. He saw the cop fire and miss.

'Stay hidden,' he called to the boy. 'Whatever happens, don't make a sound.'

He watched Jones aim again, and then The Caped Lady was there and the gunman started screaming.

How the feck is she doing that? Keenan wondered as the monster pulled the huge man into the branches of the ancient oak. As he watched, an enormous knife – some kind of old-style hunting blade – appeared in her hand, and in a series of rapid movements she stabbed her captor in the belly, the neck, the chest, through the right cheek (he saw the point of the blade emerge from the other side of the man's face).

The wounded man's legs were kicking and beating a furious rhythm in the air, and despite his wounds he still made the most pitiful wails. The blade slashed across his throat, and the keening stopped in an awful gurgle. Joe, forcing himself to move, pulled open the door of the van.

'What kept you?' Jones greeted him.

With a sound like the wind, Mother Joan was on the ground at Jones's feet. She smelt of earth and woodsmoke and something sour, almost like spoiled milk. She leaned down over the injured policeman and seemed to be examining his injury.

'Do your fucking worst,' Jones said, his voice trembling, trying to raise his gun and dropping it again as his remaining strength ebbed away.

In a flash of black cloth and bitter anger the spectre was gone, disappearing into the darkness as if she was a part of it.

'Can you move at all?' Keenan asked.

'I don't know.'

'I'm going to see if I can find something to bind that scratch, alright?'

'Thanks, mate.'

Keenan was taking a clean sheet from the cupboard where he kept their linen when Rufus started to growl, a low, rumbling sound. Another man had come from the trees – Keenan noted a familial resemblance to the mangled corpse still seeping red into the earth outside. Luckily, the sight of his mutilated brother absorbed Klaus Voors long enough for Joe Keenan to train the revolver on him. 'I'd drop the gun if I was you, lad.'

The gangster, a look of fury on his face, turned with his weapon levelled, and Keenan shot him in the chest.

'Don't say I didn't give you a chance.'

When he started to tear the sheet into strips, Keenan saw the policeman had – mercifully – passed out.

13

DIANE'S HOPE WHEN SHE OPENED FIRE WAS THAT Dunnigan would duck back under cover but the criminologist had other plans, and with a roar he charged at Chechnik. Beth made a bolt towards the woods, but the mop-topped Zeb grabbed her before she could get more than a few feet, and dragged her back, kicking and screaming.

Dwight, the outrageously pumped-up muscle-man, saw Dunnigan coming and shot once, then a second time, but his target was moving at such speed he missed, the bullets veering off into the trees. Realising his attacker was beyond both fear and any sense of self-preservation, the huge mixed martial artist stepped into his path, and Dunnigan, all fists, legs and fury, barrelled into him.

Diane, meanwhile, had reloaded, and she fired again over their heads this time, still afraid of hitting Beth. Zeb shot back, using the muzzle-flash as a reference point, but Diane had already moved away.

Dwight had Dunnigan in a death grip and was squeezing the life out of him – the criminologist could feel his ribs starting to pop and was sure his arms would break. In a final, desperate attempt to save himself, Dunnigan pulled his head back and butted his opponent as hard as he could directly on the bridge of the nose. The first blow seemed to simply surprise Dwight, but at the second he heard a *crunch*, there was a gush of red, and the man let him go. The criminologist sank to the ground, gasping for breath.

Diane broke from cover – Zeb fired, and she rolled out of the way and came up with the shotgun cocked, only for Dwight to blunder into her, blinded by his own blood. Diane grappled with the huge man, and Zeb saw his opportunity and dragged Beth and Chechnik, who had been on his knees through all of this, to one of the cars, a big Volvo.

'They're making a run for it!' Diane shouted at Dunnigan and tossed him the shotgun (she was not in a position to take the shot herself), which he caught stiffly with his still-healing arm.

Dunnigan, still struggling to breathe, blew out one of the car's rear tyres, but it made no difference: with a screech of brakes the Volvo tore down the forest road around a bend and out of sight. The criminologist stood up, strode over to where Dwight was choking his former girlfriend, and cracked him over the back of the head with the shotgun's long barrel.

Not pausing to watch the giant crumple to the ground, Dunnigan ran to the second of the cars and climbed in. Diane followed.

14

JOE KEENAN FINISHED BANDAGING JONES'S wound as best he could, and then, with Finbar's help, dragged the man into the Transit and laid him flat out in the back.

'Try to keep him from rolling about,' he told his son. 'If he's got any chance, we need to get him to a hospital, and that means I am going to have to drive like hell's hounds are chasing us.'

He realised as he wove the van through the trees that the lights from the forest road had diminished.

'I'm gonna hop out for a second and see what the story is,' he said to Finbar. 'I won't be long.'

He climbed down, Rufus following, and crept through the darkness. One car was parked in the middle of the road, its full lights on. Two men were on the ground, one of whom had no head and one whose nose was at an angle that was never intended for it. Of Dunnigan, Diane and Beth, there was no sign.

'I don't reckon there's much more we can do here, Rufus,' Keenan said to the dog.

He made the trip to Hawick, the closest hospital, in forty

minutes. The doctors told him Jones would have died if he had arrived five minutes later.

As things turned out, it might have been kinder to let the Welshman perish in the woods.

15

BETH HUDDLED IN TO THE BACK OF THE VOLVO next to Chechnik, who was beginning to regain his composure, although she was pleased to see he was still very pale. The weird-looking man with the strange haircut was driving. The flat tyre in the rear meant they felt every bump and crater in the road, but Zeb kept the accelerator hard to the floor, regardless.

'D'you want me to park somewhere and go back for the uncle?' he asked. He had a cockney accent.

'No,' the Romanian said, his voice still hoarse with pain. 'There will be another time.'

'What'll we do with her?'

'Put some distance between us and them, then we will take her into woods and finish her.'

'Why not just cut her throat right now and dump her as we drive?'

'I have ruined a pair of shoes today on account of this bitch. I do not want to mess my suit also. Take her in the trees, shoot her, and cut off her head. I will want to show it to her uncle while I have him skinned.'

They drove on in silence. The Romanian had only a loose grip on her arm, and Beth was considering opening the door and throwing herself out when Zeb slammed on the brakes.

'What the fuck is this?'

The girl peered around the headrest in front of her to see what had caused the unexpected stop. Standing in the middle of the road, still, huge and terrifying, was the cloaked figure of Mother Joan. As they watched, she raised a pale hand, and pointed at them.

'Am I dreaming this?' Zeb asked.

'Run it down,' Bradislav said.

'With pleasure.'

Zeb gunned the engine, spinning the wheels in place until they smoked, letting the bizarre apparition standing in the road know that he was in earnest. It did not move.

'I said run that thing over!' the Romanian shouted.

Zeb released the break and the car shot forward. Mother Joan stayed precisely where she was for a long moment, the Volvo bearing down on her. Then, like dark water, she seemed to roll sideways.

'Fucking tricky cow,' the cockney said, and swerved so as not to miss her.

Except suddenly, Mother Joan was no longer there. Zeb spun the wheel to right their trajectory, but it was too late: branches scratched the windscreen, and the next thing Beth knew the car was bouncing and careening over the soft ground of the forest floor at sixty miles per hour. The front axle broke across a tree stump, and the vehicle flipped onto its side, sliding for ten feet before crashing into the trunk of an elm.

The three occupants were knocked unconscious. Had they not been, they would have seen a tall figure, wreathed in shadow, step out of the darkness and approach the prone automobile.

Part Nine

WHERE THE BAD CHILDREN GO

1

ZEB CALLOWAY WAS A BAD MAN BY ANY DEFINITION of the term.

He had been expelled from every school he attended: not because he was academically challenged or could not follow instructions; psychological testing at the remand home he had been sent when he was eleven deemed that he did not have attention deficit hyperactivity disorder, nor was he at any point on the autistic spectrum. Social workers spent hours with his mother (his father had left when he was eight, and good riddance to *that* piece of bad rubbish) and could not identify anything in his past other than the breakdown of his parents' marriage that might cause his behaviour to be so extreme, and in truth, his appalling conduct had been the main contributing factor to his father's decision to go.

Zeb, it seemed, was just angry, which was a diagnosis that also seemed problematic.

Because he didn't *seem* angry.

When he was six, Zeb beat Tristan Maynard until he vomited blood, and he laughed and smiled through the whole thing.

His mother got him a dog when he was ten, and he nailed the animal's tail to the wall of their shed and threw rocks at it until a neighbour, disturbed by the animal's cries, called the police. Mrs McQueen told the officers who arrived that when she peered over the garden wall to see what was going on, Zeb had waved and smiled pleasantly before continuing to torture the poor creature.

No, he didn't appear to be angry.

If anything, he seemed happiest when he was causing pain to someone or something.

Zeb found, when he got too old to be locked away in children's institutions, that there were plenty of people ready to pay for his particular brand of mayhem. A teacher had once told him: if you find a job you love doing, you'll never work a day in your life. And as much as he had detested that teacher, this particular little nugget of information turned out to be true. His work was also his passion, and he took pride in it. His calling mostly involved making people do what his bosses wanted them to, and paying for the privilege.

If they had a problem with that, Zeb would make sure they saw the error of their ways. Sometimes, if they refused to conform to common sense, he got the opportunity to be creative, and that was his favourite thing.

'Conform or die' was his catchphrase. And Zeb Calloway could dream up *all* sorts of interesting ways of dying.

It was an odd thing, then, that someone on such close speaking terms with death had rarely considered what his own might look like when the time came.

Zeb drifted back to consciousness before Beth or Bradislav. For a moment he could not work out where he was, or why his ankle hurt. Gradually, memory returned: he was in the woods; the car had gone off the road – he could smell petrol, and knew he had to get out quickly.

He fumbled about and unlatched the safety belt, then made to push himself out of his chair towards the passenger side door, which was now above his head. The pain that shot through his ankle when he put pressure on it almost made him pass out, and he had to close his eyes and breathe deeply to stop the world from spinning. Reaching down and feeling the joint, he knew right away that it was broken – it must have happened when the car tumbled.

The other one seemed alright, which was just as well. If he found a decent stick (which in fairness shouldn't be too much trouble) he would be able to hobble back to where they had left the other cars, and get the fuck out of this hellhole.

He took a deep breath and started to push himself into a standing position, favouring his good leg. He reached up for the latch but the door opened all by itself. He thought it must be one of the others – the Voors maybe, or Dwight – come looking for them, but then a clawed hand was reaching down for him, and there was no time to look for his gun.

His death was quick but creative and he screamed until the end.

2

BETH WOKE TO SILENCE AND THE SIGHT OF DARK tree boughs waving above her head. She was lying on a bank of moss and she had no idea how she came to be there. The last memory she had was of being in the car with the two gangsters, but everything after that was blank. She patted herself all over, and only when she was satisfied that nothing was broken or out of place did she sit up.

The Volvo was lying on its side, its bonnet crumpled like an accordion, fifteen yards away. There was no way she could have been thrown clear and landed where she was – someone had pulled her free and placed her there.

'Davey?' she called, using a nearby branch to help her to stand.

No response greeted her cry. She began to walk towards the car when a splash of red to her left made her turn. Zeb was lying with his back against a tree stump ten yards away. Someone had decapitated him, and placed his head, complete with its pudding-bowl fringe, on the log. It must have happened recently, as blood was still pumping steadily from the severed neck.

It was then she heard a muffled voice. It took her a moment to realise it was coming from the car. Cautiously she crept closer. It was Chechnik, and he seemed to be in some distress.

'Help me! Please, I can hear you out there – I need help!'

As she approached the vehicle, the smell of petrol became almost overpowering. She could see it dripping from the fuel tank, which had a gash in it, obviously caused by a rock or branch during the crash.

'Who is there? I … I am hurt. Please talk to me!'

Beth clambered up using the lower branches of the elm that had arrested the Volvo's progress, and peered into the wreckage. Bradislav Vaslav Chechnik was still in the back. Somehow a long branch had gone right through the passenger side window – it was still protruding above the frame – and impaled him through the shoulder. The limb had been driven with such force, it had gone through the glass of the window on the other side, and was pinning him to the ground.

'Beth – it is you I can see, yes?'

She did not answer, just looked at the man who had wanted to take her away from the life she had managed to reclaim.

'I know you must be angry with me …' he said, trying to keep his voice steady. 'And you have reason.'

'You were going to have that scumbag take me into the woods and shoot me,' she said through gritted teeth. 'And then he was to cut my head off.'

'These words I spoke in haste,' he said, moderately.

'You said you were going to fucking *skin* my uncle!'

'He killed my little brother!' Chechnik spat, and the charade ended. 'He and I were the only ones left! What would you have me do?'

Beth waggled a finger at him, as a mother might scold a child. 'I would have you die,' she said, and, with his roars in her ears, she climbed down and began to walk back towards the road, following the furrows left by the car. She had only gone a few yards when she heard the gunshot.

3

DUNNIGAN DROVE LIKE A MAN POSSESSED.

Diane had never seen him manoeuvre a vehicle like this before (he treated his BMW as if it were made of stained glass), and she hung on for dear life and prayed that they didn't encounter any hairpin bends.

'Stop!' she shouted as they rounded a corner and their headlights revealed clear tyre marks in the road: someone had skidded, and the ploughed-up verge showed they had plunged into the woods.

Dunnigan left their car in the middle of the road, the engine still running, and the two ran towards the break in the trees. They had barely crossed the threshold when something colossal flew out of the darkness and landed on the criminologist, knocking him off his feet and backwards across the roadway. With the black creature straddling him, he came to a bone-jarring stop against the front grille of the car they had just exited.

For a moment Diane had no idea what she was seeing. Dunnigan had talked about Mother Joan back in Dublin, but she had no reference point for what she was dealing with: this was something that seemed to have escaped from a fever dream, and for a brief second she considered turning tail and running as hard and fast as she could.

The thing that was on her friend reared up, and suddenly it had a blade in its hand.

Her hands shaking with terror, Diane closed the breach on the shotgun she was still carrying.

'Hey,' she called, but the creature did not even look in her direction – it was as if Dunnigan was all it could focus on. 'Hey! I'm talking to you!' she shouted, and now she was angry as well as scared.

Slowly the hood turned and Diane perceived the darkness within – a strand of white hair hung lank below the hemline, but inside all was black.

'I don't know who you are or what your problem is,' she said shakily, 'but I have no argument with you. Go on now, and let's pretend this never happened.'

The hood swayed rhythmically, but the knife remained steady.

'What do you say?' Diane added, more gently.

Dunnigan, his eyes wide, began to push himself away from his attacker, and this movement seemed to bring the spectre back to itself. She made to lunge for him again, and Diane fired.

There was an ear-splitting screech, and Mother Joan fled back into the trees in a flurry of dank air.

They found Beth walking slowly out of the forest five minutes later.

'Where's Chechnik?' Dunnigan asked, once they had hugged and cried and been reunited for the second time in only a few months.

'He's dead,' she said. 'They're all dead.'

4

DUNNIGAN WANTED TO HAVE BETH CHECKED
over, so they went straight to the hospital Keenan had brought
Jones to, in Hawick.

'I can't believe you all made it out,' Keenan said when he
saw them.

'We nearly didn't,' Diane said ruefully.

'You know you had help, don't you?'

'I cannot thank you and Diane enough,' Dunnigan said.
'And Finbar and Rufus, of course.'

'I don't mean us,' Keenan said. 'I mean Mother Joan.'

Dunnigan looked at Beth, who had gone very quiet. 'She
tried to kill me,' he said. 'If it hadn't been for Diane, I know
for a fact I'd be dead.'

'I don't want to talk about it,' Diane said. 'I'm going
to be seeing that every time I close my eyes for a *really*
long time.'

'She was in the woods when they attacked the van,' Keenan
told them. 'She dealt with the bloke who shot Jones.'

'Did you see her, Beth?' Dunnigan asked.

The girl shook her head.

'Like I said before,' the criminologist sighed, 'she is one very confused ghost. Or whatever the hell she is.'

And he would say no more on the matter.

*

The police came and interviewed them. It was long and tedious and they were all very tired.

Beth barely said a word through the whole thing. 'Can I go and sit with Inspector Jones?' she finally asked Dunnigan when the police had gone and she had been given the all clear by the medics.

'Why? You don't know him.'

'I feel responsible. He wouldn't have got shot if it wasn't for me.'

'I know he won't see it that way.'

'Well, I do.'

'As long as the doctors don't mind. I'm going to book you and Diane rooms in the Travelodge. We could all do with some sleep.'

'Where are the Keenans going to stay?'

'I offered Joe a room and he declined. They're going to the Fens in East Anglia in the morning – he says this has drawn too much attention and he's not comfortable here anymore. For tonight, the hospital staff have indicated they'll turn a blind eye if he uses the carpark.'

Beth went to Jones's room. He was hooked up to an antibiotics drip – the real threat to a person who has been gut-shot is peritonitis, a bacterial infection caused by the bowel dumping its contents into the abdomen. Jones had been lucky – he would recover, although he had a long road ahead.

She'd been sitting there for an hour when Diane stepped in. They sat together quietly for a bit.

'Do you think we can go home soon?' Beth said after a bit.

Diane sighed and shook her head. 'I'm not sure Davey's ready.'

Beth looked at her, aghast. 'You don't mean …'

'I do. He's not finished with the case. He won't be content until they find a body.'

Bradislav Vaslav Chechnik

He drifted into unconsciousness and was troubled by dark dreams: his brother – half his face missing – was taunting him from somewhere among the trees, calling him a coward and a failure for not avenging him. He came back to awareness and realised he had been thrashing and twisting against the branch that bound him in place – his whole body throbbed with agony, and he knew he would die in that car if he did not manage to free himself.

Dragging his body off the shaft of wood was not a possibility – it was so long he would never manage it – the pain would be unimaginable. That left two options: break it off or pull it out.

The lance was as thick as his arm, so breaking it could also be crossed off the list.

Which meant his decision was made.

He girded himself, taking his wallet from his pocket – it was leather and strongly made – and placing it between his teeth to bite down on. Then he put one hand on the pole, gripped it firmly, and placed his other just above it.

His mouth was dry as bone (he knew he was dehydrated from loss of blood) and every movement left him sweating and panting with exertion. However, there was no way he was going to die in this godforsaken place, alone and pinned to the earth like a bug to a piece of card.

He counted in his head: one, two, three … and pulled with all his might.

The pain, despite the fact he was expecting it, was so great he felt himself drift away from his body, and seemed to be looking down on his prone form from above. Just before the darkness cascaded over him, he thought he felt the barb give beneath him.

But then he was gone.

Sometime later – he knew not how long – he came around, drenched in sweat and blood. He thought he was going to throw up, and dry-heaved, but he was so dehydrated nothing came. He lay there, a voice in his head telling him it was a waste of time – why not just allow death to come? It would be so much easier.

But his brother's face hovered above his vision, and he could not bear it: how could he meet Yuri in the next life if he had not striven with his last breath to avenge him?

He grasped the wood of the rough-hewn javelin and, with every piece of anger and hatred and fear he possessed, he heaved.

And this time, it came away.

Wheezing with excruciation, he managed to turn on his side and dragged the last few inches from his body, and then drifted some more.

When awareness next came, he knew he was almost gone. The window above seemed an impossible distance away, and the effort felt like more than he could endure. But something in him – a vestigial survival instinct – took hold, and before he even knew what he was doing, he climbed up the very post that had pierced him, using it to drag his wasted body out of the petrol stench and into the cool night air.

In a final, agonising movement he hauled himself out onto the side of the Volvo and stood, victorious, like Hillary on Everest's summit. He raised one hand in a signal of victory, and was suddenly aware of a warm breeze just below him. Turning stiffly, he saw the same cowled figure that had caused the crash, a burning piece of pine in its claw. In an act that looked to be almost of sublimation, the spectre leaned towards him in a low bow and then tossed the fiery brand into the dry bracken she had piled below the sundered petrol tank.

The car exploded in a column of yellow flame. The clock on the dashboard read 3.33 a.m.

5

THE SUN WAS STARTING TO RISE ACROSS KIELDER when Dunnigan finally got back to his room in the Travelodge (he had booked rooms there for the others as well). Beth was scarcely talking to him (he sensed Diane might have had something to do with this), but he was too tired to care.

He went into the bathroom and switched on the shower. He was just taking off his shoes when he felt a breeze that shouldn't have been there. All the hairs on his arms stood on end, and, somehow, he knew she was in the room.

He walked slowly back in, and found her, a pillar of darkness in human form, standing by the window, which she had left ajar.

On top of the smell of earth and smoke he could also get the copper of blood, where Diane had found her mark. For the first time he could discern features within the cowls of the hood – a sharp nose and prominent cheekbones, and hollow, pained eyes.

The woman behind the monster.

Her name, Dunnigan thought desperately. *The secret is in her name.*

'Hello, Hester,' he said, trying and failing to keep the tremor from his voice.

She reared up, seeming to become twice as big, and then like a thing with no skeleton she was flowing out the window and was gone in the gathering dawn, leaving a sense of grief and loss in her wake.

He closed the window and locked it, then sat for a long time watching the light come into the sky, as if it was the first dawn he had ever seen.

6

THERE WAS ONLY ONE MEMBER OF THE KITT family still living. Hester's older brother Malachi owned a thatched cottage just outside Newcastle, in a hamlet Dunnigan would have considered very pretty if he had been in a better mood.

At seventy-three years he was still sprightly and had most of his own hair, although the same could not be said of his teeth, the majority of which seemed to have given up the ghost.

Dunnigan, who had been unable to sleep despite his exhaustion, called on him at nine that morning as the oldster was arriving back at the tiny house after his morning stroll.

'I was just about to take some tea if you'd like to join me,' he said, his accent a gentler shade of Geordie – he had been living in the area for forty years.

'That would be very nice.'

'You're Irish,' the older man said, as the kettle boiled.

'I'm from Dublin, yes.'

'My sister loved Ireland. She told me she could spend days travellin' around, lookin' at the old churches and goin' to the sites of the ancient monasteries. Said it calmed her.'

'Your sister?'

'Oh, you know I've got a sister.' He poured water into the teapot to scald it.

'I do,' Dunnigan admitted.

'I knew it. You're here about Hester, aren't you?' Malachi said while the tea was brewing. He rolled a cigarette one-handed as he talked, an act that fascinated Dunnigan, who had been forced to do a lot of things one-handed during his recent convalescence.

'When did you last see her?'

'I'd say it's been three years. She in trouble?'

'I need to speak to her.'

'You're polis, right?'

'Yes.'

'Only reason polis want to talk to ordin'ry folk is 'cause they're in trouble.'

'I want to help her. She's injured and I think she might be very confused. I'm beginning to believe she is a good person who has been through a lot of pain.'

Malachi nodded and lit his smoke. 'Last time I saw Hester she was really sick. The voices had got so bad, she couldn't hear much else. There was a time when I used to be able to keep them quiet, make her relax some. Not this time. I was worried she'd finish herself.'

'She had medication, didn't she?'

'Made her sick. Gave her convulsions – her face would all crunch up and her arms would herk and jerk. Caused her discomfort and made it so she couldn't work no more.'

'Do you know where she might be, Mister Kitt?'

'You can call me Malachi.'

'Malachi, then. Can you suggest somewhere I could look for her?'

He nodded at the mantelpiece. 'See that picture?'

It was of a group of soldiers, all dressed in sandy-coloured camouflage. Dunnigan looked more closely, and saw one was Hester. She looked young and happy and full of exuberant life.

'That was taken in Israel, which means it was two years before they sent her to Uganda.'

'The army?'

'Naw. She was only in the army a wet weekend. After they threw her out of the convent she went to college, got a couple of degrees. I think she always wanted to belong to somethin', though. She needed a structure to her life, so if the church wouldn't have her, the army was the next best thing. When she went to sign up, they sent her straight to officer school, and it was there she met Christopher Wayne. He spotted her talent right away, and she was recruited by Maylor before she knew what she was gettin' herself into.'

'What was her role at Maylor Consulting?'

'She called it counter-insurgency, but from what she told me, it was mostly how to spy on the other side. She was always good with languages, and she's strong and fit, physically, anyway. They took her out to New Guinea or somewhere and taught her survival stuff – she lived with some tribe that spent half their lives up the top of trees. I'll tell you, she could do things with rope you wouldn't believe. Maylor trained her up with all kinds of technology too. She did classes in computers and surveillance and the like – such as it was in the 1970s. She always kept up to date, though – she could tell you all about clouds and trojans and that. She helped me fit out this place with alarms and cameras, even though I hardly ever use them – usually forget. She told me once that if they wanted to, there could be some bloke in Land's End listening in on me farting right at my dinner table. Proper upset me, that did. But it was what her job was, so I tried to understand.'

'Maylor informed me she taught military history.'

'They lied to you, then.'

'You say she got sent to Uganda?'

'Israel first – that's where that photo was taken. They was an ally of our great nation, and Hester was sent out to help train their troops. She loved it – the Holy Land and all that – she wasn't a nun anymore, but she was still religious. Then everything went tits-up in Uganda, and Maylor moved their people lock, stock and barrel to Kampala. Officially Maylor was there in an advisory capacity, but the truth is they were intelligence-gathering, all in a bid to protect British interests. By 1978 it was clear Idi Amin was going to lose power, and there were a lot of sides MI6 wanted to play off against one another. The mutiny was in full swing, and the opposition were picking targets. Maylor, who were there to maintain the status quo, were an obvious choice. Amin's government was carrying out wholesale ethnic cleansing, so those who stood against him hadn't too many scruples about who they hit. Can't really blame them, when you stop to think about it.'

'Objectively, I suppose not.'

'A group of rebels stormed the offices Hester was working out of on the morning of December the third 1978. The men were shot outright, and the women taken as hostages. Hester and two secretaries – one was an Israeli girl, the other was American – were taken to a shack on the Tanzanian border.'

'You must have been sick with worry,' Dunnigan said. The abduction of a loved one was something he understood all too well.

'We didn't know,' Malachi said, sadly. 'This was before the days of mobile phones and emails. An international call cost so much money, you saved them for Christmas and birthdays. We hadn't a clue there was a problem until it was all over.'

'What happened?'

'I'm not one hundred per cent sure of the details,' the older man said. 'I bet you can imagine how three foreign women, working for an unsympathetic opposition state, would have been treated, though. I know she was beaten. I know she was raped, multiple times. I know she thought she was going to die, and that the Israeli girl was murdered right in front of her.'

'I'm sorry,' Dunnigan said.

'She had been in captivity for a week when, somehow – whether it was carelessness or mercy or she managed it herself, I don't know – one of them left her hands untied. That was a mistake. She broke a guard's neck and escaped into the hill country. A week later she was found by government troops who were in the area driving mutineers over the border. Luckily, they had photos of the women who had been taken, and they recognised her. Apparently, it took three of them to subdue her.'

As Malachi Kitt talked, Dunnigan understood: Mother Joan had been hewn out of the ravages of a nightmarish war. Hester Kitt was trained to survive in the harshest of circumstances – and that was what she had done. It didn't excuse her crimes, but it explained them.

'Despite all that, she stayed working for Maylor?'

'She wasn't fit for anything else. She couldn't hold down any other job, and they gave her something she couldn't mess up – some kind of corporate work, team-building and conflict resolution; helping managers be better bullies, was what she used to call it. But they sent her to Ireland a lot, to work with companies over there, which she did like, so I always reckoned it was six of one and half a dozen of the other, really.'

'She must have hated the work, though. And the managers who were still punishing her years later.'

'She was not happy – remember, security and surveillance was her job, and she had warned them the offices in Kampala weren't properly equipped. She begged them to put in proper alarms and security doors, but the board wouldn't approve it.'

'The board that was headed up by Grant Noble?'

'He was chairman at the time, yes.'

'So she was forced to do what amounted to menial work for the men who had sentenced her to torture and rape, all because they didn't want to spend a few pounds on equipment they could have taken with them when they were leaving.'

'Exactly. She was never given a penny in compensation.'

'She got nothing?'

'They gave her some sort of ceremonial thing – she used to laugh about it.'

'What was that?'

'It was a collection of antique knives.'

Hester Kitt

She was Hester.

Somehow, when the man Dunnigan had spoken her name – the one her mother gave her when she was an infant – a lifetime she had suppressed came rushing back in a flood of mixed emotions.

She was a child, playing in a sunlit garden with her brother.

She was a girl dressed in white making her First Communion.

She was a smiling teenager, being kissed by a sweet boy for the first time, and then she was a sobbing young woman whose heart had been broken, but it was a wondrous sadness for all that.

She wandered for miles through the foliage, losing herself in the cool shade, by turns laughing and crying and wailing and hollering, for when she had remembered who she was, she remembered she had a voice, and she wanted to speak her truth. The warrior woman had wounded her in the side, but she had sustained worse harm over the years. It would heal, given time.

So it was with a sob of joy that she came to the walled garden on the edge of the forest as the sun was setting, and found Phillipe waiting there for her.

'My dear, you look so sad.'

'I ... I am ill.'

'Nothing we can't fix. You look half frozen to death.'

He gave her some of his whiskey and she drank deeply while he put more wood on the fire, then wrapped his arm around her. He smelt of clean sweat and a hint of expensive cologne. It was intoxicating.

'My dear, I must speak to you of something important.'

'Yes?'

'David Dunnigan is still alive. You permitted him to slip through your grasp.'

'Phillipe, he is not an evil man.'

'Come, my precious girl. What do you know of evil men?' He stood up roughly and pushed her aside. 'I asked you to do me this one thing.'

'But the girl – he loves her. He would have died for her!'

'Then why did you not let him?'

He said the words with jovial tones, but there was an edge to his voice that made her uncomfortable. The room seemed to have become smaller and the smoke from the fire made her eyes swim. The floor had started to buckle and tilt, and when she looked at Phillipe, she saw who he really was and she knew he had poisoned her. Far away, in the darkest part of her mind, the voices were laughing. Suddenly she was very afraid.

'Yes, my lady. I can see that you are ill, indeed. Permit me to help you.'

She tried to bring the knife up, but he stopped her hand with a deft movement, and gently removed the leuku from her grasp.

'Time to say goodbye,' he said, and took her in an embrace, plunging the point of the blade deep inside her.

7

'THEY FOUND A FAKE WALL IN HER ATTIC IN the place in Montague Street packed with surveillance technology, some of it of 1980s vintage,' Dunnigan told Jones, who was sitting up in bed eating jelly and custard. 'There were hard drives with enough photographs to fill a hundred Black Bibles, sound files of plainchants, sonic projection equipment, which would explain how it seemed to be coming from everywhere and nowhere, and a Bluetooth hijacker, which is how she made music come out of your car radio.'

'And you're telling me she was basically a spook,' the policeman said around a mouthful.

'If by that you mean she was trained in black ops, then yes. It's how she could get into places that seemed impregnable and how she was able to move the way she did in the forest. As part of her training with Maylor, she lived for six months with a tribe called the Korowai – they live deep in the Indonesian rainforest, in houses they build on platforms high up in the jungle canopy. These people can move through the trees carrying items many times their own weight using a particular form of rope craft they share only with tribal members. It's remarkable they taught her, but it shows how singular a woman she is.'

'And lucky me, she's still at large,' Jones said.

'I'm afraid so. We've been dealing with an incredibly skilled operative. I was working on the premise she had been tracking her victims for years – decades, sometimes – and often across several continents, which seemed virtually impossible, but no other explanation seemed to fit. The tech guys tell me, though, that she had been able to hack into security systems for all kinds of organisations – law-abiding or otherwise – from all over the world and retrieve footage and images which she then reproduced in her Black Bibles. It meant she could make her victims believe she was always watching, when in fact she was simply using the fact that *someone* is always watching. She's a smart woman. It's no wonder we couldn't catch her.'

'You did all you could. Go home, mate. Look after Beth. Make up with your sister. And have a bloody rest! You look like you're ready to keel over.'

'I *am* worn out.'

'Half the coppers from here to John o' Groats are looking for her. We've got photos of her now as a nun, as a soldier, as a sales executive, and as Mother Joan. Unless she decides to become a punk or change her gender, I think we've got it covered.'

'I don't like leaving a job undone.'

'Davey, I promise you that Her Majesty's Royal Constabulary will manage to keep ticking over without your support, welcome though it has been.'

Dunnigan laughed. 'Are you telling me you've had enough of me?'

'Yes!'

Dunnigan extended his hand, and they shook. 'Thanks for everything – mate,' he said, trying out the word for size.

'Thank you,' Jones said. 'The upside of all this is that no one thinks I'm mad anymore. I owe you one for that!'

'I think you've amply repaid me. Beth wants to come in and say goodbye, and seeing as they're insisting on one visitor at a time, she's getting rather impatient. Oh, and Diane has picked up your car – you left it parked in the woods. She's bringing your bag in from the boot – I don't know if you want anything from it.'

'Tell her to pop in after Beth goes. I'd like to say goodbye. She's a pretty fucking amazing woman, isn't he?'

'She is. I'll tell her.'

Beth was virtually hopping from one foot to the other when he got out (she and Jones had become fast friends) and she gave her uncle a stern look as she went inside. Dunnigan took the chair she had just vacated. Diane arrived a few minutes later, carrying a gym bag and a set of car keys.

'Mission accomplished,' she said. 'Beth in with the DI?'

'Yes.'

'I'd murder a Coke. Will you join me for a stroll as far as the vending machine?'

They walked down the corridor, through some sliding doors and into the main lobby area.

'Got any change?' Diane asked him.

'You decided to go to the vending machine and you don't have change?'

'I knew you would.'

Dunnigan took a fistful from one of the capacious pockets of his coat. Diane put a pound coin into the machine and punched the appropriate number.

'I didn't just bring you down here to borrow money,' she said.

'What ulterior motive do you have?'

'Open the zip on Jones's bag.'

'That's not really appropriate, is it?'

'I put something I found in the glove compartment of his car in there. Don't worry, it's right at the top. You won't need to dig any deeper into his unmentionables.'

Dunnigan did as Diane said. There, sitting on top of a pair of washed-out jeans, was a Black Bible. Dunnigan held the bag open, staring at the tome. 'Did you look in it?'

'I'm sorry to say that I did.'

'Is he in the photos?'

'Yes.'

'Do I want to know what he's doing in them, seeing as he's alone in a room with my niece this very minute?'

'Roughing up a female suspect. Planting evidence. Taking bribes. It's not pretty.'

Dunnigan heaved a bitter sigh. 'Do you think he knew it was there?'

'If he did, he never let on.'

Diane popped the ring on her can and drank deeply. Suddenly, the tin still at her lips, she froze. 'Davey,' she said.

'What?'

'We're being watched.'

Dunnigan turned, expecting to see Mother Joan. Instead, dressed in the clothes of a surgeon, complete with blood stains, was the ruby-cheeked visage of Phillipe Ressler. He articulated a theatrical bow, and was gone into the crowd.

'Beth!' Dunnigan gasped, and the two of them broke into

a sprint, bursting through the double doors and down the corridor to Jones's room.

The criminologist didn't stand on ceremony, and flung the door open. What he saw inside made him freeze instantly. The room was covered, floor to ceiling, in blood. Alfie Jones was dead, his carotid artery open and his throat slashed to the bone.

Standing over him, a familiar leuku knife in her hand, was Beth Carlton.

'Oh my God, Davey,' she sobbed, her eyes wide with horror, her hands scarlet with viscera. 'What have I done?'

ACKNOWLEDGEMENTS

ONE SEPTEMBER AFTERNOON IN 2015 I WAS teaching a social care class in Waterford College of Further Education. At the beginning of the year, lecturer and students are still getting to know one another, and as much of the material we cover is sensitive in nature, this can be a tentative process.

I wasn't surprised when, at the end of the session, one of my group, a young woman who was already showing a keen interest in the course and genuine talent as a carer, asked to speak to me.

I assumed she would want to discuss some element of theory we had just covered, but as soon as the other students filed out I could see she was upset – another common enough occurrence in the first few classes of child protection training, where many find themselves unexpectedly triggered.

I sat her down, offered her a box of tissues, and asked what was wrong.

'I'm afraid you won't believe me,' she said.

'I promise you that there's nothing you can say that will surprise or shock me,' I assured her, 'and there's nothing I haven't heard before.'

'Promise?'

'I promise.'

'I'm being haunted by Slender Man.'

I was both surprised and shocked – you'd think I'd be used to being proved wrong at this stage of my life, wouldn't you?

That was my introduction to the world of modern online mythology and the phenomenon of creepypasta. I was amazed that, as someone who considers himself to be reasonably au fait with the World Wide Web and who spends his working life in the company of young people, I had never heard of this unusual subculture, and found myself immediately fascinated by it.

My student was not psychiatrically ill, nor was she suffering from a delusion in the strictest sense of the word – she had simply fallen for what had, by 2015, become a layered and complex thread of digital folklore. Bright as she was, it didn't take me long to prove to her that this eerie character she was so frightened by had a very definite fictional origin (his creator, and the circumstances of his genesis, are widely known, as McSwain explains to Dunnigan), and the next day, some research under my belt, I could show her, step-by-step, how he became such a successful bogeyman. The 'signs' of his haunting were easily explained away, and she left my office a more relaxed and happy young woman.

But something about Slender Man stayed with me long after I rescued that poor girl from his clutches. I've always had an interest in fairytales, and stories are, as a writer, my stock-in-trade. As a folk musician, I've always been entranced by the way songs and stories are transmitted – passed from one person to another down through the years.

Creepypasta is the perfect example of that in the modern world.

When it came time to find a new protagonist for Dunnigan and company to do battle with, Mother Joan slid from the shadows of my subconscious, and I knew right away she was going to be a lot of fun to spend time with.

The creepypasta stories about Mother Joan that populate the first half of *If She Returned* are all developed from well-known creepypasta tropes – in some I've taken the general concept and thrown Mother Joan into the mix (*The Woman in the Oven*; *The Thing Wearing Mummy's Skin*), from others I've taken the loose idea and atmosphere and gone off on my own tangent (*The Seed Eater*; *The Thing You Should Not Name*). If you're interested in reading more, there are (as Dunnigan found out) literally thousands of stories of varying length (and quality – you may have to wade through a few duds but it's worth it when you find some really good ones). But be prepared to sleep with the light on afterwards – I scared myself while researching this book, and I'm not ashamed to admit it.

Mère Jeanne des Anges was a real person, and the Loudun Witch Trials happened as I have described. Probably the best-known work on the case is Aldous Huxley's *The Devils of Loudun*, but some of you may be more familiar with Ken Russell's controversial film about the events in that rural French town, *The Devils* (not a movie for the faint-hearted, so be warned!).

Obviously, I owe a debt of gratitude and a huge thanks to all the authors who have developed and evolved these stories over many years to create a new mythos for the twenty-first century. I hope Mother Joan is a worthy addition to your canon of monsters.

My wife Deirdre Wickham was, once again, an invaluable resource while writing *If She Returned*. I composed the first draft of the book over ten feverish days in July 2018 and arrived in Kielder Forest with Dunnigan, Diane and the Keenans as they faced off against Bradislav and his thugs with only a loose sense of how to choreograph the action that would bring the story to its conclusion. Deirdre very patiently sat down with me, listened to my ideas, found the holes in them, suggested some possibilities (far more bloodthirsty than me – my darling wife proposed that Rufus should meet his demise during the fracas; you can thank me, gentle reader, that he survived!) and helped me map out the movement of the various players one step at a time.

Without her, I have no idea how the whole thing would have panned out, and I am very grateful for her indulgence and common sense.

My son Richard, my daughter Marnie, and my grandson Rhys had to put up with me disappearing into my newly established writing shed and refusing to come out until the task was done. (I will never forget poor, neglected Rhys sitting on the step outside my Man Cave while I clattered away on the keys – Lulu, one of my dogs, perched beside him – bemoaning to his furry friend the fact that Grandad never seems to stop working! Now *that* is how you lay on a guilt trip.)

Before this book was begun I had the unenviable task of seeking a new agent. After one very stressful false start with an individual I was clearly not cut out to work with I found myself sitting in the offices of the amazing Marianne Gunn O'Connor, who swept into my life and wiped away all the worries I had been harbouring about the future of my literary career. The support and feedback from her and her reader Alison made rewrites a pleasure, and *If She Returned* is largely the book it is because of their generosity of spirit.

And this is a good time to thank the outrageously talented Carmel Harrington (if you haven't read her books yet, you're missing out), who is always at the end of the phone and was there for me through the most difficult ten months of my writing career. I'll always be grateful, Carmel.

David Dunnigan would not exist without Hachette Ireland. Ciara Doorley's confidence in me as a fiction writer is something I am eternally thankful for. Ciara, Joanna, Breda and all the gang are simply a pleasure to work with.

The incredibly gifted Liam Hourican has given Dunnigan a voice, and his remarkable readings of the first two novels for Audible (I assume he'll make it a hat-trick by doing this one, too) have found depths of emotion and aspects of the narrative I never even knew were there. I am very thankful to have him as part of the creative team behind the series.

If She Returned is a book about family, and just as I was sitting down to plot this novel, my younger brother Karl passed away after a long battle with cancer. People who knew us have commented on the fact that Dunnigan contains traits of both our personalities, but I think, in retrospect, that the lion's share of him is Karl. As heartbroken as I am, I like to think my little brother will live on through these stories. My love to his wife, Liz, and my niece and nephew Ellie and Thomas. This book is for all of you too.

Thanks as always to my sister Tara, to my big brother-in-law Gerry, and to my nephews Jack and Conn, who, in league with my grandson, offered me a welcome distraction during revisions of this book by insisting I compose some rude songs for their entertainment (you'd be surprised how many words rhyme with 'fart').

Finally, my gratitude and my undying affection to you, dear reader. Thanks for coming back time and again. And feel safe in the knowledge that the story's not over.

We have quite a journey still ahead of us.

Wexford
August 2018

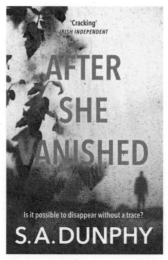

AFTER SHE VANISHED

Five people living on Dublin's streets have gone missing and criminologist David Dunnigan has been tasked with finding them.

His search leads him to ten-year-old Harry, living alone in an abandoned warehouse, who has been waiting days for his parents' return ...

Dunnigan knows more than he would wish to about unexplained disappearances. Almost twenty years ago, his young niece Beth vanished during their annual Christmas shopping trip. No trace of her was ever discovered. And the tragic mystery has loomed over Dunnigan's life ever since.

As his current investigation draws him deeper into the city's dark underbelly, Dunnigan's resolve to help Harry and unravel this mystery grows stronger.

And could it lead him one step closer to finding out what became of Beth?

Also available as an ebook

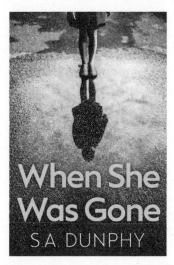

WHEN SHE WAS GONE

David Dunnigan's niece has been missing for eighteen years without a trace – until now.

Someone has sent the criminologist a shoe – one Beth was wearing the day she disappeared – and the investigation is swiftly re-ignited, along with Dunnigan's hopes of finding her alive. But is he ready for what else he might find?

As new evidence starts to link Beth's abduction to a series of apparent suicides and a horrifying people-trafficking network, Dunnigan furiously chases down leads before the trail goes cold once more and Beth is lost forever. But when the search brings Dunnigan, accompanied by his loyal friend Miley and ex-soldier partner-in-crime Diane, to the frozen north of Greenland, the hunt starts to become more and more dangerous.

But where will it end?

Is it a journey Dunnigan will survive? And will it lead him to Beth, after all this time?

Also available as an ebook

Coming soon

WHY SHE RAN

David Dunnigan and his niece Beth are on the run.

Beth, it seems, has killed a British police detective and her criminologist uncle, now more aware than ever of the terrible legacy of her experiences at the hands of the After Dark Campaign, will stop at nothing to protect her.

With the help of long-time allies Father Bill and Miley, Dunnigan and Beth set out to track down the man responsible for her abduction and end the Campaign once and for all. But while they're frantically evading capture by the police, they can't shake the feeling that someone else may be hunting them. And as events push them towards a terrifying confrontation, it becomes clear to Dunnigan that not all of them will make it out alive …

Now available for pre-order